When we are in desperate need and acknowledge God humbly without pride,
God can be found everywhere.

Sophia K. Nnah MD

1

COVID-19

Gripping novel inspired by real events

From the Unseen Doctor

Cover Design by Sophia Apple and Hal Apple
Production and layout by Stephanie Robinson

For inquiries contact unseendoctor@gmail.com, or visit
https://Doctorsophiaonline.com

Author credentials and personal history

Sophia K. Apple, MD

Emeritus Professor, David Geffen School of Medicine at UCLA. Dr. Apple is the author of over 70 professional original medical research papers, and is on the editorial board for Modern Pathology, which has the highest impact factor of all Pathology medical journals, and a primary editor and author of Breast Imaging, a seminal medical textbook correlating Pathology and Radiology findings in the diagnosis of breast cancer. She has taught hundreds of medical students, over 100 Residents and Fellows in Pathology, and many other physicians-in-training from Radiology, Surgery, and other disciplines. Dr. Apple is an internationally recognized expert in Breast Cancer, having spoken at numerous conferences and venues.

Personal history

Dr. Apple and her husband currently live in Southern California and have been married for 33 years. She contracted the polio virus as an infant in South Korea. Her family moved to Japan after her fourth grade, where she lived for almost four years but was unable to attend school because of the stigma from her disability. The family later moved to New York City for better education, becoming one of the first Asian families to live in Queens. She came to America with no knowledge of English, and later graduated from NYU with a BS and MS in Biochemistry, completed medical school in Ohio, and six years of residency and fellowship training at UCLA. She came to know Jesus as her personal savior at the age of 17 when she was hit by a car while crossing the street, and God changed her life perspective of who she was and the purpose of her life ever since. Her perspective of life and as an author is unique, as an Asian American immigrant and female physician with a physical disability. She continues to practice medicine as a pathology physician.

Prologue

The Severe Acute Respiratory syndrome COronaVirus 2 (SAR-COV-2) and the disease it causes is Coronavirus disease 2019 (COVID-19).

A devastating pandemic occurs about every 100 years. Living through the pandemic could be viewed as hell but in many ways, it could be viewed as a privilege.

Introduction

COronaVirus 2 (SAR-COV-2) entered our globe silently in the late winter of 2019, and flipped our norms upside down, causing the pandemic. The definition of pandemic means a disease is prevalent over an entire country or the world. The definition of epidemic is a widespread occurrence of an infectious disease in a community at a particular time.

The coronavirus started as an epidemic in Wuhan, China, and became a pandemic. Coronaviruses are a large family of RNA viruses that cause common colds in people, but they also infect other animals and different species. Throughout history, we know that viruses mutate constantly, and they can become highly infectious and virulent. Corona means the upper portion or crown of a part, as of the head, as the coronavirus appears when viewed through an electron microscope. The most common symptoms of COVID-19 are reported as fever, dry cough and shortness of breath. The virus is tested by polymerase chain reaction (PCR) from a nasopharyngeal swab.

As of 5/22/2020, there had been more than 5.1 million infections with the virus and a death toll of over 335,000 globally. Just within the US, confirmed deaths caused by the coronavirus surpassed 95,000. These numbers were expected to rise and affect every corner of the earth. On 3/1/2020, The New York Times headline reported, *How prepared is the US for a Coronavirus outbreak?* and within 12 weeks we knew we were not prepared.

According to the Center for Disease Control and Prevention (CDC) records, flu seasons in the US run from October through May and claim 29,000 to 59,000 lives, with common causes of death mostly from complications such as pneumonia, heart attacks and strokes. Last year, an estimated 80,000 Americans died of flu, which was the highest annual death toll in at least four decades. The death rate from influenza (flu) is generally a fraction of 1% (0.1% to be exact), but the coronavirus induced death rate is over 1% (reaching 4.7% today worldwide), so it is at least 10 times more deadly than the seasonal flu. The US initially underestimated this formidable enemy by considering it to be just a mere flu, which was a mistake.

It could be helpful if we trace through the histories of pandemics caused by viruses to predict when and how this COVID-19 will be over. In 1918, a flu pandemic caused by an H1N1 virus lasted nearly 2 years and killed more than 50 million, and infected 500 million (1/3 of the world's population). It was reported that H1N1 virus originated from genes of avian (bird) origin. In that era, there were no vaccines, antibiotics or medical facilities with ventilators like today, and the only way to combat the pandemic was by isolation, quarantine, good personal hygiene, use of disinfectants and limitations of public gatherings; non-pharmaceutical intervention.

In 1957-58, a new influenza (H2N2) virus emerged in East Asia, spreading to become a pandemic (Asian Flu). This virus was first reported in Singapore in February 1957, then Hong Kong in April 1957, and in coastal cities in the US during the summer of 1957, according to CDC records. The estimated dead numbered 1.1 million, with 116,000 of those in the US. This virus originated from Avian Influenza A.

In 1968, Pandemic H3N2 virus comprised of a new mutated Avian influenza A. And again in the spring of 2009 a novel (new) influenza A (H1N1) virus (H1N1)pdm09 arose, otherwise known as swine flu, implicating its origin from swine.

The current COVID-19 is thought to have arisen from smuggled pangolins used for both food and medicine. Another possibility is bats. Both animals have similar genetic codes as in the coronavirus. Exactly how the virus jumped from a wild animal to other animals or humans remains a mystery.

According to a recent publication in JAMA, the mechanisms leading to death by coronavirus is by filling the lungs with fluid as seen in congestive heart failure symptoms. The human lung is like a tree branching with the end of the tree twigs having grapes with empty sacs. These sacs have a thin membrane which transports oxygen molecules, which are absorbed into the blood flow to provide life to all cells within the body. With COVID-19 infections leading to death, these grape-like sacs are filled with fluid which leads to inability for oxygen transport. By imaging, the radiologists describe the condition as ground glass opacity. The ventilator is the only way to deliver some oxygen by pushing positive pressure into the lungs. The strong pressure can cause these sacs to pop (causing atelectasis) which will damage the lung permanently. A more chronic consequence is the fibrosis/thickening of sac membrane. COVID-19 infection causes this kind of dire situation very fast (within 1-3 days). As in all flus, the most devastating effects are seen in elderly, diabetes, immune deficient populations and other pre-existing medical conditions.

Knowing these facts, and the history of pandemics, what can we deduce, and what do we do now? We wait for the specific vaccine against COVID-19. Until then, we go back to what we know in how to combat the virus; non-pharmaceutical intervention. As we change the lifestyle of our norms, it is perhaps easy to blame others—governments, organizations such as CDC, WHO, the people of Wuhan, China, or the US President by saying, only if...

Strangely, we are so connected by a few people in Wuhan, China; their business of what they eat and do is no longer just their business, but we are so intimately affected. Their business is now our business whether we like it or not. So, shall we blame the Chinese? What if the next strain of virus comes from a pig farm in a small town in the US?

When one thinks like a virus, success depends on reproduction, increase in potency, and easy transport to new vectors by new and clever mutation of genetic codes. It has nothing to do with boundaries, races, ages, and genders. The question we need to ask is when will the next pandemic be, and not if.

As we fight against this virus today, the only logical ways are to physically distance from each other and wear masks to stop the spread, which will also lessen the burden to our health care workers and their resources. Most health care workers are prepared to fall and are ready to die for the sick. It is their dedication to people who are sick and their promise to the professional Hippocratic oath.

Our action today will affect others tomorrow. COVID-19 is not a joke or fake story. It is real. What's unseen is more deadly than what is seen.

Table of Contents

COVID-19

CHAPTER 1

Hart Island

March 31, 2020

It was a drizzly and cold rainy day. Samantha was sent to Hart Island for observation during the forensic pathology rotation in her third year of residency. She was dragging her feet as she was asked to report to Hart Island a day early before her rotation started on April 1. She had never been to Hart Island.

She was already regretting her decision to be a pathologist, and in residency training during the pandemic with COVID-19. With her luck, her autopsy rotation in April is when the death rate is expected to have a surge. She had several choices for her autopsy rotation, and she chose the Long Island Hospital associated with the coroner's office because her friends in residency said it was the least busy morgue and it would be easier than going to any of the other New York City morgues where the death rates were at least 10 times higher. This estimate was during the non-pandemic time. If she had a choice to switch her rotation schedule now, she would jump on it in a heartbeat, but the schedule was done in June 2019 for the entire year. No one in her class would switch their autopsy rotation with her during the pandemic. Who would have guessed last year that in April 2020 there would be a surge in death rates due to a pandemic in the US?

The boat ride was only three miles, crossing under the Pelham Bay Park Bridge and the City Island Bridge, but it felt an eternity. The boat she took had only five other people, and the captain. They all appeared to be physically fit, rough-looking men. She felt out of place. The boat was open with no roof to avoid dreadful rain, so she stood the entire time holding on to her parka hood over her head. Her hands were getting so numb with cold even though she had gloves on. It was dreadful to even think to sit on the cold and wet iron seats in the boat.

She did not understand who these men were in the boat with her. They were watching her uncomfortably, likely wondering why an attractive young female was going to Potter's field, a burial site. That was the same question Samantha had in her mind as she rode in a run-down old peeling-green colored boat with rough looking guys who are probably going there to dig burial sites. Why did she have to go there when she signed up to attend the Long Island Hospital coroner's office? What would she learn about autopsy there? Would she have a decent and safe place to stay? Where would she stay; in a decrepit old prison? Would she be able to meet her attending doctor from Long Island Hospital? Who in their right mind would ask a pathology resident to join them at Hart Island for training? In fact, no one should do autopsies on the dead due to COVID-19. Why a week there? Why did they summon her a day earlier?

No one in her residency could help prepare her or answer her questions because no one had ever gone to Hart Island for an autopsy rotation. They gave the assignment to her a day before by her hospital in the Bronx, New York, her home hospital. *Let's just hope that it will be just one week*, she thought.

The fog grew more dense as they approached Hart Island. The men around her became more and more apprehensive as they were approaching the port, but they seemed to know what to do. They pulled the ropes to tie the boat. They were moving rapidly as the captain carefully parked the boat. Samantha felt her chest getting tense as one man extended his hairy hand to her so she could jump onto land. She took it. The boat was bobbing as she took a faithful jump at least three feet away to land. She grunted as she safely landed on the grass. Thank God she only had a lightweight duffle bag.

A disappointment settled in as no one was around the port to greet her. It appeared to be an empty grass field for miles with the eerie sound of wind blowing. Most of the shoreline was black rocky cliffs. No one else was there, and no other boats were parked around the island. It was not a tourist destination by any means. She could make out some faint building structures in the midst of the fog. Everything looked dark and gloomy.

Sad feelings arose from the entire island, as if all those buried bodies were crying. It was matching the history of Hart Island, 45 acres, a mile-long island which took bodies of people with no known next of kin since 1869. Back in that time, they forced the people with tuberculosis to live there as infection spread in New York City. The tuberculosis cases were rampant and afflicted one in seven Americans. The New York City government bought the island and built a few rehabilitation places for the people who were exiled from the city due to their diseases.

This remote island was a perfect place to separate the diseased people for quarantine. They allowed no family or friends to visit. They faced lonely deaths, buried without funeral services. In fact, no one knew when they were dead.

They buried the diseased bodies from tuberculosis on the northern tip of the island. In 1985, the AIDS epidemic drove the funeral homes to close their doors to those who died of the disease. The island buried the bodies stricken with AIDS, and most likely became the single largest burial ground in the country for people with AIDS. They buried the bodies in the middle section of the island. Now, the island was being used to bury the COVID-19 infected corpses. The Department of Corrections now controlled the cemetery. The city hired contract workers, who along with the inmates buried the dead as more bodies piled in from the city in refrigerated trucks. The workers dug several large linear holes, 12 feet deep, for the COVID-19 inflicted dead bodies on the southern part of the island.

The whole island had been used as a common public burial ground for over 150 years, containing over one million unclaimed bodies.

Samantha was walking toward the faintly visible building structures without knowing exactly where she was going. Men from the boat were also walking toward the buildings. No one talked.

No one asked her where she was going. The wind swept and the icy rain blew in all directions as she tried to catch up with the men. There was no point opening up the umbrella as the sharp rain was painfully hitting her face, fogging up her glasses There appeared nothing to ensure hot meals as she was approaching the crumbling buildings. She regretted not packing at least a peanut butter sandwich for lunch.

In front of the building site, a signpost stood with the inscription: POTTER'S FIELD. RESTRICTED AREA.

She could not tell whether she was entering the prison or a cremation memorial service center.

She was merely following men. She did not know the exact purpose of their trip to Hart Island, but surely, it was for a different purpose from hers. They all entered the white painted door with another sign, RISTRICTED AREA. In front was a desk attended by a uniformed male guard or police officer; Samantha could not decipher.

"Can I help you?" asked the guard.

"We are from Gabby construction in the Bronx. I am John, he is Brad, that guy over there is Scott and that punk on this side is Ted." All eyes went to the punk and some chuckled.

"Ok. We were expecting you. You can go next door here and get yourself a hazmat suit. Change your clothes and we will give you a locker to put your belongings. Then someone there will tell you where to go."

Then the guard looked at Samantha, momentarily hidden by bulky men. "What about you? What are you doing here?" the guard said.

"Um, I am, I am here to, to meet Dr. Falkner?" Samantha said timidly. All the guys were still there, hanging around to see Samantha as they were curious to see what this girl was all about.

"Oh, yeah, I heard about you. He is not here yet. You can sit there and wait for him." The guard was pointing his finger at the chair at the end of his desk.

Samantha moved toward the chair to sit when Ted, the punk, said, "Who is Dr. Fucker? What is she up to? Is she digging the graves with us?"

"Hey guys, move and mind your own business," the guard said, pointing to the next door where they should go. Reluctantly, the guys moved and opening the door, looking back at Samantha, obviously not satisfied to know why she was there. The door finally closed, and all the men went somewhere else where Samantha could not follow any longer. The room became uncomfortably quiet.

The guard was staring at the computer monitor and avoided eye contact with Samantha. She wanted to ask a million questions but decided to be quiet for a while. A clock on the wall sounded louder as the room became eerily quiet. She looked at the guard, hoping to find a friendly gesture or eye contact at least, but to no avail. He was just looking at his computer.

"Do you know when Dr. Falkner is coming to meet me here?" she mustered some courage and asked.

"He should be here soon. I thought he is coming with you. Next boat is due in about an hour or so."

"Do you know what I am supposed to do here?"

"You tell me. Your guess is good as mine."

Samantha was hoping he would divulge more information, but it was hard to get anything out of him. She wanted to know so many things; did he ever meet Dr. Falkner? What is he like? Does he come here often? Did any pathology resident come here last month with Dr. Falkner? Where is she going to stay for a week? Is she able to commute back and forth from her apartment in the Bronx? Are there boats coming and going and if so, how frequently? When is her next meal? Was she supposed to dig burial sites as those construction guys? Are they staying on this island for a while or are they commuting? She regretted not asking all these inquiries before she came here.

The instruction she received a day before just said that she was to report at the Bronx port to catch a boat at 10:00 am and meet Dr. Falkner, a medical examiner on Hart Island. Room and Board were to be provided for a week. She realized there was no ticket to board the boat. She did not see construction guys paying for the ticket either.

She sat there twiddling her thumbs and regretting not bringing a book or journal article to read. The rain was hitting the window next to her very hard now. She was glad that she was not riding in the boat now. She could see nothing through the window. It should face toward the water and she could not make out anything.

It would be the longest hour she would ever experience in waiting.

CHAPTER 2

Dr. Falkner

Samantha took her cell phone out from her purse and looked at it. It had no cell coverage, and no Wi-Fi. She immediately looked at the guard to ask if there was a Wi-Fi connection, but she refrained. She was not sure why she was refraining to ask the question. She got up from the chair and walked around the office to gather any information she could muster. But there were no signs, posted notes, advertisements of any sort, pictures of anyone, or even graffiti on the walls. Just old peeling yellowish-white walls. As she was walking around, the guard glanced at her but said nothing.

"How long have you been working here?" Samantha tried to make small talk.

"Are you staying here for a week?" the guard asked her without answering her question.

"Yes, do you know where I am supposed to stay?" she asked firmly.

"Not sure, but probably the prison. That's the only building with any accommodation and food around here. It's probably the safest place … unless you want to be with the dead bodies."

What a pleasant thought—to be with the dead bodies. But come to think of it, the dead cannot hurt her. It is the living who can hurt her. It was also dreadful to think she might have to stay in a prison cell for a week with all the male criminals. She now imagined the worst; iron bars, being locked inside a cell with only a toilet and a lousy bed with a thin wool brown blanket. All the inmates howling and making sounds to haunt her with their insatiable desires to have long overdue sex with a woman. Indeed, she was doomed. She thought about her parents. If they knew where she was now, they would say, "Forget about the residency and get out of there!" She was the only child from a long journey of infertility problems. They had her when her mother was 42, after many episodes of miscarriages, artificial inseminations, numerous attempts for ova preservations, and even embryo adoption surrogacy. Luckily and finally, Samantha was born on their final try. They were going through the adoption application process when her mother found out she was pregnant with triplets. The other two embryos didn't make it past the first trimester.

Samantha was deep in her thoughts, contemplating to quit the residency, when the door opened and a tall man walked in, folding a black umbrella. The rain drenched him, and water was dripping from his long, tan, London Fog raincoat. "It's horrible out there!" the man said.

"Hello, there, Dr. Falkner," the guard said.

"Is this the resident from the Bronx?" Dr. Falkner asked, looking at Samantha.

"I am Samantha Parker, the resident." She extended her right hand to greet Dr. Falkner, though, disappointed to be referred to as *the resident.*

"We don't shake hands during the pandemic," he said to her rather coldly. "Did you tell her where she is to reside?" Dr. Falkner asked the guard.

"I don't know, Doc. You tell me. Is she staying at the prison?" the guard said.

"Well, it is a bit complicated. I thought the resident is a guy. We have a problem now."

They were talking as if Samantha was not there. She went back to thinking how this whole thing was a big mistake. What could she do to get out of this quickly and get back to her apartment? They were speaking to each other in indistinct voices, and Samantha looked around to the window to avoid their eye contact.

"Well, it is what it is," Dr. Falkner said, "Follow me, I will show you where you are settling in for a while. Your assignment is to help me in the morgue for a week."

Samantha quickly put away her cell phone in her purse, picked up her duffle bag and umbrella, and followed Dr. Falkner.

The chilling rain was now pouring, adding to her misery. She did not have enough time to cover her head with her hood or open her umbrella.

Asphalt quickly dissipated, followed by a gravel road, and then mud as they walked. Samantha almost jogged to keep up with the tall man as his long legs moved with ease at mere walking speed, his black umbrella bouncing by the wind. She saw a searing and grim scene. At least two large trenches had been dug. Inside were cheap coffins stacked at least three piles deep, two coffins long per trench. One trench was completely dug, and the other trench was half completed. A third of the completely dug trench had cheap coffins. Black, wet soil was running down into the trench, covering part of the tops of the coffins. Mud around the perimeter was at least knee high. About ten feet away were several run-down brick buildings, all painted in a faint reddish-orange color without many windows. She followed Dr. Falkner as he entered one of the unmarked buildings.

"This is where you are going to stay for a week. Over here is the morgue where you and I will work during the day, and over there is lodging for you. There is a shower, and a studio with a bed and a small kitchen. You will find some food in the refrigerator there. The building connects to the prison," Dr. Falkner said pointing to the places.

"Where are you staying?"

"I am not staying here. I will commute from Long Island. I will come with bodies in a boat every day about this time. The problem is, I was staying here when I could not catch the boat back, but since you are a girl, I cannot stay here."

Samantha now understood why she was problematic for him. "What will we be doing in the morgue?"

"We will do a partial autopsy. Other than that, we will count, identify and tag the bodies. We will document the names, the origin of the hospital the bodies came from, and cataloging the specifics of the dead, among other things. Your job is to help me. Like any other day, I came with a lot of bodies from New York City today and we have our work cut out for us. Get yourself together, change, and come out. You will need to gear up to protect yourself. I will meet you here in five minutes."

Samantha quickly went into the studio, seeing a door leading directly to the morgue. It looked rather gloomy with just bare essentials; a twin-size bed, a small desk, a rotary phone, not really a kitchen, but a two-coiled electric stove on a kitchen table, and a small refrigerator with a freezer on top. She did not have the time to open it to see what was inside there. She put her belongings on top of the bed. She saw that she had a lock from inside the door which made her feel somewhat relieved. She quickly left to gear up.

She saw Dr. Falkner zipping his space jumpsuit gown with a tube sticking out toward the back, an N95 mask, bonnet, face shield, shoe covers, and double gloves. He looked like a person about to walk on the moon.

"Hurry, get on with it now! The bodies are coming in," he urged, looking at an unprepared Samantha.

She was frantically trying to figure out what to wear first. She had some experience putting on a surgical gown when she was a medical student in her surgery rotation, but not to the extent of what Dr. Falkner was wearing with all the additional personal protective equipment (PPE). She never wore a space jumpsuit gown with a tube coming out of the back. During her training, she did many of the monkey see and monkey do procedures. Unfortunately, there wasn't time to explain things and give proper instructions in medical training. She was quickly observing how Dr. Falkner geared up and tried to replicate it as quickly as possible.

"Does this morgue place have negative pressure?" Samantha asked hesitantly, and then immediately regretted asking the question since the building looked so old, and rather obvious it did not have a negative pressure facility.

"No, can't you see they built in the 1920s, maybe in the 1890s, who knows?" he shouted out to her, rather irritated at the question.

Luckily, the extent of anger from Dr. Falkner was muffled and barely audible because of the mask and face shield. In fact, his body language such as eye signals, creases of the eyebrows and smiles were not possible to see through the protective gear. Samantha was already sweating, and her glasses fogged up every time she took a breath.

She was barely putting on her gloves when suddenly a garage-like door opened from the opposite side of the morgue with a loud creaking sound, jolting her. She had no idea that there was another door to the morgue. Two men in black hazmat suits and facial masks came in with a dead body on a gurney. They wrapped the body in a white plastic bag tied with ropes around the neck, mid-body and the feet to carry it.

"Put it on the table here! And put the rest of them in the drawers as usual," Dr. Falkner ordered them.

He was pointing to a typical morgue table made of stainless steel with a running water faucet at one end. Next to the table were the usual tools for autopsy; several scalpels, a ruler, different scissors, formalin glass, plastic jar containers, forceps, a large stainless-steel bucket to weigh the organs, a scale, and an electric saw to open the skull. She also noted several aseptically prepared plastic bags containing long, automatic, spring-loaded needles. They consisted of an inner needle connected to a trough, or shallow receptacle, covered by a sheath and attached to a spring-loaded mechanism normally used by interventional radiologists.

The two men grunted as they put the body on the morgue table. The body appeared heavy, not just for dead weight, but obesity. The plastic bag was stretched fully, barely covering the body with the zipper almost torn away. Dr. Falkner waited and looked to make sure Samantha was fully covered and protected with her gear.

"Are you ready?" he asked, "Open it!"

CHAPTER 3

"I need a guy resident!"

Samantha hesitated. She looked at Dr. Falkner to see if he was joking. He was not. She knew part of the job in her pathology residency training was to perform the autopsy. But this was not just an autopsy—it was a COVID-19 case. In fact, all the bodies the men were bringing in and stacking up were all COVID-19 cases. Soon the room would be full of COVID-19 dead bodies. She couldn't imagine that she would open all the bodies from the plastic bags and doing the things Dr. Falkner expected her to do. What did he say? Counting, identifying, tagging, documenting the names and the origin of the hospital and cataloging the specifics of the dead? Samantha was gifted in remembering and memorizing things, but she was not sure whether those were the only things Dr. Falkner said.

As she was trying to untie the ropes around the head of the dead body, the two men came back again with another body on a gurney behind Dr. Falkner. They were doing their own work without paying too much attention to the two doctors, all suited up as if they were used to their routine jobs. They did not look like the construction workers Samantha traveled with on the boat, although it was very difficult to tell who was who, with masks covering most of their faces. The ropes and the plastic bag were soaking wet from the rain, and it was difficult for her to untie the rope.

As she finally pulled the rope around the neck toward her, the head moved in her direction. She wanted to scream.

She had heard the horror stories from her friends who had done autopsy rotations before her, so she was somewhat prepared to face this. However, when she touched the dead body through the plastic bag, she was very tense, scared and horrified.

Dr. Falkner looked at Samantha. He was disgusted. He took over and untied the ropes himself. Then he unzipped the plastic bag. It revealed the head of the dead. It was a morbidly obese Caucasian male. Big fat face, gray, thin unwashed curly hair all tangled up, eyes closed, mouth biting the cut-out ventilator tube and the thick, hardly recognizable neck due to fatty tissue all around.

As Dr. Falkner unzipped the bag all the way to the toes, Samantha recognized there were pink fluids under the shoulder and along the side of the body where she was standing. The body was clothed in a hospital gown with spotty wet areas. She could not tell whether it was water from the rain or body fluid. A cut urinary catheter was attached to his penis. The right toe had a toe tag with his name, birth date, and a medical record number.

"Now I want you to take the plastic bag out, but carefully. Make sure the fluid does not get on you," Dr. Falkner said to her. "On my count of three, must pull the bag away. Got it?"

As soon as he said that, he was already moving the dead body toward him by grabbing the arm of the dead from Samantha's side with the intravenous (IV) needle still stuck in the arm with blue tape, rotating and lifting the body as if he was hugging the body. Rigor mortis had already set in the body, and it was turning toward Dr. Falkner as he moved it. Samantha grabbed hold of the plastic bag and pulled it toward her, hoping not to spill the pink fluid collection on her jumpsuit.

Dr. Falkner grunted, "Now pull... pull!" but Samantha could not get a firm grip on the other side of the plastic zipper to pull the bag out.

"Oh, shit! I need a guy resident!" it frustrated him, putting the body back into the supine position. He stood there for a minute, then asked one man who was transporting the bodies to help. Samantha moved to one side, letting the other guy to come over and take her place.

"I am not going to do that, Doc!" the man responded. "You guys are all geared up, and I'm just wearing this piece of shit—what do you call this? Hazmat suit? No way, José! You think an inmate like me has no value? I am not dying with the virus!"

It shocked Samantha to hear that those men were inmates. She knew Hart Island had a correctional facility, a prison, but she didn't make the obvious connection that it was the inmates who were working to move the bodies and digging the mass graves on this island.

"All right, all right!" Dr. Falkner said. "Get back here! We are going to do this slowly. What was your name?"

"Samantha."

"Yeah, Samantha, Sam. I am going to call you Sam. You are going to pull the bag out on my count of three. Ready?"

Samantha got closer to the body and this time she was grabbing the bag on two sides, one from the head and the other from the mid-body.

"Okay. One, two, three!"

She pulled the bag out, and the pink fluid spilled all over her arms and on Dr. Falkner's abdomen and pelvic area.

"Shit!" he said, letting the fluid drip all the way down to his foot. "Fucking fat people!" he added. The plastic bag was pulled only partially; a job halfway done.

"One more time, Sam. Ready? One, two, three!" Samantha successfully pulled the plastic bag all the way to the groin area, spilling some more of the pink fluid on the floor.

"Okay, well, the rest is easy," he said, while he was putting the body back on the table. He walked around toward the feet of the body and pulled off the plastic bag.

"Don't worry, the serosanguinous fluid won't penetrate through your jumpsuit. It is air and liquid tight."

Oh no, it is serosanguinous fluid, Samantha thought. It was most likely contagious, filled with the COVID-19 virus. In fact, it could be in highly concentrated form.

"Wait a minute, Dr. Falkner. I am not ready to do this," Samantha said.

There was a moment of silence after that. He looked at her intensely through his face shield and waited for her to say something more.

"I am not ready to do this. I know I am supposed to go to a morgue for autopsy rotation for a month, but this is not what I expected," Samantha said, mustering up her courage. She was in fact very upset with the current situation. She did not sign up to be a physician, a pathologist when she had to put her life in danger by taking the risk of getting infected with COVID-19.

"You think I like this?" Dr. Falkner responded angrily. "Who the hell do you think you are? We are in this shit now, and even I have no choice. We have to bury these bodies as fast as we can before they become more infectious. God knows what would happen if the bodies get blown up with intestinal bacteria and aerosolize all over the world." He paused for a few seconds, then continued, "You are doing a service to this world, and to New York City. Now, get back to work!" He was shouting by this point, and even startled some inmates.

Samantha wasn't sure what she did afterward. They were quietly doing the work. She cut open the hospital gown using scissors, and inscribed the weight, characteristics of the dead body, name, age, gender, and race onto a piece of paper Dr. Falkner provided. It was difficult to find the name of the hospital where the body came from. There was no time to pull the IV line from the dead man's arm, or the intubation tube out of his mouth as they struggled to place the body into a coffin. The inmates had brought in a cheap, light colored wood coffin. One job for Samantha was to print the name of the dead in large letters using a magic marker on all sides and the top of the coffin.

"There are 22 more coming, Doc!" one inmate called out.

CHAPTER 4

The research

It was one of the most exhausting days, Samantha thought. They had not eaten the whole time. It was hard to take a break and eat because the physical protective gear was difficult to get on and off. Also, all their gear must be so expensive to stock since everything is meant for a onetime use and then thrown away. Samantha had to be mindful of every step she took, like touching her face to scratch it. Eating felt foreign to her. The last meal she had was a dinner the night before, and she hardly had an appetite since she was worried about the unknowns in the day ahead of her. *If only she had a good meal,* she thought. She was almost fainting due to hunger, and her stomach made constant noises. She could also hear Dr. Falkner's stomach growling across the table. *The living have to eat to live,* she thought.

They did not talk much throughout the day except for the commands he had to make for her to jot down the results. The inmates took the bodies in the caskets away after she wrote the names of the dead on the coffins. Around 4:00 pm, they both carefully removed their jumpsuits without touching any part of the body, especially their face. Samantha watched how Dr. Falkner undressed first, and then she did the exact same. It was rather hard to get the jumpsuit off of her because she was soaking wet with sweat. The airtight jumpsuit and N95 mask made her body sweat an embarrassing amount. She recognized how heavy everything was when she was finally free of the extra weight from the gear. They put all the used gear in the red biohazard garbage can. He washed his arms first, as there was only one clean sink in the morgue.

"You should have changed into scrubs," he said, noting that Samantha was still wearing her street clothes. She did not even have time to change into scrubs before they started. Typical male doctors, she thought. They never tell the critical information to others. She didn't even know where the scrubs were kept. She felt filthy in her own sweat and angry, which made her even more hot.

"You should take a shower first," he said, probably noticing her sweat.

She did not hesitate. She went into the studio, locked the door behind her, took off her clothes and put them into the garbage basket in the kitchen. She did not want to even keep her clothes. She went into the shower without checking to see if there was even a towel to dry off with or soap available. She just wanted to get all the germs off. To her surprise, there was a big soap bar, shampoo, and several towels. It took a while to get the hot water, but she just stood there happy to be under the water spray, even if it was cold. She felt violated against her wish to be there. She began to cry while the hot water was hitting her face, and soon the crying led to sobbing. She could not control herself. She thought about all those people who died with the disease, and no one claiming the bodies for proper funerals. How futile life was…people were dying left and right regardless of their age, young and old alike, and she lamented for the futility in life and the miserable condition she was facing with such an unfriendly attending doctor.

Self-pity usually leads to a downhill spiral and lands in depression.

She was angry. She couldn't understand why she wasn't allowed to go back to her apartment. She felt trapped. She got out of the shower and couldn't wait to confront the nasty doctor with all the questions she formulated in the shower. She wrapped herself with a big white towel and began digging through her duffle bag. She had packed lightly for five days; underwear, socks, some thin sweaters and a pair of jeans. She was putting her bra and underwear on when she remembered seeing some scrubs and a large dirty linen hamper in the bathroom. She went back into the bathroom and got the ugly green-colored scrubs. Of course, they were all large size, probably for Dr. Falkner. She wore the scrubs anyway because she did not want to contaminate any more of her own clothes and have to throw them out in the trash. She smelled like a man, thanks to the Irish Spring deodorant soap and cheap men's dandruff shampoo.

Samantha walked out, opening the door with such a force that it made a loud noise. She was ready to confront the doctor.

"I am taking a shower too!" he said, coming in without her permission before she could say anything to him.

She had her bras and underwear all spread out on the bed. She didn't think that he would come in to take a shower. He didn't care that she was staring at him, flabbergasted as he went into the bathroom and ran the shower water.

"Open the refrigerator and make some sandwiches! There is a rotisserie chicken and bread!" he shouted.

What a gut he had to command her to cook for him, Samantha thought.

But she was starving, so she did as he commanded. There was even a microwave oven she used to heat the chicken. She normally did not eat like this. Her parents brought her up like a princess, but there was no time to complain about the food. She found some paper dishes and bottled water. Dr. Falkner came out, dressed in new scrubs, and sat on the only chair at the table. Samantha grabbed her sandwich and sat on the bed, moving her duffle bag to the other side of the bed. They ate the dry sandwiches quietly.

"I have some wine; do you want some?" he asked.

"No, thank you."

"Hey, I am sorry. I think the whole thing sucks too." There was silence for a while.

He got up and found a wine bottle from the kitchen drawer. He poured red wine into a paper cup and sipped it.

"Hey, I am a bit worried about you staying here at night," Dr. Falkner began. "The inmates will be locked in after 5:00 pm. The only people who are free to walk around after that are the prison wardens. I do not like the idea that you are here alone. They might have a key to this room. I don't know."

Oh great, Samantha thought.

"The last resident was a guy from a Brooklyn hospital, and he stayed for a week and nothing happened. You must input all the data of the dead into my laptop at night. You can even start writing the manuscript. The problem is there is only one boat going back to Long Island around 5:30 pm, and they don't wait around for me. One time I missed the boat, and I slept here with the resident. Do you live on Long Island?" Dr. Falkner asked.

"No, I live in the Bronx," Samantha replied.

"Yeah, that's the problem. Do you want to go back to Long Island and catch the train to the Bronx?"

"Why do I have to stay here? I don't understand."

"Well, it is not a regular ferry that comes to this island. I have to arrange every trip here, and there is no boat that could come back and forth from the Bronx unless they pick up the contractor guys to help out with the digging. And that's not every day."

Samantha didn't respond. She again felt trapped. What could she do?

"Where do those contractor guys stay?" she asked.

"Not sure. I think they go back, but much earlier than when we are done," he said. "Hey, thanks for helping me, but there is one more thing I need to tell you. I need to do a partial autopsy and get some samples from the lungs, heart and other organs. I need a young subject, male and female, an infant, and a skinny person in their 40s. Today, I did not get any ideal subjects. I am doing research on the different types of people who die from COVID-19. You will be helping me to procure these samples. You can be a co-author of the study if you want. I need this to get a promotion this year."

"Is that what you care about, a promotion?" Samantha was in shock. She noticed Dr. Falkner kept calling her "hey." He probably forgot her name—co-author's name.

"Yeah, a promotion. I have just this year to get promoted. I already burned eight years as an assistant professor but did not get enough papers published to get the promotion. Otherwise I will be kicked out from my academic place, and then who knows where I will end up getting a job. I want the Chief Deputy Coroner job in Long Island and need to publish so I can replace that bitch. I bought a house on Long Island and have an 18-month-old son and a wife to support, and I do not want to move to

New York City for a new job. Can you imagine being in New York City now? I would kill me doing the medical examiner's job."

"I will stay here tonight. Why don't you go? You will miss the 5:30 boat." Samantha said, disgusted at him.

The Long Island Medical Examiner's job would be easier than the New York City Medical Examiner's job, and she could understand that he has a responsibility to support his family, but to jeopardize his life and hers to publish an academic article for his promotion? And eventually get a position he wants by pushing out some woman? He was rather selective in picking his sample subjects. Is he targeting an epidemiology study by doing that?

What a stupid idea, she thought. She didn't want to see his sight even though he had beautiful, mesmerizing blue eyes, while he was eating his sandwich like a pig.

"Just give me your laptop and tell me what to do." Samantha said irritably.

"Okay. I just want you to know there is no cell tower or Wi-Fi unless you go to the prison where the wardens stay. There is only one area you can go in the prison to get a connection, and I do not recommend you venture out there tonight. They have a cafeteria, but it's a lousy one. If you have a cell phone, forget about calling. There is a phone here—you have to dial 9 first to call out. The prison wardens have to connect your call to the outside, and they might listen to your conversation, so be careful what you say."

He packed his belongings quickly and instructed her to input all the data into his laptop computer. He already had many columns of data in his excel sheet, dating back from late February 2020. The numbers of the dead were steadily increasing by the day.

"Do you want me to call anyone for you once I get to Long Island? Your parents, a boyfriend?"

"No, they know where I am," she lied.

"Well, you still have some same food left over, as you saw. There are some instant cup noodles in that kitchen drawer. I will get something else tomorrow. What do you want to eat?" Samantha could not think fast enough. The whole thing was so surreal and hard to digest, let alone decide what to eat the next day.

"I don't know," she said.

"Okay, I will get something. Oh yeah, clean up here and make sure the garbage bags are all out there near the garage door tomorrow morning, including the scrubs," he instructed, and left, closing all the doors tightly from the outside.

CHAPTER 5

Panic

Samantha could not believe he actually just took off. "Bastard!" she said out loud. She looked around and saw that there were still a few bodies left in the morgue they had not finished with. The morgue was not refrigerated, and the bodies would decompose. Samantha went into the studio and locked the door behind her. She sat and stared at the empty paper dishes Dr. Falkner left on the table. She was not sure how she could fall asleep here, all alone in such a strange place. This was a nightmare! Who could imagine what she was going through?

She moved the kitchen table and the chair against the doorknob to block the entry way from outside. She couldn't get over how insensitive Dr. Falkner was being, not knowing if the prison wardens had a key to the studio. This must have been his temporary place until he finished his autopsy research project. She figured all the items in here must be his own stuff that he brought in. Samantha untied and flipped over her large scrub pants to see the inscription, LONG ISLAND CORONER.

Of course, it is his!

She was eating his food, wearing his scrubs, using his towels and soaps. It creeped her out to be borrowing his stuff. This was classic. Medical professionals never tell residents the details they need to hear, even what to bring for survival. Wouldn't it be helpful to tell residents what to expect, what we need, where it is, and what the accommodations would be?

She thought about the guard who she met earlier that day. He must have been a prison warden. He saw her and asked her where she was going to stay. He could probably find out where she is now. She wondered how many prisoners and wardens were on this island.

Samantha got up quickly and moved the kitchen table and chair away from the door. She had to secure the garage door and the entry door from inside of the morgue better. She went out of the studio and picked up some ropes to tie the garage door. There was a loop in the middle of the garage door, but the rope was not long, unable to attach to the side of the door where a piece of iron was sticking out. She connected a few ropes and tied them together to make one long rope. She secured the rope, securing the garage door to prevent it from being opened from the outside. She then moved the morgue table to the other door she and Dr. Falkner had entered through and pushed it against the doorknob.

It did not look too secure. Someone could easily push the door open from the outside. There wasn't any way to lock it from the inside, so she opened the door again to see if there was a key lock from the outside. There wasn't one, so she rearranged the morgue table again. Samantha looked around to see what else she could use to help secure the door shut.

There was not much except for the dead bodies, and there was no way she was going to move the bodies.

She could not believe she was actually amongst the dead. In fact, there were more dead bodies than alive ones on the island. She reminded herself that the dead could not hurt her, except what if the virus was seeping out of the bags and being emitted into the air?

She ran into the studio, locked the door, and pushed the chair and table against the door again. She was breathing hard. The green scrub pants were covering her sneakers and dragging along on the floor, so she changed her scrub pants again, and folded up the bottom to fit her leg length.

She sat on the bed and took out her cell phone, only to notice she had no cell coverage or Wi-Fi connection. She wanted to call Ed Liu, her boyfriend. He should arrive to the CDC in Atlanta by now. He was going there to join the folks in the infectious division to travel to Wuhan, China, to investigate the origin of the virus.

Samantha and Ed met in college at Cornell and maintained a relationship, even though they were diverging in their career paths. She went to medical school, and he joined the Army ROTC as they paid for his college tuition, then attended a PhD program in DC to be a scientist in bioweapons.

I will worry him sick tonight, she thought. They contacted each other regularly, especially when she was changing rotations.

Samantha scrolled through the contact list on her cell phone. She thought about using the rotary phone to contact her parents. They were traveling and having the time of their lives on a cruise celebrating their 50th anniversary.

They left a month ago for the Mediterranean, and the entire trip was about two months. Samantha had been anxious about their trip from the beginning, but her parents were adamant that they would be fine. When they left on the cruise in late February, the virus was not defined as a pandemic yet. It was on March 11th, 2020 when the World Health Organization (WHO) officially declared COVID-19 a pandemic. The cell coverage for them was spotty, and her parents usually called her when they landed somewhere while touring. Besides, she could not tell them where she is now as they would worry sick. It would be even harder for them to understand why she was here at Hart Island. They were not happy that she became a doctor, anyway.

Samantha wanted to talk to Dr. Wells, her resident director, to update him about what was going on, but there was no way to contact him as she did not have his direct phone number. This experience here on Hart Island was so upsetting. It was absolutely inappropriate to put any resident here, exposing them to the deadly virus for the sake of a stupid doctor, or whoever it is for a stupid research project. Samantha planned to report this abuse to her residency director the next day and go back to the Bronx by catching the boat with the contractor guys. She was fuming in anger the more she thought about her conditions. She was ready to attack Dr. Falkner and even take his medical license away for abusing the trainee. She would also contact the resident union representative in New York City to report this doctor.

After contemplating many tactics of revenge against Dr. Falkner, she looked at his laptop and input the data she wrote on the paper that day. She had nothing else to do that night. She looked into other files on the laptop and saw that he had begun the manuscript; explaining the methodology, an introduction regarding the COVID-19 infection, and his findings of how people died with it. She had to admit; it was a very interesting article that he was writing. It was methodical, and well written.

She couldn't believe how he could write so well with full details but cannot communicate with her the same way.

In a separate file, he had his family photos. She saw what appeared to be his house, his wife and his son. His wife was beautiful, blonde, just like him. Samantha felt like she was intruding into his personal life, but the more she looked at the personal photos, the more interested she became about Dr. Falkner. Her anger subsided, and the desires to get him into trouble were dissolving.

She got hungry as the night deepened. A small window next to the kitchen was still dripping with the rain. She found the cup of instant noodles Dr. Falkner told her about and ate it. It was getting cold, so it was nice to eat something hot. Samantha wore her parka hood and wrapped her body inside the bed. She wondered if the sheets and blanket were clean and if Dr. Falkner or the previous resident had slept there, but she was too tired to change the sheets and she didn't even know if there was a clean sheet for her to use.

She still smelled the Irish men's soap but could not tell if it was coming from her or from his blanket.

Samantha fell asleep in an infant position with her parka overcoat and blanket warming her head and body. She dreamed about the heavy, dead body falling onto her in the middle of the night.

It startled her awake, so she got up and sat on the bed. The bedside light next to her was still on, illuminating the studio, so she turned it off. She looked at the window for a while, making sure no one was coming, then she went back to sleep.

CHAPTER 6

Centers for Disease Control and Prevention (CDC)

Ed Liu was constantly calling Samantha, but his cell phone calls did not go through. It just said, NOT AVAILABLE. He left multiple voice messages. Texts did not go through either and kept saying, DELIVERY FAILED.

Where the hell is she, he thought. He knew she was rather apprehensive about the new autopsy rotation and mentioned something about Hart Island. He did not even know where that was. He thought it was some autopsy place in the Bronx near her apartment. It had been a long time since he last saw her because he hardly had time and they lived far apart.

He lived in Washington DC, had finished his PhD in infectious diseases in the pandemic division and worked at Abby Laboratory as a scientist focusing on virology. The last time they saw each other was right before Christmas time when he stopped in New York for a few hours before he took off to Ohio to visit his parents. The CDC sent him to Atlanta multiple times during his internship year, and to South Africa once last year to visit their lab for a collaborative research project on the Ebola virus.

This time, he was back at the CDC where several people with expertise in virology gathered to visit Wuhan, China to determine the origin of the coronavirus. He could not believe they had chosen him to represent the US group. His boss, Dr. Allen, trusted Ed more than himself to represent Abby and to understand the virology, and often said Ed "is the guru of viruses." Ed had extensive expertise in viruses and was widely recognized for his intelligence. Dr. Allen trusted Ed exclusively, and made him the Associate Research Director only after a few years.

Dr. Allen was the company CEO who dealt with the financial and overall control of Abby Laboratory and did not have the technical and scientific knowledge as Ed.

There would be ten people going to China. The World Health Organization (WHO) went to Wuhan, China in early January 2020, but they had failed to return fully informed about the magnitude of the contagious nature of the virus.

In fact, it was reported as an epidemic only in the region of Wuhan and was not expected to spread like SARS in 2002, which spread worldwide within a few months and then was quickly contained. Now, the CDC did not trust WHO reports for obvious reasons. COVID-19 was thought to have arisen from a seafood market, perhaps in smuggled pangolins used for both food and medicine.

Another possibility was bats, because these two animals have similar genetic codes as what we find in the coronavirus. Exactly how the virus jumped from a wild animal to other animals or humans remains a mystery. It amazed the CDC group China already had the full genetic code for COVID-19. Their speed in research was impressive. However, there was a rumor now that the virus may not have originated from the seafood market.

The Wuhan Institute of Virology (WIV) lab is located just three miles away from the seafood market. A scientist from the WIV said that COVID-19 was most likely spread from a bat since its genetic makeup is 96% identical to the sequence of COVID-19.

There was speculation that patient zero in Wuhan did not contract the virus from the seafood market, but from within the lab led by a local scientist who also worked on bats at the Wuhan Municipal Centers for Disease Control and Prevention. The Chinese government withdrew this from newspapers as speculation and stated that there was no evidence the virus came from laboratories in Wuhan. They emphatically denied any link to the institute and proclaimed that they have a strict regulatory regime and code of conduct for research.

The WHO also supported the Chinese government, stating that COVID-19 did not come from the laboratories in Wuhan. They added that the only reason the Wuhan lab knew so much about the coronavirus was because of Dr. Shei, the Director of the Institute, had studied the topic for most of her life since SARS in 2003.

Ed did not think he was qualified to be there. They chose him to visit Wuhan, China, along with other gifted scientists from all over the US to determine several things; the origin of the virus, its evolution in nature and spillover to humans, and whether it was an accidental or deliberate release from a lab, or a genetic manipulation of a pathogen as a bioweapon. He was excited for the opportunity even though only reason they chose him was because he is Chinese, but he hardly spoke the language. At least he could speak some and communicate the basics.

He was born in Ohio to Chinese parents who immigrated there as scientists. They were both PhDs at Ohio State University and worked in the research laboratories in the medical field. It disappointed them that Ed did not go into medicine, but his younger brothers saved him by becoming medical doctors.

The middle brother was already practicing, and his youngest brother was in residency. His parents always said that Ed was the smartest, tallest, and most handsome of all his siblings. Ed was fit, especially after his ROTC military training, and he maintained his muscular and fit body and postures. Ed was not satisfied with simply learning medical knowledge, but he had to dig deeply with one focus—he preferred to understand viruses that can cause pandemics, devastating the entire globe much more than any human diseases. To develop a vaccine against a specific virus could be more powerful and heroic than what any medical doctor could achieve, in his opinion. Ed was proud of his accomplishments and confident in his own ability to save the world when the time came to show his heroism. His parents had an innate bias that Ed should be a medical doctor or lawyer, but Ed knew a PhD can discover cures for diseases more than medical doctors. Ed did not want to argue against his parents for he was an obedient and honorable son who would never lecture his parents.

They were not too happy about Ed seeing Samantha for many years. They wanted their firstborn male child to carry out their names and maintain their Chinese heritage by marrying a Chinese girl. Also, they were devout Buddhists and Samantha and her family were Christians.

Ed was a source of disappointment from his parent's perspectives. His parents expected too much of Ed, maybe because he was a first-born son. No woman was good enough for Ed because he was "so smart, tall, physically fit, stunningly handsome, kind and gentle" as his parents always put it. Deep down, Ed was confident his parents accepted him. Perhaps his parents worried most about his future income as a scientist, just like themselves, who were less than medical doctors.

Ed thought going back to Wuhan, China as a virologist expert would make them even more proud. They indeed were immensely proud and joked with him over the phone about getting a cute, young Chinese wife while he was visiting China.

They expected the trip to be at least one week, depending on the progress of their findings. They were all staying at the same hotel near the Wuhan lab. Wuhan still had a strict lockdown and curfew orders from the government in place. So, unfortunately, a tour was not on their agenda. Also, the Chinese government was reluctant of their visit to the WIV, and Ed was not sure how they would treat a bunch of US scientists. After all, the WHO scientists came, checked and approved of all the findings from the WIV.

They were all expected to fly to China late tomorrow evening, and it frustrated Ed that Samantha was unreachable. He did not have much more time to call her since there were a lot of meetings scheduled before their departure.

CHAPTER 7

Baduk (Go)

January 6, 2020 (85 days earlier)

Mrs. Emily Lee Parker was excited to see her neighbor Mrs. Kong finally come back from Wuhan, China on January 6, 2020. Mrs. Kong was there for almost two months. She left right before the Thanksgiving holiday to visit her sister's family. Mrs. Kong lived alone in San Francisco after her husband passed away about two years ago.

She was becoming more and more lonely living in a big mansion all alone, so the trips to China became frequent and routine. She was even contemplating a permanent move to Wuhan, China, where her sister and sister's family lived.

What am I going to do in a seven-bedroom house by myself? The kids are all grown up and have their own families to look after all over the States, and they're not even visiting me in San Francisco, she thought.

The only friend she had was Emily, who lived next door to her, and they played the game Baduk regularly; on Mondays, Wednesdays and Fridays. Mrs. Kong, like Emily, was a woman of means and lived in a quiet residential area in Potrero Hill.

The Potrero Hill neighborhood house, affectionately known as the NABE, sits at the top of De Haro Street at Southern Heights Avenue, and has an incredible view of San Francisco, both the Bay and East Bay. It is also next to the Mission District in downtown, where there are ample restaurants and shopping, providing convenience to those living in a busy city.

When Mrs. Kong goes to China, Emily takes care of looking after her house. She opens the house for the cleaning lady, Bita, who was from Iran. When Mrs. Kong was in China, Bita came to clean the house only once every other week. Bita took a bus or train to get there and needed the money to live. Neither Mrs. Kong nor Emily knew exactly which neighborhood in San Francisco Bita was commuting from. Bita was a sole breadwinner of the house, and her parents, two small children, and husband all lived in a small apartment crammed up like sardines. Bita often talked about her living situation with Emily and wanted to clean Emily's house when Mrs. Kong was out of town. But Emily already had a cleaning lady from her church, a Korean woman who also cooked Korean meals. Bita could not help Emily since she is Persian, not Korean, and Emily politely declined the offer but felt guilty.

Like Mrs. Kong, Emily married a wealthy Caucasian husband. Even though Emily was living and loving the American life, she missed Korean home cooked food terribly, and had to eat rice and a Korean dish for at least one meal a day. Luckily, her husband also acquired a love for Korean food after living with her during 50 years of marriage and did not argue too much about the kitchen table every day. He quietly wished, however, not to smell kimchee in his milk and cheese in the refrigerator.

Emily kept her life fairly busy after her retirement as a research coordinator under her husband's laboratory, where she met Samantha's father, Dr. Robert Parker. He was a renowned obstetrics and gynecology doctor at the San Francisco Medical School, and now he was an emeritus professor, enjoying his fully retired life playing golf. They had ups and downs in their marriage just like any other couple, but the most difficult problem they had to go though was infertility.

Luckily, much of the financial and medical access burdens was somewhat eased because of the position Robert had in medicine. They had only one child in their 40s, Samantha, whom they raised like a princess. They thought about adopting another child, but the application never went through, and they did not see the need as Samantha kept them very busy along with their professional careers.

Emily was enjoying her retired life with Robert playing golf and traveling around the world. She also attended the California Culinary Academy, which was located a few blocks away at 350 Rhode Island Street. She really enjoyed international cooking classes. The facilities included professional kitchens, student-staffed restaurants, lecture classrooms, a library, and a culinary laboratory. Emily's hope was to learn more about Korean cooking, but the curriculum of the school had not reached Korean food yet.

Another activity Emily enjoyed was playing Baduk with Mrs. Kong. They usually met in Mrs. Kong's house because sometimes they got noisy playing the game, especially at the end, and they talked endlessly over tea and cookies. Emily did not want to bother Robert, who read his books quietly.

Baduk (Go) is an abstract strategy board game for two players. It has two different colored stones; one set white and the other black, and an empty board which is a 19 x 19 grid. Players take turns placing one stone at a time, and the aim is to surround more territory than the opponent. The person with the black stones plays first, and Emily and Mrs. Kong often fought to have the black stones. Although China invented the game 2,500 years ago, it was Emily who taught Mrs. Kong how to play, and since then they were both hooked. They played the game for hours. Sometimes, Emily experimented in cooking international food she learned from the culinary school with Mrs. Kong, but Emily truthfully did not really have much talent in cooking. Mrs. Kong usually ended up cooking delicious Chinese food, but she let Emily try out a few dishes to spend more time with her.

Emily was picking Mrs. Kong up from the San Francisco airport that afternoon, as she had done for years now. Her drives to the airport had become more routine. It had been two months since she saw Mrs. Kong, and she missed her and was looking forward to having her friend back to play Baduk. Emily would also demonstrate her ability to make crème brûlée, a dessert dish she recently learned.

"Ne hou, Emily! Long time, no see, xie xie," Mrs. Kong exclaimed as she came out from the narrow terminal to where the luggage was being picked up. Mrs. Kong spoke increasingly more Chinese mixed with English when she came back from China. Emily also spoke "Konglish," a mixture of Korean and English to her many times. Between the three languages they often mixed, they understood each other fairly well and had no problems communicating.

"I worry, you come from Wuhan. You okay? Many sick from Wuhan," Emily said. She could speak perfect English, but for some reason, when she was with Mrs. Kong, she did not want to speak English perfectly.

"Okay, okay, no sick."

"Your family okay? Your sister?"

"Shi, shi." Emily gathered that meant *yes* in Mandarin.

"Miss you. Your house ok. Bita came yesterday—clean your house," Emily said.

"Xie xie, let's play Baduk. No people, family play Baduk. I miss playing."

They drove back to the NABE. Emily noticed Mrs. Kong was sniffing and coughing a little. Emily gave her the Kleenex tissues from behind the seat while she was driving. It was a very long reach to get the Kleenex tissue box. *It is rather common to have sniffing after a long flight,* Emily thought.

CHAPTER 8

Bita

January 20, 2020 (71 days ago)

Bita went to back to her bed in the morning. Her body was aching, and she had an irritable, dry cough that would not stop. She was chilled to her bone, and she kept adding more blankets over her. She had no appetite ever since she lost her sense of taste and smell for a few days ago. She had to go to work every day to clean different houses, but she knew she couldn't that day.

Most of her clients lived in San Francisco or Palo Alto areas. She enjoyed being in their mansion houses or penthouse condos, wondering what it would be like to live like that. She imagined one day she and her family will live like that—rich and famous, the American dreams. Maybe her grandkids would grow up in this country and let her live in a luxurious house like that someday. As she sat and watched the Bay views during a short lunch break in the middle of cleaning, she imagined herself living in luxury and chuckled. But she took pride in doing a good job cleaning, as if all these places are hers.

All her business was referrals from rich doctors. Her first cleaning job was from a rich doctor in the Palo Alto area, referred by her friend who could not add any other houses to her full list. After about two years, she was introduced to other wealthy people connected to the Palo Alto doctor, and she now had a good solid clientele for herself. Her schedule was full for every weekday and even every Saturday.

She did not have a car to drive. If she was going to San Francisco to clean a house, she had to take the Caltrain and Bay Area Rapid Transit (BART) for an hour and a half each way. Palo Alto was a much shorter trip. Because of the long train rides, she could only clean one house per day. On Sundays, she took her family to the nearby park and sometimes, actually rarely, they went to the Islam mosque during Ramadan.

She called the doctor's wife who lived in Palo Alto that morning and told her she was too sick to clean her house that day. She realized she had never called in sick and missed her work before. She needed the money.

Last November, she got a flu shot from the nearby drugstore, but she didn't because it cost $20 per person. She had her two grandkids and elderly parents get flu shots, but her husband, Payman, and Bita decided to tough it out and save the $40 to buy more food they needed. She now regretted that decision. She thought maybe it was just the flu, and she would get better tomorrow or the next day if she just rested and slept.

They lived in a small one-bedroom apartment. The grandkids and her parents slept in the living room, and she and her husband in the bedroom. The bathroom was almost always occupied by someone throughout the day, and especially in the morning. They all took turns going into the bathroom, and often interrupted by someone who had an emergency, which was guaranteed to be followed by a fight.

About three months ago, Payman lost his job at the San Jose Airport. They lived close to the airport, and Payman used to work in airport security for a while, but they fired him. He had a fight with his senior colleague who joked to him, "you look like a terrorist and shouldn't work in airport security," because he had a long, bushy beard.

His nationality as a Persian with dark-colored skin did not help him. Ignorant Americans call all Arabic-speaking people middle eastern regardless of the nationality, and to some people of these nationalities all looked like terrorists. Payman didn't even speak the Arab language. He spoke Farsi, but some Americans did not care to know the difference.

Bita was told by her husband he was sorry about the whole thing, and he regrets punching his senior colleague in his face, which cost him his job. But she knew that he was secretly proud of himself. Bita was concerned about his bad temper and drinking habits, which became more frequent these days. He could not find a decent job, especially one with medical insurance benefits for his family like the previous job he had.

Their grandkids were growing up; the six-year-old boy needed to go to public grade school soon, and the four-year-old boy should be in kindergarten, but they couldn't afford the school fees. They weren't able to afford kindergarten for the first boy either, even when Payman was working at the airport. He could not keep his job for over one or two years at a time. He worked many odd jobs; picking almonds in the orchards, seasonal grape picking for a winery, keeping beehives, janitor jobs at schools and offices, and sometimes helping Bita clean houses. He always had many excuses to quit or get fired from his jobs. It seemed to him people did not like his looks, and he had no luck.

Bita's clients also did not like to have Payman in their homes, even though the cleaning time was much faster when he was there to help her. Her clients told her they just wanted Bita to clean the house alone, and not to have a man with a beard touching their property.

As his self-pity deepened, Payman was drinking more heavily, and behaving poorly by verbally abusing her, his grandchildren, and even her parents. He did not hit anyone or throw things, but she was afraid of Payman hitting her, or even worse, hitting their grandkids in front of her parents. His ugly side showed when his temper flared.

Bita and Payman had one daughter, who left her two kids when they were two years-old and six-months old. Her daughter was not married when she had her two children. Bita was not even sure if these two kids had the same father. Her daughter became a drug addict and had been fighting depression since her teenage years. She hung out with a wrong crowd. No matter what Bita did—and she tried paid counseling and strict disciplines—her daughter would not stop doing drugs, mostly methamphetamines.

Payman beat her severely once when she was sixteen because she was pregnant. Bita had to take her to the abortion clinic and paid cash for it.

Soon after that, her daughter ran out of the house and did not come back until she had her two kids, now without their father. She showed up to Bita's apartment one day and left the kids. She took off saying nothing. Bita and Payman adopted their grandchildren shortly after that.

Bita's parents came to live with them while they were visiting them from Iran in their tiny apartment two years ago. At first, the whole family was excited to have them visiting and helping with the chores while they were working, and there was the added benefit of having reliable and permanent babysitters, but now, Bita and Payman were worried about the undocumented nature of their stay in America. They had just a three-month visa to visit their family in America, and that time had well passed.

Bita lectured her parents to not to go outside too much or cause any problems with their neighbors or with Payman. She was afraid her parents would be deported back to Iran if they were caught. She was also afraid Payman would lose control of himself and display violent behavior in a small contained space with her parents when she was out working. She was also scared about not having enough money, or the ability to pay for medical bills if her grandkids or anyone got injured. She was concerned about the lack of food in her refrigerator to feed six people, a large family, if she couldn't work like today. She had to spend an enormous amount of money filling the refrigerator every fourth day or so.

Today, she couldn't think or care about the whole family dynamics. She had to sleep off her flu. She closed the door behind her and slept the whole day. Periodically her family checked on her, encouraging her to eat at least some soup, but she couldn't get up to eat. Payman went out to the drugstore and got her some Theraflu powder, dissolving it in warm water as a tea, and she drank that, then went back to sleep. She was thinking in between her dreams, where did she get this flu from? She has so much human contact from her train rides and in her close neighborhoods, but she remembered when she worked at Mrs. Kong's place on the last two consecutive Fridays, she noticed Mrs. Kong was hacking with the same dry cough she had now. But Mrs. Kong never lay down in her bed with a fever or any other symptoms. At least, Mrs. Kong never told her she was very sick.

Bita would know because she changed Mrs. Kong's bed every week, and the sheets were not soaking wet with sweat like hers are now. She thought she should go next Friday to see Mrs. Kong and ask her if she was very sick like she is at some point.

CHAPTER 9

Santa Clara County Coroner

February 6, 2020 (52 days ago)

Payman found Bita dead in their bed on the morning of February 6, just 17 days after Bita could not go to work. Some days, she said she was feeling much better and ready to get up and go to work, but she noticed as soon as she got up she felt too weak, and would fall over.

She spiked a fever again and found herself in bed the entire day. Payman wanted her to go to the emergency department in a nearby hospital, but Bita refused because it would have cost a fortune, and they wouldn't have been able to pay it. She told him she would be okay if she just rested.

Payman noticed that Bita had stopped coughing and waking him up constantly that night. He had a good night's sleep for a change, without being interrupted by her movements or coughs. Now, he found her dead, not moving at all and already cold to touch.

Sheer panic set him off, and he ran around the apartment, not knowing what to do. Bita's parents said to call the ambulance. The kids were dumbfounded and kept shaking their grandmother to get up. Payman called 911 and frantically reported that his wife was dead. The 911 dispatcher sent the ambulance within 10 minutes. The ambulance workers then called the county coroner's office and the police department.

Soon the whole apartment perimeter became like a crime scene with yellow tape all over the place, a few neighbors gathering to see what was going on in their building, and a white truck with a huge CORONER sign parked nearby. No one could go into Payman's unit.

Bita's parents went outside, escaping from the sight because they couldn't distinguish whether these police officers and other people from the coroner's office were from the immigration office. All government agencies in uniform were a danger sign to them, and they ran as far away as possible from them.

The kids and Payman were standing outside when the investigation began, not knowing where exactly Bita's parents were. *They probably went out to the nearby park,* Payman thought.

One police officer asked Payman for the details of how he found his wife dead. He thought they were treating him like he was already a criminal who killed his wife. Somehow, he was stuttering like a guilty person answering the questions. The police made him come back into the bedroom where Bita was still lying in their bed. Payman worried his grandkids would run somewhere to find their grandparents while he was trying to answer what happened that morning when he found his wife dead.

The coroner workers were wearing white coverall suits and taking photos as the police officer directed. Then they moved the body and took Bita into the coroner's truck. Payman signed the paperwork to give permission to conduct an autopsy at the county coroner's office by the medical examiner. All these steps were new to him. He did not know why she had to get an autopsy. The police officer said all deaths occurring at home need examined by the medical examiner for possible homicide, or suicide. There was no other information given to Payman as to when he could get the body back for funeral arrangements, and he couldn't think about asking appropriate questions. He did whatever the police and coroner's officers asked

By the late afternoon, they were all gone. Bita was also gone. The only remaining thing was the yellow tape around his unit, and a part of his building entrance. He went out to find his grandkids and in-laws. Luckily, they were standing across the street and Payman went to them, hugging all of them, and cried. They all joined in and began to wail.

The Santa Clara County Medical Examiner-Coroner was Dr. Melissa Jordan, who conducted the full autopsy on Bita, including her brain. She signed off on the cause of death on the certificate as pneumonia. Bita's lungs were heavy and congested with serosanguinous fluid within the pleural cavities. It fit well with a flu caused by influenza, as per the patient's history of symptoms. Influenza causing pneumonia claimed thousands of lives per year. Dr. Jordan did not see any telltale signs of murder. She sent the blood sample and pieces of lung sample from Bita to the CDC as a precaution to rule out other possible infectious etiology. Bita was only 57 years-old when she died.

CHAPTER 10

Having the time of their lives

March 1, 2020 (30 days ago)

A week ago, Emily and Robert departed from San Francisco harbor for a two-month cruise to the Mediterranean on a luxurious ship. It was to celebrate their 50th anniversary. The only sad part about this trip was that Samantha was not a part of their celebration. They wanted to re-do their wedding on the cruise and brought a new white tuxedo and a white wedding gown. The priest was on board, and they arranged a very small wedding.

Samantha had to be at the hospital, continuing her residency training program, and to leave for a two-month vacation was not possible. Her father, Dr. Robert Parker, always wanted Samantha to have a better and easier life than a physician, because he went through a tough time as a doctor; all the long hours of working, night calls, heavy burdens and responsibilities, making tough decisions, and of course the medical malpractice lawsuits. They had plenty of money stashed up for Samantha to have a comfortable living without her being so tough on herself.

Emily always told her to marry a decent man and be a nice housewife with a couple of kids. That is the best way to live as a woman. Samantha then challenged her why she worked until her 60s in the laboratory. Emily said it was because Robert needed her to help him with his research, and it was not really her choice to work. She always gave Robert a hard time, poking fun at him, saying that he used her as a slave and free labor. Overall, Emily and Robert had a good life together despite their differences in race, culture, (particularly food) and their ways of thinking, (western versus eastern) and infertility in the beginning of their marriage.

While they were boarding the cruise ship in the last week of February, Emily was having some flu-like symptoms; headaches, body aches, sneezing and coughing. Robert thought they should cancel the trip, but Emily insisted they go. After all, they paid $30,000 per person and if they did not go, she was afraid that they would not get a refund. It was their one-of-a-kind trip to celebrate, and she would not have it any other way. The trip was indeed extravagant; going to 15 different countries, all-inclusive land tours, specialty wineries, Micheline star restaurants, opera and classical music performance tickets. Emily had so much fun shopping each night for dresses, long evening gowns, jewelry, and shoes to match her clothes, which cost more than the two tickets for the cruise combined. They even took ballroom dance lessons; cha-cha, tango, classic waltz, foxtrot and salsa for six months prior to the trip.

With all those preparations and investment of their time and money, Emily would not miss out on the trip. Samantha was a little concerned about the COVID-19 situation in a tight space on a cruise ship, but both parents were looking forward to this trip so much, and she knew she was not going to stop them.

Robert and Emily took many pictures on their trip, including at the 50th anniversary ceremony on February 28 with her wedding gown, and the wedding cake they shared with the people on board. Every time they landed in the ports in different countries, they called Samantha and shared some pictures. Neither of her parents were savvy with an iPhone, and Samantha had to remind them how to send the pictures via texting. They sent the photos in such a big file that she had to wait forever to download them and see their happy faces and elaborate clothes.

Every night, the cruise had all the happy and delighted guests watch the famous champagne waterfall; a golden bubbly poured atop a pyramid of 300 glasses. Drinks were passed out, hand to hand, as guests clinked the champagne glasses and posed for photos. There were a dozen different restaurants, a countless multitude of bars and nightclubs, three large pools, a spa, a casino, a 350-seat theater where the entertainment and shows occurred every night, dance floor and a hundred crew members ready to serve. The dining room had at least two buffet style meals, open and ready 24/7. The guests shared the buffet utensils, some picking up food with their fingers to taste, and having casual conversations with each other in front of the buffet trays, not knowing their droplets had landed on the food.

Two days after their 50th anniversary, Robert developed a fever of 100.8 F degrees. He felt lousy with muscle pain and irritating dry coughs that would not stop. He stayed in his bed. Emily on the other hand, felt so much better than when she started the trip. Emily felt terrible transmitting her flu to him.

But Emily never had a high fever like Robert. She realized the hacking coughs might have started with Mrs. Kong when she picked her up from the airport, and the repeated visits to her house to play Baduk games. Mrs. Kong never complained about anything other than coughing and sneezing. Emily did not see her in bed with muscle aches, or fever, or hear her complain about a loss of taste or smell. In fact, she was cooking and eating with Emily. She brought new spices and ingredients she found in China and was cooking up a storm. Emily brought home many leftover dinners for Robert. Mrs. Kong even liked the crème brûlée Emily made. It was puzzling to Emily why the flu symptoms were all so different.

"Robert, do you think you got this flu from me?" Emily asked him.

"I don't know. Did you have muscle aches and a fever like me?" he asked.

"I had headaches and muscle aches but not a fever."

"It might not be from you, darling. We have so many people aboard this cruise ship. Who knows? I must have gotten this from someone else."

"Robert, honey, do you think Mrs. Kong had COVID-19? She recently came from Wuhan, China after all."

"Maybe, maybe," he paused for a long time. "Maybe we are all infected by COVID-19," Robert said.

"Honey, don't say that. I am scared. What do we do then? This is what Samantha was afraid of."

"I know, darling, let's not go there. It's probably nothing, just a flu. I will be all right tomorrow, I am sure. Let's just sleep it off, okay?"

"Okay, sweetie. Feel better tomorrow." Emily was still worried, but smiled gently to Robert.

"We will pay more attention to the COVID-19 stories tomorrow. Let's read some newspapers," Robert responded.

They were not paying much attention to news these days. They were too busy following the land tour schedules, nighttime entertainment schedules on the cruise ship, had a wedding to conduct, and were exhausted. They were actually having so much fun socializing with other guests they had just met. Most of the guests on the cruise were rich, and some were famous people in their retirement. It was known that most people on the ship were loaded with money to pay for such an extravagant trip. Their conversations, therefore, did not focus on the money. It was very easy to have a commonality amongst them.

They all knew that no one would try to take advantage of them due to their richness.

CHAPTER 11

Santorini, Greek Island

April 1, 2020

Robert was facing a dire situation as he had shortness of breath, cyanotic (blue) face and fingertips, and was needing an oxygen tank or ventilator to breathe. He could not talk at all because he was spending all his energy to just breathe. The cruise ship had 27 more days of traveling, but the captain detoured the ship to a nearby Greek Island, Santorini, to dock there longer than scheduled for medical help.

Santorini is part of the small islands to the west, with beaches made up of black, red and white lava pebbles. It was devastated by a volcanic eruption in the 16th century BC, forever shaping its rugged landscape. It overlooks one of the Cyclades islands in the Aegean Sea and enjoys exquisitely clear waters while perched on the rim of a massive active volcano in the middle of the sea. The whitewashed, cubiform houses of its two principal towns, Fira and Oia, cling to cliffs above an underwater caldera (crater). The bright blue painted roof tops perched high up on the edge of the Caldera accentuate the spectacular beauty.

Almost all guests from the cruise ship did not mind spending more time exploring Santorini, tasting the local wine and eating exotic Greek food.

The captain and crew members were calling the local medical hospitals for help. There were a few doctors on the ship, but they could not do much, because the ship did not come with ventilators. They were thinking of transporting Robert by a helicopter to a local hospital for the treatment and then continue their scheduled trips. Emily would stay with him and discontinue her trip.

Emily had been trying to contact Samantha for several hours, but she had not picked up the phone for two days now. At first, Emily thought maybe Samantha was in a deep sleep, so she was trying to count the time difference. It would have been March 31 in America the first time she tried to call. Emily had to leave Robert in his cabin alone and go to stores or coffee shops to connect to strong Wi-Fi to call Samantha, which was not an easy task for her. She called Samantha at various times during the day and night, but she did not pick up the phone. This made Emily even more worried something might have happened to Samantha.

Now Emily had two people to worry about. She was in tears, but she could not talk about Samantha to Robert. He was struggling severely, fighting for his dear life, trying to breathe.

No hospitals would admit him, for they feared that he would bring COVID-19 to their communities. Soon, the local Santorini government asked the captain to have all the cruise guests board the ship as soon as possible. The local government ordered the local businesses to be closed for tourism. The local people were shutting down their bars, coffee shops, gift shops and restaurants, quickly turning away all the guests.

The captain sent his crews to gather all 272 guests scattered about the island of Santorini, and by the sunset, all guests were on board. In the meantime, the captain contacted one of the large hospitals in Athens, who agreed to take Robert. The captain made an announcement through the intercom that some guests were extremely sick and needing medical attention. Hence, he will detour the ship to Athens, 297 kilometers away, arriving in eight and a half to nine hours, which would be the next morning.

Many of the guests were disappointed and did not know how bad the situation on the ship was, nor the magnitude of the COVID-19 situation globally. Secluded from the realities of COVID-19, many did not care that much because it was not in their own reality.

Many rich and famous people sometimes do not think any of the news, particularly pertaining to the bad news, has anything to do with them. They think they are somewhat immune to tragedies of the world.

They think their wealth, positions, and power of influences can help them escape many troubles of the world, even the pandemic.

No one predicted that within the luxurious cruise ship many were already facing the epidemic of the COVID-19 infection. Emily returned to the cabin where Robert was, after a brief dinner alone. No one sat next to her to eat together. No one knew Robert was the sick one, but people just did not pay much attention to her sitting by herself eating. The mood was a little somber. Rare jokes and laughs came from the far side of the table occasionally. Emily just felt guilty eating alone.

Robert could not eat much for about 10 days now, and he was losing his weight quickly. He must have lost about 15 pounds already. He had been taking blood pressure pills and high cholesterol pills for more than 10 years now, after his mild heart attack incident. That incident was the culprit of him retiring from the stressful job he had as a physician. Misery always compounds, and he was facing a lawsuit at the same time. Maybe the lawsuit caused him to have his heart attack.

Robert was sleeping most of the time because the doctors on the ship put him on a morphine drip to calm him down. Emily sat next to him, holding his hand, crying softly. She woke Robert by her cries. "Darling, did you speak to Samantha?" he asked. Emily cried more loudly without answering him.

"Tell her I am okay, I miss seeing her," Robert said, fighting for breath.

CHAPTER 12
Another day on Hart Island

April 1, 2020

Samantha got up early to bring the trash and dirty linen hamper out close to the garage door of the morgue as Dr. Falkner instructed her to do. She untied the ropes and moved the table away from the door. She ate the left-over rotisserie chicken and bread again for the breakfast. She realized the next meal might be 4:00 or 5:00 pm if she ends up doing the same thing as yesterday with Dr. Falkner.

She determines to get out of the place as soon as she finds out the boat schedule back to the Bronx and report this bastard's behavior to her residency program director, Dr. Wells.

She looked out her window from the studio and was surprised to see sunshine hitting the island and the sparkling blue ocean. She took a walk as she had another hour to kill. It might be a bad idea walking around to check out the island, but she wanted to locate the area where Wi-Fi was working to call her boyfriend, Ed, and her parents.

She went outside. The air was still crisp and chilly, about 55 degrees. The wind was blowing with a noisy sound in her ears. The distance between the trenches to her studio was closer than she thought from yesterday. She saw nine inmates wearing black colored hazmat suits, and four construction workers wearing gray colored hazmat suits, already digging. They all turned to see Samantha as she was walking.

One prison warden, the one whom she saw yesterday at the office, turned his head to see what all the men were looking at. Some inmates were making whistling sounds and stopped working. The guard called out, "Back to work, back to work. You over there—stop where you are!"

He walked toward Samantha, almost running. "You are not supposed to walk around here. Get back to the morgue!" he said to her.

"I need to make a phone call," Samantha protested.

"You have a phone in the morgue. Use that phone."

"I need a Wi-Fi connection to leave a message for my mom."

"Alright, I will take you there. Follow me." He was rolling his eyes at Samantha.

She followed him while the other men were still making funny noises toward her. She arrived at a rather small prison warden's room next to the cafeteria. The coffee smelled so good as she walked in.

"Want some coffee?" the warden asked her.

"Yes, thanks." She grabbed the coffee cup before he finished his sentence, was already pouring the black coffee into it.

"This area has Wi-Fi. You have your cell phone, I presume."

"Yes, I do, if you can excuse me. Oh! by the way, when is the next boat to the Bronx?"

"Don't know, ask the Doc."

"Are you having more construction workers coming in today?"

"Nope, not today."

"The other construction workers who came with me, did they stay last night here?" Samantha asked.

"Why, is one of them your boyfriend?" he scoffed.

Samantha decided not to continue talking to him.

She dialed Ed first. The phone rang, but he did not pick up the phone. She left a message. "Hi Ed, I am all right. I am at Hart Island doing an autopsy rotation. I know you probably are in Atlanta. Are you going to China today or was it tomorrow? I can't remember. But I just want to say hello, and I am okay. I plan to go back to the Bronx today. Love you. Talk to you soon."

Then she immediately called her mom's phone, and she too did not pick up the phone. "Mom, Samantha here, I am doing okay. I am doing the autopsy rotation. I am sorry if you tried to reach me, I couldn't get to you. There is a situation here, I will talk to you soon about it. But I just want to tell you I am okay. Hope you two are behaving well and having a fun time. Congratulations on your anniversary again. I saw your wedding picture. You look beautiful, Mom. That wedding gown was two thumbs up! Love you, see you soon!"

The prison warden was watching and listening the entire time and said nothing. She felt awkward; he was eavesdropping on her private conversations.

"Do you want to pick up some breakfast?" the prison warden finally asked, after a few silent moments.

"No, thanks."

"Well, are you done with all the phone calls?"

"Yes, but I need to read my emails."

She was frantically trying to open her email, but the Wi-Fi was not speedy, and the wait sign was going around and around on her phone. She breathed out hard, frustrated at the whole situation.

"It may take a while. It is not fast enough to download things. And young lady, you need to get back before one of the inmates comes looking for you."

That startled Samantha. She closed her cell phone and asked, "Do you have the key to the morgue?"

He did not answer that, unfortunately, but only chuckled.

Another bastard, she thought.

She walked back to the morgue, and the prison warden was chaperoning her. She realized that he had a gun in his belt. Another bout of whistling occurred while she was going back to the morgue. As she was walking, she saw a fairly large boat docking toward Hart Island, the same spot as she came in yesterday. It must be Dr. Falkner. He arrived earlier than she thought this morning. She waited for him inside the morgue, practicing what and how to say things to him. She then realized she had not even washed her face. No makeup, nor had she brushed her hair.

"You can't drink your coffee here in the morgue. You should know better," the prison warden said.

"Oh! Yes, thank you." Samantha quickly trashed the unfinished coffee cup. The prison warden picked up the garbage and dirty laundry hamper and left the morgue after putting on some gloves.

Dr. Falkner walked in and immediately said, "I was worried sick about you last night. I couldn't sleep at all. I am so sorry; I should not have left you here. Are you okay?"

It shocked Samantha to hear this, and she just stood there looking at him for a minute before she said, "I am fine."

"Did anyone come into the morgue last night?"

"No." Not that I know of, she thought.

"Oh! Good, I am taking you back home tonight."

"Is there a boat going back to the Bronx today?

"I don't know. It depends, but we could go back to Long Island, and then I can drive you to your place in the Bronx."

"How long would that be, to drive from Long Island to where I live?"

"Not sure, maybe an hour and a half to two hours without traffic. These days there is very little traffic."

"Where do you live in Long Island?"

"I live in the Mastic Beach area."

"How long will it take you to go back to your place after you drop me off in the Bronx?"

"That will depend on where your place is. How close do you live from Queens?"

"I live near Morris Park."

"I am not sure where that is, but I am sure I can take you. We will need to finish the work here as quickly as possible. We have 41 bodies today. There are more and more bodies coming in. We will not have enough time to jot down all the specifics. We will need to just write the names of the dead and bury them. New York City is expecting more deaths, a huge surge, but not all the bodies will come here. They are already bringing in more parked refrigerated trucks for the bodies. There are not enough funeral homes to store the bodies until the family can claim them. The New York City funeral director is announcing only 15 days to claim the bodies from the families, not the usual 30 days because they are running out of spaces to store the dead bodies. Some of them are coming here to be buried. We need to keep good records for the dead, because some families will look for the bodies in a later time. Maybe they will exhume the body to have a special funeral later when this crisis is over."

Dr. Falkner started dressing in his space jumpsuit while he was talking, and suddenly said, "Oh! Yeah, I almost forgot. I left the grocery bags in the office."

He took off his jumpsuit and ran out before Samantha could respond to anything he said. He came back with two bags of groceries and went toward the refrigerator. "I don't know what you like. I just grabbed everything I saw from the grocery store last night. I even went to the local restaurant, my favorite one where I live. Hope you like seafood stew! I got them with flat noodles," he said enthusiastically, occasionally looking at Samantha.

She could not figure out how to behave. Why was he so friendly today? Why did he buy so many things when he said he would take Samantha back to her home tonight? It looked like he and Samantha could live here for a week or more with the amount of food he bought.

"Do you want to eat something now before we start?" he asked.

"No, thanks, I ate breakfast."

"Okay, then let's get started. Hope we have a pediatric case today." He came out of the studio and put on the jumpsuit, smiling at Samantha. "Oh! About the autopsy, I don't know if…"

"Look, I know how you feel about this whole thing. I told you also, I do not want to be in this position. We are in a crisis. Do you understand? People are dying with COVID-19 right now. The doctors and nurses, in fact all the health care workers, are facing an enormous pandemic not knowing whether one of them will face death and be transported to this island. You are a pathologist! For God's sake, you are a doctor who needs to have responsibilities and callings in this pandemic time!"

The usual Dr. Falkner's rudeness came back, she thought.

She took the jumpsuit and put on all the PPE quietly and quickly alongside Dr. Falkner.

"That's more like it!" he said, and they began to work, starting with the bodies from yesterday.

"We need a forklift. I brought several of them in the boat today." As soon as he finished saying that, the garage door opened. An inmate was bringing in the dead body on a forklift.

"Doc, why didn't you have this before? Much easier!"

"I heard there are 41 today, Doc?" the other inmate asked.

"Yes, we have 41 today. Look, I don't think we can register all of them. Can you just bring some light-weighted and younger ones? Otherwise you can write their names on the coffin."

"How are we to know who is young unless we open the zippers? We are not supposed to open the zippers, Doc."

"Don't you have some paperwork with the body? Their names, ages?" Dr. Falkner said.

"No sir, there is no paperwork. There are just bodies piled up!" the inmate said, with a disgusted face.

The other inmate said, "Can we have lunch with the young doctor here?" pointing at Samantha.

"NO!" Dr. Falkner said loudly. "Now, get out and do your work! We got it! We will do the work ourselves!"

"All right, all right, Doc. Have it your way!"

The inmates were still staring at Samantha up and down as if she was a piece of meat, waiting to devour. Samantha was disgusted at their behaviors. She could not see their smiles at her due to the masks covering half their faces, but she was sure they were showing their teeth looking at her body.

With that, the miserable work started. Samantha reluctantly participated in her service to the society, risking her life and also the humiliation of mockery she faced as a female physician. No one took her knowledge or her medical doctor degree seriously, she felt. Whether it was the prison or in the hospital ward, men just looked at her as a cute resident and an object to be possessed.

At least, the inmates are honest about it and say like it is, she thought.

Several hours later, they found a pediatric case—a 12-year-old Hispanic boy who died of COVID-19. Dr. Falkner was so excited to have the case, and it was out of context to have such joy.

He performed several biopsies from the boy's lungs, liver, kidney, and heart, using the long needles percutaneously. He opened the skull, reflecting the skin off of the boy's face using the electric bone saw, and performed several biopsies on the brain. While he was doing all the procedures, Samantha was helping him to label the formalin containers, and shifting the body into the various positions for needle access.

She thought he was quick with his hands doing the autopsy procedures, and his skills impressed her. On the other side, she was concerned about the virus spreading through the entire room from aerosolization. How dangerous was their work really, she wondered? How can they possibly take off their protective gear and eat later next door? The place was not under negative pressure, and the autopsy table was not ventilated to protect the risk of exposure from airborne pathogens and odors.

None of the circumstances was Occupational Safety and Health Administration (OSHA) approved. She felt like she was living in the first pandemic time in 1918.

Dr. Falkner was truly inhumane. He didn't even go to the bathroom. Samantha had to break out of her PPE several times to go to the bathroom and drink water. He finally stopped around 4:30 pm. They decided not to do such a thorough job with each dead body. They just copied and wrote the name on the coffin from the toe tag. The sheer amount of the dead bodies was overwhelming. They took showers just like yesterday, in the same order. They ate, and devoured the seafood noodles he brought after microwaving them, without talking.

"Pack your things and let's go," he said after eating.

Samantha did as she was told without an argument. Dr. Falkner took his laptop computer and the biopsy samples in an air-tight biohazard bag with him. They quickly left and got onto the boat leaving for Long Island. Dr. Falkner held Samantha's hands, and helped her to get on to the boat.

Samantha felt a little awkward to be so close to Dr. Falkner. She did not really need his help to get in, and she never asked to be helped. She thought maybe her bags were tipping over and it made her look vulnerable.

The cool air was refreshing. It was still very windy. Samantha was taking in all that fresh, cold air. She was wishing all the COVID-19 viral particles in her lungs would be replaced by the fresh air. The boat was going to the opposite direction, away from the Bronx, she noted. She stood, getting all that cold air as the boat picked up some speed.

Dr. Falkner came over to her. "Aren't you cold?" he asked.

"No, I am fine."

He stood next to her, looking at the land approaching. The sun was slowly setting.

"Do you have a car parked near the port?" Samantha asked.

"Yes." He glanced; Samantha's wisp of hair touched her cheek.

"How long is this boat ride?"

"About 40 minutes. It does not go very fast, as you can see," he said.

"Then, it will be around 6:15. Then to my place is, let's say two hours, that makes it 8:15. Then back to your place in another two hours, which is 10:15 pm." Samantha was worried.

"Yep."

"How do I come back tomorrow?" Samantha could not believe she just asked that question.

"Do you want to come back? I am surprised you said that," he smiled.

Samantha had never seen him smile. It was a beautiful and warm smile.

"I suppose you can catch the boat from the Bronx just the way you did before. I am not sure if they will pick up additional construction workers or inmates from Rikers Island in the morning. I haven't checked. There will be more bodies tomorrow, I am sure."

Rikers Island is a 413.17-acre island in the East River between Queens and the Bronx. It is home to New York City's main jail complex. It is technically part of the Bronx, although the bridge access is from

Queens. It has been described as New York's most famous jail, home to one of the world's largest correctional institutions and mental institutions, composed of a staff of 9,000 officers and 1,500 civilians managing 100,000 admissions per year, and an average daily population of 10,000 inmates. Recently, Rikers Island has attracted the media for its reputation for violence, abuse and neglect of inmates, and judicial scrutiny that has resulted in numerous rulings against the New York City government.

With recent increase in the death toll due to COVID-19, New York City funeral homes had reached full capacity to bury the dead. This forced the funeral directors to order more refrigerated trucks to park in the city streets to hold the bodies and shorten the time span to 15 days for the family to claim the dead for their private burials. If no one claimed the body within 15 days, then the body would be transported to Hart Island. New York City was taking prisoners by the old school bus and the boat to dig the mass graves at Hart Island. The media was expressing more concern about abusing the inmates to do these jobs, and hence, the government was hiring more construction workers to continue digging the trenches for burial.

"Do you mean you checked to see if there was a morning boat ride on March 31st for me?" glancing at his blue eyes.

"Oh! Yeah, I've arranged it for you. I arranged nothing for tomorrow though. I will have to make a phone call. You might have to wait for the boat for a while. I'm concerned about you taking the boat with the prisoners from Rikers Island or the construction guys. I don't know. Or maybe you will get lucky and tell me that there is no boat tomorrow, and not show up at all," he chuckled. Samantha did not answer. There was a quiet moment after that.

Then he asked, "Do you want to sleep over at my place? I have an extra bedroom. My wife and my son are in Italy visiting her family. They have been there for a while now. Now, they are stuck there. I've also encouraged them to stay in the villa for now. Italy as you know is the epicenter for COVID-19 in Europe. They are staying in Tuscany, in a small village, and they are safe for now. They are in strict lockdown."

"No, I want to go to my place," Samantha said nervously.

"Okay, I will not push you on that. But it will be safer than the studio at Hart Island, I will assure you." Long silence followed this.

"Listen, I am sure many pathology residents in New York City are facing an incredibly difficult time now. The morgues are filled with dead bodies stacked up everywhere. All hospitals are filled with the COVID-19 cases, and they are panicking about where to store the dead. I heard hundreds of health care workers are getting infected with COVID-19. Even the hospital transportation employees who move the bodies to morgues are getting infected with COVID-19. They don't even have the proper PPE. It's a real bad time to be in your shoes now, doing autopsy service during the pandemic time. I am a medical examiner, and this is my job, whether I like it or not. But you, I feel bad. I think spending time on Hart Island is not as bad as doing the autopsy rotations in the New York City hospital now, I would think."

"Why would you think so?" Samantha asked. "Well, for one, the virus does not infect the limited amounts of inmates and wardens. At least not yet anyway. Who knows how many hospital workers and patients are lurking around the hospitals where you work? They are all vectors for the virus, is how I see it. If you are the virus, the main goal is to infect as many vectors as possible to replicate the viral genes so you can reproduce and maintain longevity. On top of that, New York City is so condensed, with people packed like sardines. It will be hard not to get infected."

"I am cold. I am going to sit inside," Samantha said as she walked.

"I wouldn't. I am not sure they disinfected the boat. This is the boat that carried all the dead bodies in the morning from New York City and Long Island."

So, they stood the entire 40-minute ride. When they arrived at the port, Dr. Falkner helped Samantha again, holding her hands. He even carried her duffle bag. They walked to his car—a black fancy looking

Audi. It was good to get into a warmer space. He took all their belongings and threw them into the back seat.

"What is your address?" he asked, ready to put it into his cell phone with GPS system.

CHAPTER 13

Tender side of human

"I will stay at your house tonight," Samantha said. It was already getting dark as Dr. Falkner started his engine.

"I can get you to the Bronx," he said.

"No, I think it is best if I stay at your place. Then we can go to Hart Island tomorrow together."

"I thought you don't like the place. In fact, I thought you were going to leave the place as fast as you could and never return. I was wondering how I was going to fill out your evaluation form from your program if you did not show up the rest of the week. Are you sure?"

"Yes, I am sure. You said you have extra room."

"Yes, I do."

"Okay. Go then."

Dr. Falkner and Samantha drove in silence for quite a while. He had classical music on. It was a beautiful and sad sound—Chopin Concerto II. The sound of this music demands the heart to be quiet, and be in the moment, mindful with one's innermost feelings.

The ride seemed like it took an hour, and by the time they reached his house, it was very dark. His house was a cozy, beautiful two-story building surrounded by many trees, providing a private and quiet setting. The other side of the house was facing the dark ocean, with the ocean waves providing a relaxing and constant sound.

"Here we are. This is my house. Your room is downstairs. Please take a shower again immediately. Put your shoes outside on the doormat. I do not want any germs in the house."

He was very methodical toward the germs as he was removing his shoes, constantly disinfecting his hands, all the bags he was carrying, and the keys. Once they went inside the house, he gave Samantha some shoe covers. She put them on around her bare feet. He showed her the room where she was to stay.

"The bathroom attaches to the bedroom. You will find a plastic bag there in the bathroom for your dirty laundry. Tie the dirty laundry tightly, and you can use the laundry machine later if you'd like," he said, and he took off to the second floor.

Samantha looked around his place. It had a modern and stylish kitchen, with a dining room connected to the living room, and an open space with large glass windows in the living room overlooking the ocean. Everything was immaculately clean. She was surprised that he was such a tidy person even without his wife around to clean things, though it would not be out of his character.

She went in her room and took another shower as he instructed her. This time, the soap bar and shampoo smelled very feminine and expensive. When she came out of the shower, her cell phone inside her purse was making all kinds of noises, full of unread texts and phone messages. She wrapped herself with a towel, and looked through the messages, sitting on the toilet seat.

Her Mom had left a voice message, "My love, Samantha, where are you? I've been trying to reach you. We are going to Athens. Your father is very ill. We have to stop the trip and get your father into a hospital in Athens tomorrow. I do not know what to do." Her Mom started to cry. "Well, hope you are okay. Call me soon." Then she hung up.

There were at least three texts and one voice message from Ed. "Hey, I got on the plane now. Where are you? Is everything okay? I'll call you again when I arrive in China."

Samantha called her Mom, but she did not answer the phone. "Mom, I guess you are in Athens now? It will be around 3:00 am your time on April 2nd. What's going on with Dad? What are his symptoms? How sick is he? What do you mean he is very ill? Is it a flu, heart problem, or indigestion? What is it Mom? Hope you are okay. Love you. Talk to you soon. Call me soon. For the next 12 hours, I should be able to get your phone call. Okay?" Samantha was crying now.

She did not bother to call Ed, for surely he was on the plane unable to get her call, anyway. She got dressed in her own clothes and sat on the chair looking at the paintings on the wall for a while, thinking about all kinds of possibilities of her dad's illness and what Samantha could do. Should she go to Athens to meet her parents?

She was checking on the flights to Athens when she heard small knocks on her door.

"Are you okay? Let's have some dinner," Dr. Falkner said.

Samantha came out the door. He saw Samantha's tears, red eyes and red nose.

"Hey, Sam, I am cooking salmon filets and vegetables. I want to barbeque them. What do you think?" he said rather shyly, ignoring her tears.

"That sounds good. I don't need to eat, but I will watch you eat." He said my name, she thought.

"No, you need to eat. Let's have some wine too. I have a chardonnay that will go really well with the salmon." Samantha watched him cook. She got up to help him clean vegetables for the salad, brussels sprouts and onions. He took some vegetables and the salmon, olive oil and seasoning powders, put the whole thing in the foil and went outside to barbeque.

She followed him outside to the patio and watched him cook. A nice breeze came in with the ocean waves. The house was on a cliff with rocks, with white ocean water breaking and making foam. The sound was so relaxing.

Dr. Falkner went inside and brought two glasses of chardonnay and gave one to her. "It's nice, isn't it?"

"Yes, thank you, Dr. Falkner."

"Call me David." He watched Samantha for a minute who was constantly looking at her cell phone and said, "Sam, are you all right? Did anything happen?"

"My father is sick. My mom called. They are on a cruise ship going to Athens, last I heard. I do not know how sick he is. I don't know what to do," Samantha began to cry. She didn't care how she appeared anymore. She just could not contain her worries any longer. He let her be for a while until she regained her composure.

"Tell me more about it," he finally said.

Samantha told him about her parents' vacation trip to celebrate their 50th anniversary. They were to be back at the end of April in San Francisco, where they live. She did not know if she should go to Athens to meet them, for her Mom could not handle all the hospital issues on her own, especially in the foreign country.

She was frustrated that she was at Hart Island without cell phone coverage during this critical time. She did not know what to do.

She added that she did not even know where to go after this week for her next rotation.

Everyone was so hectic with the COVID-19 crisis, no one was communicating to the residents about what to expect.

Teaching and guiding residents were the last thing on their mind. It frustrated her at not knowing what tomorrow would be like. Everything seemed messy and abnormal to her with COVID-19.

It scared her to death about contracting the infection while she was doing the autopsies with Dr. Falkner. And why did he care about his promotion and research papers during the unprecedented time like this?

She could not believe she just let it out to Dr. Falkner.

He listened quietly, not interrupting Samantha. He said, "Fish is burning. Let's eat."

Samantha laughed and followed him inside to eat what he cooked. He clanged the wine glasses with her, and they ate quietly.

"Are you going to say anything, Dr. Falkner?"

"David. I know, Sam. Well, I am glad you are eating. I was just thinking about the whole thing. How this COVID-19 violated our norms with so many people. It's been a month since my wife and son went to Italy. I am not sure if they are coming back to me. I was going to go there to bring them back last week. She left me suddenly. She took our son with her. I am a workaholic she said. I gave her this beautiful house, and everything she asked for. What else can I give to her? Then this stupid COVID-19 happened, and I am stuck on that terrible Hart Island doing the worst job because I am the youngest medical examiner who can be abused. I couldn't get a ticket to Italy. Both New York and Italy are now the epicenters. Sometimes I think about quitting everything and settling in Tuscany with my wife and drinking wine all day. But then, I do not think I would be happy," he said.

Then he added, "You know Sam, I heard the 4th year medical students are graduating early this year and they are putting them to work in the hospitals, dispersed all around the COVID-19 patients. Can you imagine what they will go through? At least you are on the pathology residency track with a solid program and curriculum. Who are they going to report to now? I am not sure if they had any choices where to have their residency training programs."

"I am sorry about your wife," Samantha said, adding, "I am sure it will work out somehow."

"Well, thanks for saying that, but you realize that is such a vain word."

"I am sorry."

"It is not your fault. By the way, if you need to go to Athens, let me know."

They finished eating. Samantha thanked him for a lovely dinner. Dr. Falkner said he would clean up, do the rest of the autopsy work, and review the data from his laptop that night. She said good night to him and went back to her room.

She waited for her phone to ring and lay in bed. She thought about David Falkner. It was such an unexpected conversation that they had and shared deeply personal and vulnerable things. She realized all humans without exception had tender spots, and he was not such a jerk after all. He impressed her with his ability to think outside of the box to mention the situations with the medical school students. She appreciated his compassion toward her, and ability to listen in quiet.

Come to think of it, he even arranged Samantha's boat ride a day earlier on March 31st, along with four other construction workers from the Bronx. He must have known that there might not be another boat from the Bronx on April 1st. Although that arrangement was beneficial to him, at least he thought through things ahead of time and prepared it. He also cooked, cleaned up, and was doing the data input work on his laptop tonight.

What he said about Hart Island being a blessing in disguise might be also true; she may end up going to the New York City or the Bronx coroner's office and handle more dead bodies than she could possibly imagine, although she still may end up going there in April, anyway.

She still was not clear whether the inmates and the construction workers stayed overnight on Hart Island, and if so, where? Were there real prison cells within the buildings she saw? Many thoughts came to her, but the main thought was that she made a good choice to stay at Dr. Falkner's house to learn more about him. She felt sorry for him.

Instead of complaining about the whole situation Samantha was facing at Hart Island and abuse she once felt from Dr. Falkner, she merely asked Dr. Wells, her program director, to provide the next autopsy rotation schedules for the rest of April via email. She also told the program director that she may have to take a few days off starting April 11 due to her family situation. Her father was extremely sick. And she apologized for such short notice.

CHAPTER 14

Detour

April 2, 2020

Emily lost all hopes for Robert to live. They could not transport Robert to the Athens hospital yesterday. The government of Athens changed their decision on disembarking the cruise ship passengers with flu-like symptoms, for they feared it would be COVID-19. The captain contacted the US ambassador to request they ask the hospital administration to accept the patients who were in dire need of medical help.

Every request was denied, except the people of Athens provided the ship with a significant amount of fuel and food, along with a few of their precious ventilators. They adamantly would not allow any passengers to get off the ship. Emily also learned there were five people or more in a similar situation to Robert who desperately needed a ventilator. The doctors on the ship hooked up the ventilator to Robert and heavily sedated him to a comatose status. Some crew and passengers were coughing with flu-like symptoms.

The captain, after finding out about the dire situations all around the world with the COVID-19 pandemic, discontinued the tour routes and turned the ship to return to San Francisco. It would take eight to nine days depending on the weather and the condition of the sea to travel 5,889.92 nautical miles (6,778 miles), despite the maximum speed reaching about 30 knots (35 miles per hour). Crew informed him that approximately 40-50 people onboard were probably infected with the virus.

The captain ordered all passengers to remain in their cabins, and limited people from gathering socially. The food and beverages would be delivered as room service by the crew members. The passengers could order the drinks and food at any time, whatever they want and need.

They stopped night programs in the amphitheater, entertainment, music and dancing. The passengers in tiny cabins without balconies to look out over the ocean were complaining, so the captain allowed them to roam around other areas of the ship in groups of a maximum of ten people at a time, keeping within social distancing parameters of six feet or more.

They did not have face masks for all passengers or for the crew members. Many passengers were getting very upset and already demanding reimbursement, and some people were contemplating a lawsuit against the cruise company.

Tensions were building up and identifying the source of the original infected person (patient zero) was becoming their number one topic of discussion. All the people—including the crew members who were supposed to make the passengers feel welcome—were now looking suspiciously at some Asian people. Emily definitely detected a tension from the people around her, and she rarely went out onto the deck even for fresh air. Luckily, she had one of the most luxurious accommodation spaces with her own private balcony overlooking the ocean anytime she needed to get fresh air.

It was early in the morning, around 8:00 am, when Emily checked her cell phone before the ship departed from Athens. They were still loading up the food and water from Athens, and the cell coverages were now available. She called Samantha immediately after she heard the voice message from her. It would be 1:00 am for Samantha, but she did not care about disturbing her sleep.

Samantha picked up her cell phone, saying with a sleep interrupted tired voice, "Mom? Where are you. Are you okay? Is Dad okay?"

"No, my love. He is in the hospital bed downstairs with a ventilator. They moved him the other day and they would not let me see him." Emily was crying, unable to speak.

"Mom, does he have COVID-19? When did he begin to have symptoms? Are you okay? Are you having the same symptoms?"

"I did, my love. I had it when we first boarded, but it went away. I think it came from Mrs. Kong. I am fine now, but Robert…"

"Okay, okay, Mom. Are you going to be in Athens? Do you want me to go there and meet you?"

"No, they would not let us disembark in Athens. We are going home, the whole boat. No more trips. We are going to go home, and the captain said we will arrive in San Francisco in eight to nine days."

"Okay, Mom. I guess we cannot talk to each other during that time. What kind of stupid boat does not have Wi-Fi these days? Do you know how to email me? Mom, you go to the business center. I am sure the boat has one. You turn on the computer and send me an email. You have my email address, right Mom?"

"Oh, yes, I do, I will send you emails, but the captain said I am supposed to stay in my cabin and not go out."

"Mom, listen! I am sure you can go once a day. Get permission or get out secretly at night and send me an email. Okay?"

"Oh, oh, okay."

"Okay, Mom, I will try to get out of my rotation to meet you in San Francisco." She looked at her calendar, adding eight to nine days quickly, "It will be the weekend of April 11th. I will go there, okay?"

"Okay, my love, are you okay?"

"Yes, Mom, I am well. Don't worry about me, I will see you very soon."

The phone was disconnected after that. Emily was sobbing out loud.

Emily was afraid to go outside of her cabin. Everyone was talking about her. The people found out Robert was sick, and since then they were looking at Emily with suspicion that she might be the culprit.

At first, she thought those rich and educated people would not give her a hard time or talk about her from behind her back. But to her surprise, the people, even the befriended ones, were suspecting Emily to be the one who started the whole epidemic on the cruise ship. Emily was wondering who the other four people were; those who were very sick like Robert, and if they were also married to Asians. Then she realized how racist that thinking was as COVID-19 does not have to come from Asian people. It may have come from Wuhan, China at first, but after that, anyone could be a victim, and a culprit to spread the virus. But she could not keep thinking about who the other Asians were. Then she remembered there were some Asians, one Chinese American couple and one Filipino couple. Both Chinese American couples were doctors, and Emily and Robert had dinner with them once at the beginning of their trip. The couple from the Philippines were rich, but she couldn't remember their line of business. It was maybe something to do with computers.

Most of the guests were Caucasians, and one African American woman who was married to a Caucasian. There were some Asian crew members, but they were a few in number. Maybe some of them brought COVID-19, she thought. Emily was, in fact, not tested for COVID-19, and she may just have caught a regular flu from Mrs. Kong. Emily never had a fever or the severe symptoms like Robert was having. It must have been one of those Asian crew members or the Chinese American doctors, she thought. Even though it did not matter who brought the virus into the ship at this point, the possibility somewhat comforted her that maybe it was not her who spread the disease. Now, she had to figure out how to get out to the business center and email Samantha to update her.

The ship began to move, a long journey without stopping to America. She would have sea sickness going through the deep ocean without land in her sight. She experienced sea sickness when the ship was going through turbulent waters in the deep water. She took one Dramamine pill with water. She flipped TV channels, hoping to see some Korean drama, but she could not find one. She found Downton Abbey, a British historical drama television series written by Julian Fellowes on TV, and decided to watch the entire series and get her mind off of the reality. She thought that by the time she landed in San Francisco, she would have finished the sixth season. She felt guilty watching the show while Robert was hanging by a thread to just breathe. If only she could be next to Robert to attend to his needs.

CHAPTER 15

Wuhan Institute of Virology (WIV) Laboratory

Ed arrived in Wuhan, China. Ed's team was heading to the WIV with the notion that the US was trying to understand and learn more about COVID-19. The team, a total of 11 people, was composed of an infectious disease medical doctor, bioinformatician in virus resources, molecular virologist, the NIH Virology Director, biotechnologist in virology, vaccine development expert from J & B Co, a CDC representative specializing in virology, the US Director of WHO, the political ambassador in China relations, a media representative with expertise in China, and Dr. Ed Liu from Abby Laboratory in Washington, DC, who was an Associate Research Director, the only Asian, and a Chinese American.

The Wuhan Institute of Virology Laboratory is China's first Biosafety Level 4 facility. A biosafety level, or Pathogen/Protection level, is set from the lowest biosafety level 1 (BSL-1), to the highest at level 4 (BSL-4).

A Biosafety Level 2 means the laboratory works with agents associated with pathogenic or infectious organisms that cause human diseases which pose a moderate health hazard. Examples of agents include equine encephalitis viruses and HIV, as well as bacteria Staphylococcus aureus.

A Biosafety Level 3 laboratory typically includes work on pathogenic or infectious organisms that are either indigenous or exotic, and can cause serious or potentially lethal diseases through inhalation. Examples of agents include yellow fever, the West Nile virus, and the mycobacterium that causes tuberculosis. The microbes are so serious that the work is often strictly controlled and registered with the government agencies. Laboratory personnel are also under medical surveillance and could receive immunizations for microbes they work with.

The Wuhan Institute of Virology Laboratory opened in 2015 and consisted of multiple buildings connected by complex structures from the lowest level of biosafety to the highest biosafety level. At the lowest level of biosafety, precautions may consist of regular handwashing and minimal protective equipment, and at higher biosafety levels, precautions may include multiple containment rooms, airflow systems, and sealed containers. The worker who needs to go to the level 4 receives extensive personal training, high levels of security to control access to the facility and needs to wear positive pressure personal suits undergoing several steps of chemical decontaminations.

Historically, the WIV evolved from the Wuhan Microbiology Laboratory under the Chinese Academy of Science, founded in 1956.

In 2015, in collaboration with the French government, it became a level 4 facility and received many grant funds, including sub-recipients of the grant funds from an NIH grant titled Understanding the Risk of Bat Coronavirus Emergency.

In January 2020, new speculations and allegations arose that the current crisis was precipitated by the release of the coronavirus responsible for COVID-19 from the WIV, and not from the seafood market just three miles away. Given these concerns, NIH suspended the WIV from participation in federal programs including the $3.7 million grant, which was spread across multiple installments over six years at sites including China, Thailand, Cambodia, Laos, Vietnam, Malaysia, Indonesia and Myanmar.

The precipitation of suspending the funding aligned with the worldview in the midst of the pandemic, including the US, who believed it could have been stopped at the source (China), and stopped quickly. Then it wouldn't have spread all over the world, killing so many people.

A team led by Dr. Shei at the WIV was the first to identify, analyze and name the genetic sequence of the novel coronavirus (2019-nCoV), and published its databases in Nature.

In February 2020, the Institute applied for a patent in China for the use of Remodesivir, an experimental anti-viral drug owned by American pharmaceutical company named Gilud Sciences, which the Institute found inhibited the virus in tissue culture (in vitro).

With the previous extensive research including the complete genetic codes of the virus, and the request of a patent for the use of a new antiviral drug specific to COVID-19, the allegation of bioweapon research including the possibility of "outbreak though accidental leakage" deepened with the financial motivation of monopolizing the treatment plans from China.

Dr. Shei also made various public statements defending the WIV and the Chinese government, adamantly denying the accusation that COVID-19 originated from the laboratory.

However, there was a rumor that the patient zero was, in fact, one young research graduate student who died in the WIV lab, which Dr. Shei denied. Dr. Shei claimed that the two samples she received to be analyzed were from the local hospital in Wuhan, and from patients with flu-like symptoms who ended up dying from the disease. Later, the Chinese government also banned academic and other research institutions from publishing their research on coronaviruses on their websites.

In addition, Dr. Li, a 34-year-old ophthalmologist, the first whistleblower, who worked at Wuhan Central hospital, recognized many patients were dying with sudden acute respiratory syndrome (SARS) like symptoms, similar to 2003 SARS, and sent a message to fellow doctors in a chat group warning them to wear protective clothing to avoid infection. Four days later he was summoned to the Public Security Bureau, in the Chinese government sector, where he was told to sign a letter to apologize to the public that he "severely disturbed the social order" and "made false comments."

Within one month, Dr. Li contracted COVID-19 and died.

There was speculation that he did not die from COVID-19, but that the Chinese government killed him after forcing him to wear a mask while he was lying on the hospital bed as one of the COVID-19 infected patients. The reason for this speculation was that he did not have any other medical conditions such as high blood pressure, diabetes, or immune-compromising status. He was a vital young doctor who did not take even a single medication and also, he was an ophthalmologist, not an emergency or intensive care doctor who faced the COIVD-19 patients directly.

On the other hand, many scientists had rejected this, noting that the Institute was not suitable for bioweapon research, and that there was no evidence that the virus was genetically engineered, stating, "The evidence we have is that the mutations [in the virus] are completely consistent with natural evolution."

Ed's team checked into a nearby hotel in Wuhan, in close proximity to the WIV. The Chinese government escorted them from the airport. The streets were empty as the lockdown order from the government was still in effect when they arrived. Food, drugs and essential needs were delivered to the civilian homes by Chinese government people in uniform. No one was on the streets walking.

It was not just the lockdown order as seen in America, but a total and strict law from the communist government. If they found a person on the street, the police or the Chinese government officers beat the person with a baton.

The team had to sign a document which stated, "No pictures, no camera, no cell phones, and no recording machines," and the Chinese government confiscated all these from their hotel. They were permitted to write their findings in notes during the stay. The team was in shock with the lack of freedom and new norms in the communist country. They were given a strict schedule when to visit the WIV lab. The team could not gather together to visit the WIV or eat meals together. The meals were to be delivered to each room by room service. They were not allowed to gather in the hotel conference room. The only group conversation all team members could have was by Zoom from their computer. The team was faced with a different set of unfamiliar rules, and challenges that they did not prepare for. But they all had to abide in this circumstance.

Personally, this meant that Ed could not contact anyone in America by using his cell phone. He could not contact Samantha and his parents. Without knowing how many days his team needed to stay in Wuhan, he was even more frustrated with the Chinese government restrictions. There was a rumor that the Chinese government would lift the lockdown order very soon, however.

Ed would be the first one to visit the WIV lab, scheduled for tomorrow at 9:00 am. Everyone from the team went inside the hotel room and decided to unwind, eat and sleep for three hours, and then have at least a one-hour meeting via Zoom.

CHAPTER 16

Vain work

April 3, 2020

The Chinese government officers escorted Ed to the WIV in a black sedan. They were wearing government uniforms and face masks. Ed also wore a mask and sat in the rear car seat. They began speaking Mandarin to Ed. He understood some, mostly common language such as how are you, what do you want to eat, how much is it, but not technical language. He understood it better than speaking Mandarin. As soon as Ed was to answer, he spoke the English language which was his natural tongue.

The trip was short, about five minutes.

They could have walked. He would have enjoyed walking, but there was a strict day time curfew. He was carrying a thin, black Montblanc leather bag with a computer, notebook and pen. It was still chilly, 60 F degrees, but sunny that day in the morning. Ed was greeted by two WIV staff laboratorians, and they took him into a small conference room. There was an interpreter who waited inside of the conference room.

"We are glad to see a Chinese person from America. Could we all speak Mandarin?" one of the lab persons said in Mandarin.

Ed recognized what he said and replied in English, "Well, I understand better than I speak it. I do need an interpreter."

"Of course, welcome to Wuhan. What can we do for you?" the interpreter translated to Ed in English.

"We would like to know the specifics and origin of COVID-19 in December 2019, and the discovery of the anti-viral drug Remodesivir, and to tour the facility."

"Well, not so fast. Let's get to know each other. After all, the American Gilud company should have told you all the details of the drug Remodesivir, since they funded the program with our scientists."

"Please educate me with the specifics of COVID-19," Ed said.

"Well, let's have some Chinese tea. Enshi green tea is the best local Chinese tea, growing 150 kilometers west of Wuhan. Let's drink it and get to know each other more."

They are deliberately taking their sweet time, Ed thought.

They chatted nonchalantly for a while, not getting into any specific business. They then took Ed into the level 1 laboratory space where a few research scientists were working. No one spoke to Ed, they just looked at him and continued the routine work as if he was not there. Ed asked to visit the level 4 laboratory and meet with Dr. Shei, but they made silly excuses and declined to take Ed on any further tours. After two hours of bullshit, Ed was taken back to the hotel.

He called for a Zoom meeting with his team. They were all excited about what Ed had to say. With disappointment, Ed did not have much to report to the team. In the afternoon, after lunch, another person was scheduled to go to the WIV. Ed told the next person in line that the laboratory researchers and staff might do the same.

He hoped that he was treated badly, or at least not taken seriously, simply because he was pretty low on the totem pole.

The schedule to tour the WIV was set as two meetings a day, one group in the morning and one in the early afternoon, and therefore the next five days were set. The remaining team members were taken one at a time to exercise; using the swimming pool or gym in the hotel which was deserted.

All meals were fairly good; a western style breakfast, sandwich for lunch with salad and a fruit bowl, and a Chinese dinner. No liquor was served at any time during the meals, but the hotel had a refrigerated wet bar with collections of alcohol.

They allowed limitless Zoom meetings. The team debriefed after each tour, but there was not much to discuss. The team members were brainstorming more creative ways to approach the stubborn and calculative WIV staff to get them to spill out their secrets.

Since Ed's cell phone was confiscated, he emailed Samantha telling her what had happened so far in China. In addition, he wrote, "I called you several times. I hope you are okay. I am sure it's very hectic now with COVID-19 in New York City. Wuhan is empty, a ghost town. No one is out. Very strange times we are living in… don't know when I will be back. Please tell me you are doing okay. Miss you. Ed."

Ed found himself having a difficult time adjusting with the time changes. He watched a movie he downloaded from Amazon Prime before he came to China and finally fell asleep at 3:00 am.

CHAPTER 17

Dr. Shei

April 6, 2020

No one was taken to the level 4 laboratory, but Dr. Shei met with a few team members, in particular the politician and the media representative. She did not say much except to emphasize that the laboratory was not responsible for the spread of COVID-19, and they did not accidently "spill the virus." They followed strict guidelines to highest level of respect and guaranteed that they were not the source of origin.

When the team asked to debrief them on the meeting with the WHO visit in January, they claimed that they showed everything, including the level 4 lab spaces. They were reluctant to show the level 4 space to the current team members because, first, they were not obligated to show it, and second, the current team came from America, who was accusatory to the Chinese government in their opinion.

There was nothing else the team could do to persuade the WIV personnel to change their mind. It was definitely a different culture. Americans had an open policy and revealed the truth to anyone who wanted the information, particularly in science, but China was not even revealing truth for the good of scientific knowledge. At the end, Ed was exhausted with the stupidity of the Chinese government, and they were ready to go back home. They were all tired of listening to each other in Zoom meetings and not being able to have dinner and drinks together.

After several requests from Ed's team to at least tour the Huanan Seafood Wholesale Market, some government agents took the team. Again, two at a time, while the other team members were still touring the WIV. The Chinese government agents argued the point that the market was closed, and they could not get inside for touring, but Ed's team members insisted to look at the periphery of the market. The marketplace was completely shut down, as the Chinese government agents said, and there was not even a single person seen around the perimeter of the market.

The Huanan (which means South China) Seafood market was located in the Jianghan District, Wuhan, Hubei, China and consisted of a live animal and seafood market. After being identified as the possible point of origin of the COVID-19, it was closed on January 1, 2020 for sanitary procedures and disinfection.

Two-thirds of the initial 41 people hospitalized with SARS-like pneumonia were exposed to or associated with the market. 33 of 585 environmental samples obtained from the market indicated evidence of COVID-19, and among them, 31 were from wildlife areas, according to the Chinese Center for Disease Control and Prevention. There were rumors that the market was in an unsanitary condition.

Numerous wild animals were found in the market for either food or Chinese medicine, including badgers, bamboo rats, beavers, camels, chickens, civets, crocodiles, dogs, donkeys, foxes, frogs, giant salamanders, hedgehogs, marmots, ostriches, otters, pangolins, peacocks, pheasants, pigs, porcupines, rabbit organs, sheep, snakes, spotted deer, turtles, and wolf puppies. Anything goes, it seemed, as long as there was an exchange of money.

They kept the livestock and wild animals alongside dead animals, in narrow lanes and stalls in close proximity to humans.

Amidst mounting criticism of the industry both domestically and internationally, the Chinese government banned the sale of all wild animal products in Wuhan in late January, and the trade and consumption of wild animals throughout China in late February. But there was talk that Wuhan would open the lockdown very soon, including the Huanan Seafood Market.

The team asked Ed to plead with Dr. Shei for a meeting, because they thought with Ed being Chinese, there could be some connection or favor if Ed pursued this request.

Dr. Shei was a woman in her late 50s, looked younger than her actual age, rather short, somewhat attractive, tough looking scientist who exhibited a no-nonsense atmosphere. She was known to be highly intelligent, determined to succeed in her endeavors and yet exuded openness and kindness to others.

Finally, Dr. Shei agreed to have a Zoom meeting with Ed's team, and gave a unique opportunity for an interview.

According to her, people knew her as the "Bat woman" in China. Her work in bats started 16 years ago during the SARS epidemic.

In 2004, Dr. Shei and her colleagues located a bat cave, and began trapping bats by putting a net at the opening before dusk and then waited for the nocturnal creatures to venture out to feed at night. Once the bats were trapped, they collected blood, saliva, fecal pellets and urine samples. Their team explored at least 30 caves, which was very difficult work that required working at nights, roaming the mountains, locating bats roosting in deep, narrow caves on steep terrain.

A bat cave in Yunnan Province, whose exact location was being kept secret, was inhabited by horseshoe bats that had "a rich gene pool of SARS-related coronavirus." There was a 97% match in the genomic sequences, and samples from three horseshoe bat species contained antibodies to the SARS virus. This was a turning point for their project.

Her researchers learned that the presence of the coronavirus in bats was ephemeral and seasonal—but an antibody reaction could last from weeks to years.

She spent the next five years in Shitou Cave, on the outskirts of Kunming, the capital of Yunnan, where they conducted intense sampling during different seasons, and their painstaking scrutiny had yielded a natural genetic library of bat-borne viruses. They discovered hundreds of bat-borne coronaviruses with incredible genetic diversity. Most of them were harmless, but dozens belonged to the SARS, which could infect human lung cells in a petri dish and cause SARS-like diseases in mice.

They speculated that the constant mixing of different viruses created a great opportunity for dangerous new pathogens to emerge. In the vicinity of such viral melting pots, "You don't need to be a wildlife trader to be infected," Dr. Shei said.

Near Shitou Cave, many villages sprawled among the lush hillsides in a region known for its roses, oranges, walnuts and hawthorn berries. In October 2015, her team collected blood samples from over 200 residents in four villages and found that six people, or nearly three percent, carried antibodies against SARS-like coronaviruses from bats, even though none of them had handled wildlife or reported SARS-like or other pneumonia-like symptoms.

Three years earlier in 2017, her team had been called in to investigate the virus profile in Yunnan's mountainous Mojiang County—famous for its fermented Pu'er tea—where six miners suffered from pneumonia-like diseases and two died.

In her opinion, with the growing dense human populations, increasing encroachment on wildlife habitats, changing the landscapes by building roads and mines, cutting down forests and intensifying agriculture, transporting wildlife and livestock across countries, and shipping their products around the world, and a sharp increase in both domestic and international travel, pandemics of new diseases were a mathematical near certainty.

China was not the only hotspot.

Dr. Shei said that she had been preparing scientific research for over the past 16 years, but last December was the most intense and the most stressful time of her life. With emerging atypical pneumonia patients and increasing death tolls, she had begun a test using a technique called polymerase chain reaction (PCR), and the team found that samples from five of seven patients had genetic sequences present in all coronaviruses.

By January 7, her team had determined that the new virus had indeed caused the disease those patients suffered—a conclusion based on results from analyses using PCR, full genome sequencing, antibody tests of blood samples, and the virus's ability to infect human lung cells in a petri dish. The virus was eventually named SARS-CoV-2, a coronavirus that the researchers had identified in horseshoe bats in Yunnan. Their results were published in Nature on February 3. "It's crystal clear that bats, once again, are the natural reservoir," and her researchers were sure that humans could have caught the deadly virus from bats.

She also mentioned approximately 500 human infectious diseases were found from the past century. The wildlife trade and consumption were only part of the problem.

The pigs across four farms in Qingyuan County in Guangdong, only 60 miles from the site where the SARS outbreak originated, in late 2016 suffered from acute vomiting and diarrhea, and nearly 25,000 of the pigs died. The cause of the illness—swine acute diarrhea syndrome (SADS)—turned out to be a virus whose genomic sequence was 98% identical to that of a coronavirus found in horseshoe bats in a nearby cave. Pigs and humans had very similar immune systems, making it easy for viruses to cross between the two species. Moreover, the SADS virus could infect cells from many species in a petri dish, including rodents, chickens, nonhuman primates and humans.

Given the scale of swine farming in many countries, including the US, looking for novel coronaviruses in pigs should be a top priority.

She mentioned that there were over 5,000 coronavirus strains waiting to be discovered and she was planning to lead a national project. They will systematically sample viruses in bat caves, with much wider scope and intensity. She was assuring Ed's team that the COVID-19 virus could not have been concocted in her lab.

Viruses are much more intelligent than humans in their mutations.

When Ed's team asked about the death of a young research student, she denied knowing that. There was a rumor that the WIV wiped out and scrapped the records of this event in the WIV. Dr. Shei adamantly denied this rumor and stated that the lab was a research facility to study the bat viruses, and incapable of being a bioweapon industry. She added that most scientists around the globe who had studied the genetics of the coronavirus said that the overwhelming probability was that it leapt from animal to human in a non-laboratory setting, as with HIV, Ebola and SARS. However, the US government needed to cover up their inadequacy and incompetence, so the president was talking about suing

Beijing to seek $10 million per every death. This was ridiculous in her opinion, especially the unproven allegation, just like the US failed to find the chemicals for mass destruction in Iraq.

The US repeatedly argued that it still had not gained access to the main campus of the Wuhan Institute of Virology, and so this time, Ed's team would not tour the place.

Ed thanked Dr. Shei profusely for her time and her generosity in accommodating the American team, and they ended the meeting. Ed was proud of the work this Chinese bat woman did, single-handedly studying and spending almost two decades of her life dedicated to the bats in the association of coronavirus. It gave motivation and inspiration to Ed that a Chinese scientist like himself could become a respective person to contribute in science. He and many American scientists could publish nothing in Nature easily. He also thought that Dr. Shei was doing this interview because Ed was there on the team, a Chinese connection, and it felt good being a valuable player on the team.

After the team ended the meeting with Dr. Shei, they continued to talk for a while saying that their missions were first; to get access to the lab itself, and two; to get the virus samples. They did neither. The team members told Ed to continue having a good relationship with Dr. Shei and infiltrate into the level 4 lab space and get the viral samples.

Ed understood their desires, actually the orders, but he could not figure out how to get these done.

CHAPTER 18

Nightmare

In the middle of the night, Emily was awakened by someone knocking on her door loudly. She put on her gown, opened the door and found the captain and a man who introduced himself as a doctor. Emily could tell something ominous happened by the look of their faces. "Are you Mrs. Emily Parker?" the captain asked.

"Yes," she said.

"I am sorry to tell you that your husband just died."

Emily could not stand any longer, so she just flopped down onto the floor. The doctor and the captain tried to hold her, but she just sat on the floor. She was in shock and could not breathe. The doctor got a brown bag for her to breathe into and out. After she gained the stability in breathing, they helped her to sit on a chair. They kept saying, "I am sorry."

They left after saying if there was anything they could do to help, please let them know. They also reminded her she could not visit her husband because the total area consisted of COVID-19 infected guests, and the captain decided to dock at the Barcelona port to release the dead bodies. Apparently, there were already three who died. They would need to disinfect the ship and release many infected patients who needed medical care and ventilators.

She just sat there like a catatonic psychiatric patient for quite a while, for she could not find the physical strength to get up. She began to cry. She could not imagine her life without Robert. It was supposed to be their once in a lifetime trip to celebrate their 50th wedding anniversary, but it ended up being a nightmare. The last time she saw Robert was when he said he loved Samantha.

She did not even know the basic things—how to manage the finances, where was the money, where were the retirement funds, which bank(s) had checking and saving accounts, where did Robert keep all the passwords for accessing the money, etc. She was relying on Robert to deal with all the money things. She was just enjoying her retired life without thinking she would lose Robert to take care of her. She did not even bring much money onto the cruise ship, maybe a few hundred dollars and her VISA credit card. There was no need to carry the cash or credit card on the ship because the cruise ship took care of everything, even the tips for the crew members.

She did not know what or how to do the next thing.

How would she get Robert out of the boat? How would she arrange the funeral? The first thing she should do was to tell Samantha what had just happened, but she could not get up, let alone find the business center and deal with the computer to email her. Sobbing began until she lost all her energy.

The captain made an announcement through the intercom that the ship would refuel in Barcelona, Spain that morning. He had received an order from Spain that the cruise ship could not allow the people to disembark, and to remain in their cabins for one day.

That morning, the cruise ship was near the harbor and several small boats were drawing alongside the hulking ocean liner. Within the ship were the rumors of many people who got infected with the coronavirus, and some had died. Two dozen Spanish health care workers in protective gowns boarded the ship, and helped by deck boys, marched directly to the captain's office.

Shortly after, the captain announced they would conduct COVID-19 testing.

Spanish officials were struggling with their response. They lacked enough kits to test everyone on board. Passengers were given N-95 masks and alcohol wipes. The crew were busy disinfecting the elevator buttons, doorknobs, common area decks and even the utensils.

Soon after Robert's demise, the number of passengers who tested positive for coronavirus grew to 69, and the next day to 135. And that number was not even a complete count because the test kits had run out. Obviously, the ship did not leave Spain after what they understood was "just refueling."

Many passengers felt under-informed, left to glean details from the spotty news reports and the Spanish officials. They were already told that the cruise line would reimburse the money for the trip and everyone would get free Wi-Fi, which was an expensive charge per day.

The captain was daunted by high-stakes challenges. This was unlike anything he had faced before. Rather than having the absolute authority as the captain of the ship, he was following the orders from both the Spanish government and his corporate command chain.

Rather than the usual bon voyage of the cruise, the captain and his crew were overseeing the logistics of food delivery, sanitation, and health care for the ship which had become a small city.

Most of the 150 crew members responded to the captain's orders with enthusiasm, delivering three meals a day to all the guests' cabins, but were ill-equipped, lacking personal protection equipment. They just had one surgical mask given to them daily and gloves with no training in dealing with a disease of this virulence. The crew members were from many countries: Mexicans, Hondurans, Venezuelans, Indonesians, Filipinos, Ukrainians, and Indians, and most of them did not speak fluent English nor understand technical and medical language, particularly.

But they could see day by day, more and more people were getting infected and dying with the disease. They had become afraid of their lives but could not talk to anyone because they needed their job and were afraid of retaliation from the cruise.

The kitchen of the ship was packed with food workers almost touching shoulder to shoulder, cooking and cleaning three meals a day for everyone. The crew were housed in quarters beneath the passenger decks, packed with bunk beds without windows, lacking ventilation. One by one, the crew members were also getting sick, and they had to divide the sick from healthy and designated the areas where the sick were quarantined for 14 days.

The sick helped the sick and isolated themselves in windowless rooms packed with more bunk beds.

The healthy crew members were taking showers immediately after working more than 15 hours a day with almost scalding hot temperature water, for they thought the virus might die faster if the water was unbearably hot to the point of skin burns. They were talking to each other secretly of the ways to get out of the boat, because it was not worth it to lose their lives working in such conditions, but they had nowhere to go other than jump off the boat and swim to the shore.

Every day, the passengers and crew members alike received a nasopharyngeal swab test and waited for a day or two to get the results. The Spanish health care officials came by every day in better protective gear; in hazmat suits with masks, facial covers, shoe covers and gloves, marching through the passengers and crew to scan their foreheads for fever with thermometer guns. They were escorting the sick people out of the ship and into ambulances, and the dead people inside hastily packed bags on gurneys by men in hazmat suits.

The people could see from the ship that their boat was filmed from afar by TV cameras set up onshore and several helicopters were buzzing around the ship.

An international conference call was arranged in the captain's office with the US President's administration, the State Department and the CDC. Several passenger-doctors joined the calls and made a strong recommendation to safely repatriate and quarantine all the people on the boat to the US by evacuating them soon, otherwise the remainder of the people onboard would all get COVID-19 infections. The plan discussed was to fly uninfected passengers out on chartered cargo jets, and those who tested positive would stay on the ship for 14 days because the Spanish government would not agree for them to disembark.

At first, the American government officers did not agree to have the uninfected passengers come out from the ship for various reasons, but the doctors made it clear their decision was unconscionable, would surely be out in the public news from inside the ship, making a threat. They argued that many passengers were elderly in their 70s and needed medications such as insulin, blood pressure and cholesterol pills, and they were the ones that would be devastated if infected. Finally, the CDC agreed to accept them in Atlanta to be quarantined for 14 days, and the US government officials agreed to send a cargo plane to the Barcelona airport.

The captain informed the passengers of their findings from the call, and within the next two days, those who tested negative with COVID-19 would be sent to the Barcelona airport by the bus to take a cargo plane to Atlanta, and into hotels nearby the CDC. All the other passengers who tested positive, and the crew, would remain on the ship and eventually go to Miami, Florida because it would be a shorter distance from Spain, and avoided going through the Panama Canal to arrive in San Francisco.

The passengers were staying in their cabins, for they feared getting infected. The crew did not have a choice but to stay with the cruise ship. The crew members were extremely disappointed they could not go with the passengers sooner back to the US. They were trapped with all the COIVD-19 infected people, and soon believed they would all get converted to positive testing, if not get sick, or die.

In time like this, life should be saved whether one is rich or poor, but the poor people always seem to get the shorter end of the stick.

Emily called Samantha with a newly gained Wi-Fi connection. It would be the middle of the night for Samantha, but Emily did not care.

"Honey, your father…" she could not end the sentence.

"What Mom, what's happening?" Samantha was almost angry because she was afraid of the next sentence her Mom was going to say.

"Your father died last night." There was a silence after this.

"I tested positive for COVID-19 testing. All the passengers are looking at me with suspicious eyes, and there is a rumor going around that I am the one who made everyone sick. I cannot go out of my cabin to face anyone because they all hate me and blame me. I cannot make it without Robert. He is gone, I mean, they took him. He is not on the ship with me anymore. I do not know where they took him. I don't know what's going to happen to him in Barcelona. I am not allowed to go anywhere, and I will not be taken by a cargo plane back to Atlanta because I am tested positive."

Emily was frantically saying everything at once, and Samantha was lost at the meaning of all the things her mom was saying.

"What is it?" Dr. Falkner said next to Samantha, and she said, "Shhh..." pointing her lips to her mouth.

"Is someone next to you, Samantha?" her mother asked.

"No, Mom," Samantha lied. "Mom, I thought you said that you will arrive in San Francisco this weekend, so I was going to go there to meet you guys there."

"No, everything is changed. We are in Spain now. It looks like we will be here for a while and then go to Miami, not San Francisco. I don't know when. Samantha, I am lost! I really do not know what to do. What are they going to do with your father here?"

"Mom, please calm down. You are making me really nervous. How did dad pass away? Did he get COVID-19? Did he get the ventilator from the boat? Were there doctors on the boat?"

"Honey, I was not even there when he passed. They would not let me go down there where they kept him. He died alone. I could not even say I love him or goodbye." Emily began to sob. Samantha was sobbing also. They talked more in a calmer way and Emily repeated what had happened more slowly.

After 30 minutes of crying together, they hung up the phone to call each other every day to update around the same time. It was 5:00 am for Samantha.

CHAPTER 19

Freedom

April 7, 2020

Samantha continued to cry in Dr. Falkner's arms in his bed. One thing led to another between them and they found themselves in his bed naked when Samantha's mother called. Samantha got up and dressed. She went out to the kitchen to brew coffee. She sat at the kitchen table watching the sun barely peeking through the horizon. She opened the window and heard the ocean waves more loudly.

She could not believe she was in this chair, sitting with a coffee mug, watching the sunrise. Such a beautiful house! And yet, she felt guilty about everything. She felt as if God was punishing her and took away her father's life because of what she did with Dr. Falkner. A married man! Adultery in his wife's bed at her house. Not only that, Samantha had a boyfriend. What was she going to do? How was she going to tell Ed what had happened?

Samantha was retracing how it happened. She spent the night in his house from April 1.

At the end of the week on Friday, April 3, Dr. Falkner took her to her apartment in the Bronx. Since it was getting late, they picked up a Jersey Mike's sandwich with chips and ate in her place. Then he drove off to Long Island. When he was leaving, she felt sad that she would not be able to see him for the weekend. She was rather surprised by her feeling and tried to explain herself; maybe it was because she had spent so much time, in fact 24/7 for a few days with him in a stressful environment that they created a strong bonding through a working relationship.

But she found herself glancing at him more, and felt attracted to his sensitivity, vulnerability, and even his handsome features. She also felt that he was watching her more than expected at times. He was paying more attention to her and occasionally found themselves looking at each other at the same time and turning away from the shock of it. Maybe it was the shyness. They worked together well without much need of communications. They were sensitive to each other's need and became aware of being together.

They went to work together and came home together. They ate together and even knew when each was going to the bathroom.

During the weekend, she got bored, and perhaps even missing Hart Island. She contacted Dr. Wells, her program director, who said that it would be better if she went to Hart Island for an additional week if she thought it was safe there. Dr. Wells also told her it would be okay with the program if she took a few days off, even the whole week to go to San Francisco for the family urgency, but she needed to fulfill and make up the time during her vacation to do an added autopsy rotation. And in the last two weeks of April, she would need to go to New York City's coroner's office in the Bronx and finish the rotation.

So, she bought a round-trip airplane ticket to San Francisco from New York JFK, with flexible dates in case she needed to change the dates.

But now she needed to cancel the ticket and maybe change the destination to Miami. She needed to figure out what to do for the week of April 12th by contacting Dr. Wells again.

She did not mind being with Dr. Falkner for another week, and in fact, she wanted to be with him. Maybe she could write the manuscript with him at his lovely house.

On Sunday night, Dr. Falkner came back to pick her up from the Bronx and she spent a night on Long Island. He said it would save some time to go to work on Monday morning and catch the boat to Hart Island. She agreed and felt excited to see him again. She wanted to deny the feeling she had for him, but she couldn't help but to recognize her deep longing to see him.

They drove without talking much and they each went to their separate bedrooms that night, feeling somewhat uncomfortable and awkward. On Monday night, when they came to his home, they had a relaxing time cooking spaghetti together and had a glass of wine watching the ocean waves.

He talked about how he met his wife in Italy.

He was traveling with his colleagues on holiday in Tuscany. His wife was a sister of one of his colleagues and they had met casually in one of the family dinners in the countryside at a Tuscan winery. They dated every day after that dinner for about two weeks while in Tuscany. She spoke particularly good English because she went to schools in the US along with her brother, who had become a doctor. Then she went back to Italy because she really did not like hustles and bustles in American life and missed her parents who were in the winery business. She had helped her parents in their business since she graduated from college, until they met.

She then came to the US to live with Dr. Falkner shortly after that time, and they got married within a year of living together. They had a beautiful life and had a baby boy together. They bought this house just last year and moved in from a small apartment on Long Island next to the hospital where he taught the medical students and worked as a medical examiner in Long Island's coroner office. His life seemed picturesque and ideal! But he said he had a new director who came to join less than a year ago from New York City. She was very unfriendly and tough on him, asking him to do all kinds of work and treated him as a minion. And hence, he called her "the bitch" and couldn't wait till he succeeded her position one day.

The pressure of the promotion became much more tangible when the university he was at notified him in a letter that this year would be his last year he could get promoted to the Associate level. He needed to write a substantial paper as a first or last author in a reputable journal this year, otherwise; he was out.

In order to make a tenure position, he must achieve the Associate Professor title from Assistant Professor within 7 years, and it was his 8th year. The university professor's life was stressful because of the demands of excellence in teaching, professional medical practice, and publications.

All required his full attention and the time for dedication. He found himself adjusting his professional and personal duties difficult, especially with a baby who required immediate and unforgiving attentions during the night, particularly. He was at his workplace most of his waking hours and dealt with the bitch who was not satisfied with his work no matter how hard he tried.

He also found that his wife was becoming more elusive, not talking to him about her unhappiness and depression. He had noticed her mood changes right after the birth of their son. He thought maybe it had to do with melancholy mood swings after the birth of a baby which was possibly due to the compression of pituitary glands which controlled hormonal changes in the brain. It is common in the postpartum time, called baby blues.

His wife had become very depressed, anxious, irritable and unable to cope with any stress. This went on the entire year and a half, until one day she just left with a note on the kitchen table saying she would be in Tuscany, back to be with her parents with the baby without a specific date of return. He had no idea she had bought the airplane tickets and packed, since it exhausted him working 12-13 hours a day.

He called his wife, but she would not talk to him. He talked to her parents, who said she needed some time to think and to let her be for a while. He felt that he failed his wife and his son.

He was also failing his career as a professor. He was in tears.

This was when Samantha was moved by his vulnerability and his total honesty, got up and hugged him to console him and they found themselves kissing, mixing his tears and the smell of wine.

They should have stopped, but she found herself getting undressed in his bedroom. Yes, it was a mutual and consensual act.

Now, she could not stop thinking about him. She wanted to be with him day and night. Whether it was on Hart Island amongst the inmates and the dead bodies in the trenches, she did not care. She wanted to know him more. She knew everything they were doing was wrong. And there were so many people who would get negatively affected by their doings. They would get hurt, including Samantha herself and Dr. Falkner. But she was willing to go through all these just to be with him. She did not even like herself thinking this way, such a shortsighted and selfish act, but the force of the desires and demands of her heart to be with him could not be stopped, disregarding the shamefulness and guilt.

Now, her father's death! It felt like God was definitely punishing her. He was a young 73-year-old man. Besides his mild heart attack several years ago, he was a vital, fun, loving father who played 18 holes of golf almost every day without getting fatigued. Everything seemed upside down. Her love life, pandemic, her parent's situation, loss of her father and how to do the funeral when his body was in Spain of all places. And yet, she was amazingly content being there with Dr. Falkner, drinking tasty coffee in his house, watching the sun rise. Shortly after, they both needed to dress to go to work at Hart Island.

Dr. Falkner came out in his boxer shorts and hugged her from behind. "Good morning, my Sam. Tell me what is on your mind. Why were you crying?"

Samantha told him what was happening with her parents and that she had lost her father. She cried and found herself unable to talk. He just hugged her in his big chest and shoulders and let her cry. All he said was, "I know, I know, my father also died."

Samantha appreciated her freedom that she found in his shoulders to be whoever she was at the moment without trying to impress him, and never even bothered to put on her makeup whenever she was with him. It was mostly because of the work she was doing, wearing the mask and face shield covering most of her face so there was really no need to put on makeup. Besides, because of the perspiration, all the makeup would be smudged. There was nothing to hide with Dr. Falkner. She felt accepted by him no matter what she looked like and that gave her comfortable freedom, which she had never felt with Ed.

Maybe because Ed's parents never accepted her, she had to put on additional makeup and additional diplomas, degrees, or credits to buy their acceptance.

She wanted to stay there with Dr. Falkner like that forever. It was the sweetest moment of her life; she felt fully content, fully happy and fully peaceful.

But as usual, the life demands everything to end, whether or not she liked it.

She had to dress and go to work. At least she was with a man she had begun to adore.

CHAPTER 20

God in disguise

April 9, 2020

Emily had cabin fever. She had not gone out for at least 3-4 days; she couldn't remember. The cruise ship was still docked at Barcelona for reasons not clear to everyone. All the actions they could see were Spanish government officials coming back to do more testing. She was told at least 150 people had tested positive with COVID-19. She ventured out at least to take a walk around the pool areas. After the passengers who had tested negative for COVID-19 disembarked to go to Atlanta by a cargo flight sent by the US government several days ago, the ship seemed emptied.

She walked out and locked the cabin door behind her. It seemed odd and foreign that she was walking around the hallways. She took the elevator to the top floor where there were at least two pools and a splendid view of the water with an ocean breeze. She took a deep breath. It felt good to be out and walking. There were several people who had the same idea as hers, circling around the pool to fast walk for exercise. Everyone was wearing an N-95 mask and maintained at least six feet of distance between them. The passengers who remained on the ship had supposedly tested positive for COVID-19, and all the crew members remained, regardless of their testing status. Emily felt sympathetic toward the crew who remained to work and serve the passengers. Overall, they appeared calm and pleasant, still serving the guests with much respect and friendliness.

As she was walking, two Caucasian ladies in their late 40s stared at Emily for quite a while. As they approached Emily, one lady said to Emily, "It's all your fault. You should be ashamed of yourself. We heard your husband died because of you. And look what happened here to all of us, just because of you. Why don't you go back to your home to China!"

The other lady said with a British accent, "Hear, hear! Go back to your home."

They were angry and shouted out to Emily. All the other people looked toward the commotion where Emily and those two ladies were located. Emily could say nothing to defend herself. She was not Chinese and how dare they say such things when everyone on board were foreigners while here in Spain.

The British lady should go back to her home, Emily thought. This ship is a US territory cruise!

Emily got so upset that she stopped walking to exercise and almost ran out of there to go back to her cabin. Her heart was pounding with anger. Not only had she lost her husband on this trip, she was getting discrimination of being an Asian person on this expensive cruise by the Caucasian women.

She always felt some protection under her husband who was a Caucasian; people treated her better when she was nearby her husband, but when she was alone, shopping or eating at the restaurants, people did not ask her, "How can I help you or do you need anything?" She had tried to deny the feelings of discrimination both on the cruise ship and in the US, even in San Francisco, especially when she was shopping at the expensive stores.

Probably, she did get less discriminatory remarks when she was with her husband. One time, she was taking a flight with a first class seat and some flight attendant called out and said, "You can't sit there, it is for Mrs. Parker." That happened when Robert had still not boarded because he had to go to the bathroom and Emily boarded alone.

Emily was now hyperventilating for a while, and then she became sad and cried out loudly. She went out to get some fresh air on her deck and sat on a chair. The sun was setting from the horizon, which made her more melancholy. She looked at the blue ocean with nice steady waves and a mild breeze. She was on the 6th floor deck and the height from the water seemed terribly tall from her angle, but it appeared to be calling her to jump over. She was lost without her husband, a constant companion, friend, confidant and who took care of her. There was no reason to go on by herself. She lost all hopes to live alone without him. She felt inadequate and incompetent to take care of the finances, paying the bills and taxes, and the immense house in San Francisco that needed much repairs.

She was nobody if she did not have Robert, she thought. The only thing that would hinder her to die was Samantha; how would Samantha handle her mother's suicide? Emily kept on thinking, what was the point of living. Samantha was now a grown woman, a doctor, and she would be better off without taking care of an incompetent mother who would constantly need her daughter to look after her wellbeing. Emily was now almost 70 years old, and she was not getting any younger. She would be a total burden to Samantha, especially with the distance of 3,000 miles apart from New York City to San Francisco to take care of her mother. Who needs that? Besides, if Robert and Emily both died, then Samantha would get more life insurance money. With that money, Samantha did not need to complete her training to become a "real doctor," but could live comfortably without ever working. They had the house in San Francisco fully paid, and it just required some constant maintenance repairs, especially the large pool which needed a new cement covering. Emily had lived a good life thus far, and there would be nothing more she desired to have.

But then, Emily thought, she really wanted to see Samantha get married and have a few children. She would love to see the grandchildren and play with them. She imagined Samantha having a son and a daughter, dropped off to Emily for a babysitter job occasionally, and she would buy toys for a boy and dolls and lovely princess dresses for a girl.

Emily smiled just thinking about it.

She would miss all the milestone moments for Samantha if she jumped off from the ship at this moment. But was that enough reason to keep living? What else was there for Emily to hope for in her life?

Then, she remembered the Lord, her God, who saved her from the eternal death. Emily was a born-again Christian. Her faith in the Lord was important to her. Robert and Emily both were devout Christians, and they went to church every Sunday; well, almost every Sunday. She still had her women's Bible studies, church fellowship gatherings to knit together, and she had Mrs. Kong to play Baduk games. She had joy in life, doing church activities, and friends she would miss terribly. She just cried and cried. Losing her life at this moment seemed unfair, but she felt unwanted. Definitely these cruise ship guests did not want her. Apparently, there was a rumor that Emily was the source of the COVID-19 infection, a patient zero on this cruise ship. She wondered how long this rumor had been going on and how many people were gossiping behind her back. What a terrible rumor that was, since no one really knew who brought that virus onto this ship.

What would Robert say if she joined him, entering the heaven today? Would she even be able to enter the heaven if she committed a suicide? She was told by her minister during a sermon if someone committed a suicide, he or she could not end up going to heaven. If this was true, Emily would be forever condemned in the hell burning for the rest of her life. That made her feel scared to death. She wanted to be with Robert in the heaven when she died. She also realized that she would need so much courage to jump overboard.

The action of jumping to release and let go of the life required tremendous hate toward herself and life, which she did not have. She did not hate herself, and she did not hate her life.

She had yet to see what life could offer to her, mainly because of Samantha. She lacked courage to commit such an act, also.

She untied her sneakers and removed her socks. Slowly, she moved toward the edge of the glass and looked at the deep blue ocean. At this moment, it looked more deep, black and it appeared cold. She imagined the impact of her body when she dropped into the cold water. It was not high enough to lose consciousness like the Golden Gate Bridge from San Francisco, which would have been better to jump off. She would rather not feel the impact and freezing temperature or go through the pain of drowning.

She wished she was at the Golden Gate Bridge in San Francisco now. She was trying to put one of her legs out and over the glass to stand on the ledge of the boat. The wind was blowing and she lost her balance, almost tipping over as she grabbed the wall and barely held on to regain her balance. She then put another leg over and now she was standing on the ledge outside the glass. She stood there and looked at the bottom of the ship. She was still holding on to the wall, crying.

She realized that she should have written a note for Samantha, at least to tell her she loves her daughter.

At that moment, one of the cleaning ladies came into her cabin and saw Emily standing on the edge of the deck. She ran to Emily and said, "Please, don't, please don't do that!"

The cleaning lady was a different person today, a middle-aged Filipino woman who extended both arms, trying to catch Emily's hands with a desperate face with tears.

"They think I am the one who brought this virus!" Emily said.

"No, they are wrong! Please step inside, please."

"I have no reason to live anymore. My husband died."

"Yes, you have reasons to live. God is watching you now, and the Lord is sad to see you like this. He has purposes in your life, please come inside."

"How do you know God even exists or cares about me?"

"I just know; you need to have faith. He is looking at you now with tears in His eyes."

"I lost the love of my life and I have nothing anymore."

"Do you have children, grandchildren?"

"I have a daughter."

"How old is she? Is she with you here?"

"No, she is not here with me. She is 30."

"Is she beautiful like you? She must be a beautiful woman, just like you, Asian?"

"Yes, she is beautiful. She is mixed American Asian. I married a white man."

"Oh, she must be really beautiful then. Don't you think she will miss you if you do this? What about her? Did you think about her if you do this? She will be so sad, so devastated."

"Yes, she will be. I want to see her getting married and have children of her own."

"Sure, you do, you must see grandchildren. They will miss having grandmother too!"

Emily was sobbing now. The cleaning lady grabbed Emily's hands and pulled Emily toward her.

"Now, careful, careful, bring your leg inside one at a time." Emily held the cleaning lady's hands tightly and did as she was told. Emily was safely inside the glass on the deck and they embraced, both crying and smiling at the same time.

"Good, good, now you are safe. I am so happy. You are an Asian! We need to keep each other safe and happy," the cleaning lady said.

"Thank you, thank you!"

"Now, you will pick up the phone and get a warm tea with cookies. Today, they cooked chocolate with peanut butter cookies. I had them already for my lunch. It's really good."

Emily continued to embrace her, for she needed someone to hug her now. She needed to be accepted by someone. Emily thought this was her Lord, her God in a woman's body revealed to her in the time of desperation. It was good to be held by someone warm and told by someone with a voice to eat chocolate cookies. She could not stop crying.

After the cleaning lady left, Emily could not figure out why she came at that hour. Usually the cleaning crew came in the morning, never in the hours of sunset. Right after dinner time, another crew comes to turn the bed over and leave chocolates and that was about 8:00 pm. Emily realized that her Lord has sent an Asian woman to console her during the darkest hour of her life. If the Asian woman had not come, Emily probably would have jumped over and by this time, she would be in the deep water. She did not even know how to swim.

Maybe it was God Himself disguised as an Asian woman.

CHAPTER 21

Ideal man

New York City claimed 731 deaths on 4/7/20, 779 on 4/8/20, and another 799 on 4/9/20 due to COVID-19. These were actual death counts just in the city of New York. In the US, a total death count was approaching 17,000, and worldwide it was 92,798. These numbers were numbing, especially the way media portrayed this as just numbers. New York City became an epicenter of COVID-19. As a result, they created more hospital beds to increase capacity to 90,000 to treat COVID-19 and recruited 7,000 additional medical workers from a reserve force of retired and out-of-state nurses and doctors to aid in the fight.

The bodies were piled up in all hospital morgues and funeral homes to maximum capacity, and the city was now storing bodies in the refrigerated truck trailers stretched for several blocks on the streets and parking lots. City Hall acknowledged that the trucks were part of a fleet being used for long-term storage of dead bodies until the family of loved ones claimed the bodies. But in reality, not too many family members claimed the bodies.

There were many reasons; funeral directors could not handle the sheer number of the dead. Many people could not afford to have a proper funeral since they lost their jobs. The fear of contracting COVID-19 from handling the bodies was real. The complexity of finding the dead body was tortuous, and a daunting task for the family. Most of the dying patients from COVID-19 died with no family members around to say goodbye and died a lonely death.

The living had to live, according to the lockdown law, and go out only to buy food from the grocers to eat. The time was truly unforgiving.

After 15 days inside the trailers, the bodies from morgues and funeral homes were sent to Hart Island or other places to be buried.

Dr. Falkner and Samantha could not keep up the work at Hart Island. Most of the dead bodies were dumped into the cheap pine coffins with the names written on the coffins, in case the family members come back to claim the body. The sheer volume of the dead was just too overwhelming for medical examiners to deal with. Dr. Falkner did not perform any autopsies recently. He decided not to continue the work at Hart Island as the danger of contracting the coronavirus became too risky for both himself and Samantha. He left all the work to bury the dead to the inmates and contract workers from New York City.

Dr. Falkner went to his coroner's office on Long Island instead, because the COVID-19 deaths had steadily increased on Long Island, needing the medical examiners there. No one wanted to do autopsy service on Long Island because the cause of death was already known and there was really no need to perform an autopsy. Dr. Falkner already had over 20 autopsies performed at Hart Island, sufficient to do his studies to publish the organ damages caused by COVID-19. He also had a variety of ages and races in the cases so he could draw potential differences in the findings.

Samantha decided to follow him to the coroner's office and help him extract data, review the slides, take pictures of interesting findings, and write a manuscript with him. She was happy to be with him, observing how he handled all the difficult issues during the pandemic time with an increased volume of deaths and the pressures in the morgue. She followed him as if she was his shadow, trying to learn as much as she could. She never imagined being a medical examiner herself because she hated autopsy, but seeing Dr. Falkner do his work as a medical examiner was educational and surprisingly pleasing to her. He did not lose his temper easily, always cool as a cucumber in dealing with difficult situations and personnel issues, and his quiet and calm nature was admirable to her, something she would like to emulate.

Samantha stayed watching him in the coroner's office during the day and at his house at night the entire week. She did not get tired of him. They worked side by side writing the manuscript. He was meticulous in writing and put the figures together to convey accurate findings to the scientific readers. He was aiming high, hoping to publish in The New England of Journal Medicine.

Dr. Falkner had a beautiful library in his house, wall to wall cherry hardwood bookcases filled with mostly medical books, and a large long table with a few chairs to study. Next to the table was a long comfortable couch, a perfect place to read and fall asleep. It was quiet, just soft ocean sounds and cool breezes from the window. She imagined living in a similar house one day after she finished her residency program. She had a beautiful ocean view house growing up in San Francisco where her parents still lived, and she was used to seeing the endless blue ocean. So, Dr. Falkner's house made her very comfortable, as if it was her house and it felt natural to stay there. An added advantage of Dr. Falkner's place was the library that she always dreamed of and the espresso machine with a wet bar and small sink, so she did not even have to walk across to the kitchen to make a cup of coffee which went so well with reading books.

And seeing such a handsome doctor focusing on reading and writing on his laptop amid all the books was something Samantha recognized she could not help herself not to get attracted to.

When her friends asked her previously what kind of man made her go wild sexually, she could not answer for sure, but now, she had found it. Some friends of hers said a cook with a white apron, or captain of the airplane, or a man with a French accent made them sexy. None of them were interesting to her, and she was not sure what made her sexy, but now she was seeing one right in front of her. She could not help herself from looking at Dr. Falkner while she was trying to focus on writing about the figure descriptions.

She was to finish all her parts by tomorrow, which was her last day with Dr. Falkner. That Friday came too soon, and she could not help feeling sad. Next week, she was to go back to her Bronx hospital and would do the autopsy rotation there. They were having a tremendous amount of people dying due to COVID-19, and she had heard they filled the morgue with bodies which no one was claiming.

Samantha was sipping her espresso coffee, looking at David Falkner. She could not believe she had slept with him. How did this happen so quickly?

She was not the type who slept around. In fact, she had not even slept with Ed, her boyfriend over several years. There were many opportunities to do so with Ed, but she wanted to keep her virginity until she got married to Ed, and that was something she was taught by her parents and her church. In an actual sense, she never had an urge or significant desire to sleep with Ed. Ed was just a comfortable friend, easy to get along with and someone she could be with, and no pressure to please sexually. They had known each other so well, almost like a brother and sister. Ed also did not pressure her to sleep with him. He was very patient with her and once said that he would wait for the wedding night.

Dr. Falkner was a totally different man. She found herself not being able to control herself. In fact, she did not even know that she had such a strong sexual urge. When she was with him, she wanted to be close to him physically, wanting his attention constantly, and sex was a natural next step. She always thought the first time would be just painful, but she did not find the intercourse painful at all with him. It was pleasurable as all the movies she watched over the years. The best part was to lie with him afterward and just talk next to him, his arms holding her.

She found him distant at times, even when he was holding her. He probably was thinking about his wife. He probably felt guilty sleeping with a young woman, a resident under him who he should not have this kind of relationship with. He probably was thinking what would happen in a worst scenario and would see the headline of a tabloid newspaper, A Medical Examiner Found Dead with Heart Attack Next to a young Pathology Resident.

They never talked about what he would do with his marriage, or his wife and son. To Samantha, she decided to just think about now, and would not complicate her thoughts with Dr. Falkner, for she knew this was just a temporary thing. He was a married man with family. She had not thought through any possible future with him, and that was okay with her. It was a few days of life with an uncontrollable strong emotion of what might be called love, that she had dreamed about having once in her lifetime. When she walked out of his place, she could never return. She would walk away from him and he would have to do the same. For Samantha, having this experience with David Falkner once in her life was enough for her. She now knew and would treasure this experience as a sparkling moment of her life. It was entirely just for her to savor. No one could steal her love for someone like David Falkner, a man of her life, despite the fact that she could not have him as a lover forever.

But having him in her life for these two weeks would be enough for her to live the rest of her life with the memory of how this love felt like. No matter who and what would be said, whether she was a sinner or had adultery with a married man, she would have to accept it as her own burden in her heart, but she would cherish the part her love was pure. And that she could have a romantic love, at least once in her life would be sufficient for her to claim that she had experienced something special in her life.

Dr. Falkner looked at Samantha watching him, drinking coffee and thinking something. He got up, pushed her to the bookcase and started to kiss her. They started to breathe heavily.

CHAPTER 22

Time to say goodbye

April 12, 2020

On late Sunday night, Dr. Falkner drove Samantha to her apartment in the Bronx. They both knew that it was the end of their short romance. There was no romantic dinner in a fancy restaurant, bouquet of flowers, or even a cheap ring. It was just work, hardship at Hart Island seeing things that no one should see, long hours and writing scientific cold facts about COVID-19, how the virus killed the hosts. Nothing was romantic about their relationship but when two people go through such a hardship for 24 hours a day, an incomprehensive and inexpressible time of life, the bonds that form were so strong, in this case it led to a romantic relationship.

They had a wonderful weekend together. They walked along the beach at sunset, collected a few lovely stones and seashells and talked about the future, how each of them would like to live the old age. His ideal life in his old age did not include Samantha, but definitely his son. He talked about being a great father to his son, and about retiring in the winery hills of Tuscany. Even though he never talked about his wife, Samantha understood that he would go back to his wife.

Samantha talked about her short-term goals, going back to San Francisco to be with her mother for a while, finding her father's body in Barcelona to cremate and flying the remains back to the US, taking care of the house from a long distance until she finished her residency, and trying to get a job near San Francisco to be near her mother.

She told Dr. Falkner about her boyfriend Ed, how they met and where they were now. Recently she did not respond to his emails for weeks because she felt they were going in separate ways. She talked about his family not truly embracing her, and there seemed nothing she could do to please them. And she was tired of trying to be accepted by them.

She naturally talked about racial issues that Dr. Falkner had probably never even thought about because he did not have to think about this. He seemed very interested in her view of the world in the eye of an Asian woman. She talked about growing up; she was ashamed of her mother being a Korean American with broken English.

She was embarrassed to have birthday parties at her house even though she always had a large beautiful ocean view house that her friends adored. She talked about getting embarrassed to display kimchee on the dinner table and talked badly to her mom about the stinky smells. She hated to have part of her face and hair looking like Asians.

It was when she went to college that she started to respect her mom, especially in the summer, as she and her mom went to Korea, saw her relatives, drove around the countryside, and spent some time to see the culture. She appreciated her part of a unique heritage, how Koreans think you were a part of them, embraced her and took her into their world, and she began to have pride in her mother's language and culture. She came to realize that if she did not accept her 50% Asian DNA, she would ultimately never learn to accept herself for who she was. She decided to embrace herself, the inevitable fact about who she really was, and from then on, she appreciated and even became proud of her heritage.

Dr. Falkner was keenly interested in Samantha cooking Korean double fried chicken when she talked about it. So, they went to get the chicken wings, and they cooked together and had a lovely time eating it with a glass of wine. The time she spent in his house was like her honeymoon. Even though she was worried about her mom's whereabouts, she had been deeply appreciating the time with Dr. Falkner. It seemed perhaps sweeter because the relationship should not have happened and knew their time would end soon.

He parked in the street and turned off his headlights. They did not talk the whole time during the drive. It was a time to say goodbye. But no one spoke to break the silence. Finally, Samantha said, "Thank you for driving me." She gathered her stuff and was ready to open the door.

"Just a minute, Sam."

"I think this is it, Dr. Falkner," Samantha never learned to call him David as he requested.

"So, what will you be doing next week?"

"Autopsy rotation at my hospital."

"Oh, yes!"

"Will you have another resident next week?"

"No, you are it for the month of April."

"Do you usually sleep with female residents?" Samantha was curious. She really did not know Dr. Falkner whether he was a playboy seducing young residents to sleep with.

"NO! I have never done that!" He seemed angry she asked such a question.

"What will you do? Are you going to go see your son in Italy?"

"I should, but I cannot. No one can travel to Italy from New York City now."

"Well, I wish you well. I finished my part for the manuscript. I think it is a very good paper. I am incredibly happy that I could be a part of it. Thank you for the opportunity and including me as an author."

"When can I see you again?"

"It's not a good idea we see each other anymore. I think you know why."

There was a long silence. Samantha opened the door and got out of the car. There was no last kiss, hugs and warm wishes. Not even goodbye. She left the car and went into her apartment. The car was still parked when she took the elevator to her unit.

CHAPTER 23

Origin of detrimental loss

Emily found herself befriended with Mahalia, a Filipino woman who saved her life. The cruise ship took off yesterday, finally, to Miami. Supposedly all the passengers were positive with the COVID-19 testing.

Many of the crew members were getting sick with the virus now, and only half were actually working in the service line. The captain was still maintaining his calmness with excellent service in mind for the remaining passengers in different stages of the viral infection. Some were perfectly fine like Emily; some were just having mild flu-like symptoms, and some were getting sick by the day. Emily did not know the conditions of the crew, how many were sick, and where they were in the ship.

Emily looked for Mahalia and found her in the laundry area where she was working most of the waking hours. During her break, Emily took her to her cabin to eat wonderfully, a beautifully placed lunch with Mahalia and enjoyed food and conversation with her. Mahalia loved to stay in her cabin, hidden from the ugliness of the crew life, momentarily forgetting her status and enjoyed eating expensive food she only could look at and never able to taste.

Emily ordered the room service more than she could ever eat by herself. She even asked Mahalia what she would like to taste and gave her the menu to order from. Mahalia was so excited to taste lobsters, T-bone steak, and even perfectly fried chicken.

They always ordered a bowl of white rice to accompany the main dish, even if the rice did not match with the main course. Since some crew members were Asians, they always cooked some form of rice every meal. Mahalia also brought a bottle of Huy Fong's Sriracha sauce with her, which Emily kept in the small refrigerator in her cabin. They took it out and smothered it on top of everything and every dish they had.

Emily wanted Mahalia to come for lunch and dinner, but Mahalia was afraid some of her workers might find out and get caught that she was going to one of the passenger's cabins to eat guest's food, which was against their policy. It was their strict policy to never join the guests in eating, drinking or any social contacts.

All they could say to the guests were, "Yes sir, yes ma'am, I will bring it to you, how can I help you?" The class difference was definitely visible between the guests and the crew workers from downstairs.

Obviously, the upstairs crew members were entirely a different story; such as captain, co-captains, even chefs and sommeliers. They got to stay in a nice cabin just like passengers, sometimes even better suites.

Emily found out that Mahalia was not an American citizen. She came from the Philippines and she was the breadwinner of her household to support her elderly mother and four siblings who were all younger than her, age between ten to college, and she was only 30 years old. She wanted to be married and have a few kids of her own but did not find a man of her dream because she was always traveling in the cruise ship.

Her time on the boat was at a minimum nine months, if not 11 months. She said she did not want to marry someone in the cruise ship because the chances were, they would not be well off and would struggle to live, just like her. She did not see herself working in the ship for more than five years. She wanted to settle down with a man, married and able to go to church on Sundays.

Emily asked how Mahalia came to her cabin on the day Emily was about to jump off the ship and she said she was told from the regular cleaning lady who attended Emily's room that she had forgotten to bring the extra blanket Emily asked for that day, and she also just had an urge to come to her cabin at that time.

They both recognized that it was God's doing to prevent Emily to do a silly thing. Emily learned through Mahalia that she has had so many blessings in her life that she was not even aware.

She never had to skip a meal because she couldn't afford the money, for instance. Emily had so many privileges and had become insensitive to recognize how much God had given to her.

Although God had taken her husband Robert, she realized that she had so much to offer to people like Mahalia. And she had a daughter to look after.

Emily was thinking a short while ago, when she was having their 50th anniversary wedding ceremony, how unknown passengers around her celebrated with them with champagne glasses raised high for them and ate their gorgeous wedding cake. But now, those same people in the current circumstances were turning their heads as if Emily should not exist and telling her to go back to her home. How easily people changed their attitudes and minds according to the situations.

There was no loyalty in its pure sense and difference between friend or foe from people were in thin air depending on the circumstances. If Emily did not have money, they would treat her like Mahalia, unseen, subservient, a mere commodity to use for their advantages.

This made Emily to realize that she needed to be strong, controlling her money tightly to make sure that she would not be treated as a naïve foreigner who they could take an advantage to steal from her, now that she had lost her husband. They would see her as a weaponless minority widow in the society without a protective husband. She also needed to be strong and clever for Samantha so that her daughter would not see her as a burden.

During the long journey crossing the Atlantic Ocean, Emily called Mrs. Kong to tell her that Robert passed away with COVID-19. Mrs. Kong was in a total shock and cried with Emily. Emily did not tell her about her suicide attempt. Then Mrs. Kong said something Emily was in shock to find out. Mrs. Kong said that when she returned to San Francisco on January 6th, her sister's family got sick, all of them.

In fact, it began on November 17, 2019, when her sister's first son died, and he worked at the Wuhan Institute of Virology laboratory. He was a research assistant or a graduate student; she was not sure. He joined the place right after finishing the college from Beijing. He was very smart, hope of the family to be the next brilliant scientist in China.

He was feeling extremely tired and sick the day he reported to work.

Her sister told him not to go to work that day, but he was adamant about his work ethic and went to work and died in the workplace inside the laboratory.

That was one reason why Mrs. Kong went to Wuhan in November before the Thanksgiving Holiday; she was attending the funeral.

They had no idea why he died, for he was only 24 years old. He was working under Dr. Shei, who was the director of the Wuhan Institute of Virology.

No one could figure out the cause of death until early December, when Wuhan hospitals were having clusters of SARS-like pneumonia cases. On December 31, the Chinese government finally admitted to WHO that they had 41 cases of atypical SARS-like pneumonia cases. China said that the very first death was on January 11, 2020, an old man 57 or 61 years of age who went to the seafood market constantly, but Mrs. Kong thought that was not the case.

The very first case may have been her nephew who worked at the laboratory.

The Chinese government had forced many doctors to not reveal their findings and also retrieved scientific papers from the scientists who wrote about the COVID-19 deaths. The people of China were living under the communist regime and had no power to defend for themselves against the government.

Chinese people did not believe their own government, especially at a time like this when China looked bad. The Chinese government should have learned the lesson from SARS in 2003 when they tried to cover up the epidemic that originated from China, and again in 2019 they tried to hide. No one from China believed the reported number of deaths from the government because almost all people had lost at least someone from their family.

Mrs. Kong had come to San Francisco on January 6, 2020 when the flights from Wuhan to US had no restrictions which made her feel lucky, otherwise, she would have gone through the strict lockdown in Wuhan.

But she admitted that she may have given the bad virus to Bita, her cleaning lady who died. Later, both her parents died also from the same disease. Bita's husband was left with two little children to take care of, and he was unemployed now. Mrs. Kong went to see Bita's husband and gave him thousands of dollars, for she felt guilty. Of course, she did not tell him she might have been the source of the bad virus.

She could not bring up that fact.

Mrs. Kong said that she was so sorry for Emily because Robert died of COVID-19. If it was a fact that Mrs. Kong was the original source of transmitting the virus to all other people around, she wanted to just kill herself. She felt so remorse and sad by this possibility that she could not face Emily anymore.

Emily said don't do stupid thing such as killing herself to Mrs. Kong. Emily could not face any further death right now. No matter what, all human lives were under God's control and not of Mrs. Kong, for she did not have that kind of power to kill other people.

When they hung up the phone, Emily knew exactly how Mrs. Kong might have felt, for Emily was facing the same accusation from the cruise ship. Being an original target for spreading this terrible disease was an unbearable burden for anyone. Emily would rather die than face the consequence of the original culprit who had brought so many deaths and illness to her neighbors.

She was sure that Mrs. Kong would contemplate suicide, especially knowing Robert also died with COVID-19. Emily also did not realize Bita and her elderly parents had died.

She was wondering how many people around her had lost their lives due to this pandemic. She was worried sick about her daughter Samantha, for she was in a frontline dealing with so many deaths in New York City of all places right now.

If she had any choice of telling Samantha what to do, she would tell her to quit that doctor thing right now, but she knew her daughter well. Samantha would not quit the doctor thing at any cost. She was stubborn as Emily, maybe more than Emily.

Emily could not help getting angry at the Chinese government; only if they had contained the virus earlier by admitting the situations in even December, the whole world would not have faced these detrimental losses.

CHAPTER 24

Residency program

April 13, 2020

Samantha returned to her home hospital in the Bronx and began a 2-week autopsy rotation. Her home hospital was affiliated with the Bronx Coroner and Medical Examiner, which was a unique situation. Samantha was in her third year of pathology residency. She was required to finish five years of training during the residency, composed of an equal number of years in anatomic and clinical pathology rotations.

Within the anatomic section, she had to take four months of autopsy rotation; three months in her hospital and one month in the coroner's office doing forensic pathology. During the medical examiner's autopsy rotation, which Samantha was doing now, they expected her to attend at least one homicide investigation, go through one ambulance pick up, and perform an autopsy on a severely decomposed body.

In Samantha's case, she already had two weeks of forensic pathology experience on Hart Island and in the coroner's office on Long Island, and would be in the Bronx coroner's office for the remaining weeks.

Samantha and other pathology residents had many options to go through any coroner's office in New York City of their choice depending on the resident's desire. Some pathology residents who wanted to be a medical examiner went to the busiest and largest facility to get more exposure. In Samantha's case, she wanted to get minimal exposure and hence she took the easier place such as Long Island, where the death tolls were typically low.

During the pandemic, because of overwhelming amounts of COVID-19 deaths, the number of autopsy requests from the clinicians had decreased tremendously. The hospital morgue was facing very different challenges; a lack of space to store the bodies. The morgue had eight refrigerated drawer spaces of dead bodies, but the bodies kept coming.

They brought small bunk beds, but they already filled those, so they began stacking the bodies on the floor.

Added to the already existing problem was that the elderly nursing home facility next to the hospital was bringing their dead bodies, which was now becoming more than 50% of their total volume.

In the Bronx coroner's office, which was affiliated with her hospital, had on average over 300 stored dead bodies, but during the pandemic, it was accumulating countless bodies every day, resulting in a horrifically overcrowded and chaotic facility.

The Medical Examiners of the Bronx hospital were overwhelmed with the pressure to move the bodies out of the morgue, and they spent all their time on the phone with funeral homes and family members to claim the bodies instead of actually doing the autopsies.

They did not want to deal with the residents in the training program and told Samantha to go back home and wait for the assignment to be called for a homicide investigation, which was a part of the training.

All the residency training programs including hers were undergoing a dilemma of how to continue the education program during the pandemic time. This was affecting not just the pathology residency, but was across all disciplines like radiology, surgery, internal medicine, etc. Exposure to the virus for all health care workers in all levels was ultimately unavoidable.

And the question was, what would be the appropriate role of trainees during the pandemics?

Historically, physicians had always been at the front lines of deadly outbreaks, and as a result, were regularly infected by the same disease as their patients.

This was true in yellow fever to cholera to typhoid fever in the past eras of unregulated medical and graduate medical education.

However, Graduate Medical Education (GME) which was the governing body of all residency training programs in the US, had been more structured to a landscape of predominantly hospital-based internships, and eventually specialty-focused residencies with a unified accrediting body.

Most physicians including residents were expected to be on duty to treat despite their fears and perceived risk, and GME had now shifted the conversation to reconsider the vulnerability of the trainee, and much wider efforts were undertaken to protect trainees from potential exposure.

In particular, during the Ebola epidemic in 2015, students were prohibited to have contacts with presumed cases of the disease and the reasons included insufficient training, liability, and a less than clear moral imperative.

To limit total number of exposures and to mitigate the potential for disease spread, faculty were compelled to care for all patients, even in the face of personal risk, by virtue of their training, their contracts, and their professional codes of conduct.

The downside to this argument was that residents would miss the training opportunity, which would put residents at higher risk, both now and in the future.

Also, the opportunity to model professionalism in attitudes and skills necessary for life as a physician would be missed.

Residency was not just about attaining the knowledge of medicine. With the COVID-19 pandemic, health care systems including GME were developing protocols ad hoc as time allowed, flying by the seat of their pants in US hospitals and others around the globe who were facing this unknown enemy.

The pathology residents in Samantha's program had 20 residents and 20 fellows and most of them were still reporting to a workplace, but the experience was severely limited because of a decrease in surgical specimens to about 20-25% of normal numbers in the anatomic pathology section.

Most of the outpatient elective surgeries and even many of the cancer surgeries had been discontinued. The cancer screenings were also stopped, so the biopsy specimens such as breast cancer using mammogram from radiologists, colorectal cancer using endoscopic procedures from gastroenterologists, and prostate cancer from urologists whose volumes had all gone down significantly.

Only the emergency and life-threatening cancer surgeries were conducted in the hospitals. All the medical cares were now shifted to the Emergency Department, Intensive Care Units, and COVID-19 beds, making those areas significantly busier.

Disproportionate shifts of the hospital business to attend to COVID-19 cases also affected the clinical pathology sections. Most hospitals were now requiring a fast turnaround time for COVID-19 testing within the hospital, so, on the clinical pathology side (often in the microbiology sections), had to come up with their own testing platforms.

The most common was the nasopharyngeal swab PCR method, which took a minimum of two to four hours to get the result. This was much faster than sending out to either the CDC or commercial laboratories, which could take days to get the results.

Samantha's resident friends in the microbiology rotation had to gear up with personal protective equipment in a negative pressure room, as in the Emergency Department because the specimens needed to centrifuge (spin down) by using Vortex mixer at a high speed which could aerosolize the virus particles in the air.

Blood Banks were a part of clinical pathology, and this business had gone down because surgeries had decreased.

Also during lockdowns, most people stayed home, were not driving, so traffic accidents and trauma surgeries had gone down, requiring fewer blood products. Blood donation had also gone down significantly because of the lockdowns.

People were also afraid to come to hospitals, even cancer patients who needed chemotherapy treatments. It was a double whammy for the cancer patients because chemotherapy would result in an immunocompromised status, yet they needed to come to the hospital to get their treatment where the COVID-19 virus was concentrated.

Many cancer patients opted to postpone their chemotherapy.

The education process had been affected because residents generally followed the attending during the sign-out of the pathology cases, but with social distancing policy, residents were not having contact with the attending, reviewing the cases alone and talking to the attending via WebEx or Zoom.

All education lectures were now conducted online. Residents were encouraged to stay home because of the compact office situations. It was not unusual for residents to work and stay close together, shoulder to shoulder, due to lack of spaces given to them. It was lucky to have a small cubicle in certain rotations during training.

Samantha walked around to check on her residency friends and found that only a third of residents were coming to the hospital in April. Dr. Wells, her resident director, also encouraged the residents to stay home unless they were involved in essential service duties. He said this was not unique to pathology residents, but all residency programs. Even faculty members were staying home because the volumes had decreased and leaders also wanted to have only half of them working in the hospital in case some faculty got sick with the virus, so the other half could later cover the service.

Dr. Wells said that the Bronx pathology group was lucky not to have involuntary furloughs like the commercial laboratories, at least not yet. The government was seeking more doctors to treat COVID-19 but many doctors including oncologists and surgeons could not work because of the disproportionate number of sick patients due to COVID-19. It was an extraordinary time for the Infectious specialty, Emergency Department doctors, and respiratory therapists.

The hospital emails were filled with COVID-19 related news, plans for surge, guidelines on how to and when to perform elective or routine surgeries, when and who to get tested for COVID-19 as directed by the hospital CEO, the president of the medical group, or other people in high power positions with impressive titles. Also published every day were updates on the COVID-19 patients in ICU on ventilator, ER admission numbers, and how many employees had tested positive with COVID-19.

Among them were also deaths of their own employees who died of COVID-19 infection, providing condolences with mourning messages about the dead. One was a man who transported the dead or alive patients to various parts of the hospital to get CT-scans in radiology or transported to the morgue.

Samantha went home to her apartment, feeling somewhat relieved to decrease the exposure to COVID-19. She was wondering what Dr. Falkner was doing today. He was probably still writing his manuscript. He was intensively interested in the skin rash autopsy case he and Samantha performed on an infant the last time they performed a limited autopsy on Hart Island, whether or not that was related to COVID-19.

CHAPTER 25

Personal interrogation

April 14, 2020

Wuhan re-opened and eased outgoing travel restrictions on April 8, after a 76-day lockdown that began January 27. The Chinese lockdown was different from the American lockdown; the people were confined to their homes, and food, medicines and essential needs were delivered by Chinese government officers.

On April 8, the people came out massively, taking highways, trains, buses and airplanes to go out of town from Wuhan and they even celebrated in the streets for their liberation. Social distance law with personal space of more than six feet was disregarded, but they all still wore masks. Wuhan was a large city composed of 11 million people and on that day, it seemed all the people came out swarming the streets, highways, and train stations as long as the government-issued app showed they were deemed virus free.

Ed's team from the US joined in the celebration with the people of Wuhan, because in a way, they too were locked down in the hotel, unable to go out without the Chinese government permission.

China had continued to face criticism at home and abroad over lack of control and handling of the virus, especially during the initial phase of the outbreak by silencing whistleblowers and delayed informing the public about the severity of the crisis.

For the people of Wuhan, the Chinese government took away their personal freedom, had a strict sense of day and night curfews, and were very critical of their own government.

During the initial outbreak in December, any patient who even had severe symptoms of COVID-19 could not be admitted to a hospital because all hospitals were at full capacity. Some patients with COVID-

19 were treated like trash as they lay in hallways, and some even lay on the street near the hospital. Some family members abandoned their loved ones because they did not want them to come back home and infect the rest of the family. The hospital emergency departments, intensive care units, and even all inpatient areas looked like war zones. Doctors and nurses were trying to control the order in their units, but countless sick patients were lying down in the hallways, blocking the passage of health care workers. This went on until at least March, and by the end of March things were a little more controlled.

Ed realized the Wuhan people did not trust their own government. The jubilee feeling of freedom from the lockdown changed after just two days.

Slowly but surely, the people went back to their confined spaces even though the lockdown was over, due to fear of getting the second wave of COVID-19 infection. The restaurants and retail businesses were open for about a week or two, but soon, they could not stay open further because the income from selling any items was less than what they paid workers. Just like in the US, unemployment rates shot up. The grocery stores lacked food, particularly rice, wheat, flours and meat products as the people were scrambling to find food. Families rationed their food. When the people went out to the grocery stores, they had to line up to buy food, and some went back home empty-handed after waiting in a long line. Everyone was fighting for the food and frequent commotions of shouting broke out in the grocery stores.

Despite heavy criticism, the Wuhan Seafood Market opened as usual on April 14, 2020. They did not change much. The exotic animals, both dead and alive, were still available to be sold when the usual unkempt market re-opened. Ed's team toured the market and secretly took some photos using a disposable camera purchased at a store in Wuhan.

Last week, Ed received a personal phone call from Dr. Shei to meet privately in her house. When Ed told that to his team, all the team members were excited and went out to the hotel bar to celebrate. They all had different ideas why Dr. Shei personally called Ed. There were a variety of potential reasons Ed's teammates were constructing; some plausible and some not.

Some said since Ed is young and handsome, maybe Dr. Shei would like to seduce him into her bed after a nice dinner; maybe she is actually horny, even though she looks tough as a nail. Others said since Ed is Chinese, there is some special treatment and comradery and nothing more than that. Some others said since Ed is young and naïve, Dr. Shei wants to invite him to dinner and interrogate or manipulate him to gather the US intelligence and know the motives of their visit.

Whatever the reason might be, they all wanted Ed to gather more information about the Wuhan Institute of Virology and ideally get an invitation to see the level 4 lab and obtain a sample of the virus.

Ed dressed up with a clean white shirt without a tie, dress pants and a blazer. It was a rather cool night. He took a taxi to Dr. Shei's house. Surprisingly, the house had a spectacular and modern architectural style. The inside was clean and a rather minimalistic style of furniture, which Ed liked. Somehow, Ed was expecting Dr. Shei to have a traditional old house or live in a multistory apartment.

Dr. Shei and her husband welcomed him warmly. The dinner was served in a typical Chinese style to impress the guest. Even though it was just Ed, they served the elaborate six course dinner by at least four maids delivering the hot, delicious, mouthwatering food in a sequential manner. Ed thought this was definitely a deliberate act to ask Ed to do their favors. While he was chewing his home style food, he was anxiously waiting for them to ask him something.

After the dinner, they had some fruits, and coffee delivered to them in a large living room. They asked Ed to join in for cognac and opened a bottle of LOUIS XIII Cognac, France, which costs $3,500. Ed thought there were definite strings attached to this one.

He took a glass and as expected it melted in his mouth.

"It is really good! What year is this from? The first one was created in 1874," Ed said.

"Impressive! Such a young age to know cognac and the year it started from," Dr. Shei's husband said.

"So. Tell us about yourself. We want to know all about your parents, your siblings, and how did you end up being an American?" Dr. Shei said.

So, the interrogation started, but to Ed's surprise, it was all about his personal life, not the American intelligence or motives and not even his work.

He answered as politely as possible that his parents are both scientists who immigrated to America when they were young and went to college in the US, received their PhDs in Science and worked in the hospital laboratories when they met. He has two younger brothers who are both medical doctors in the US and he is the only one who does not make much money; his family gives him some pressure about this. In fact, Ed makes the same salary as the youngest brother who is still a resident and his salary is a joke amongst his family. He works at Abby Laboratory as an assistant research director. Next year, he will work as the Associate Director of Virology section, hoping to develop a vaccine against the current coronavirus.

"Are you married?" Dr. Shei asked. Such a direct and personal question, Ed thought, but nothing unusual for Chinese people, just like his parents.

"No, not yet!"

"Well good, we were hoping you were not married." They both laughed, relieved to see Ed was still a single. "We wanted to know if you want to meet our daughter. She is a young lady, born in the Year of the Rat in 1996, just 24 years old. She works at one of the British laboratories in London after graduating from Oxford College last year. She is our only child. She is actually here visiting us now. Today, she is at her friend's house, but tomorrow, she will be here. We'd like you two to meet," Dr. Shei said.

Okay, that was the string, Ed thought. Finally, it came out.

"I am much older than her. I am 30," Ed said somewhat shyly.

"Oh, that's a perfect age. Just six years older, that's great!" Dr. Shei's husband said.

They were busy talking about their daughter, mostly how great she is, how pretty she is, and all kinds of nonsense things that Ed was simply not interested.

Ed thought about Samantha and wondered why she would not respond to his emails. Last he heard from Samantha was that she was going to Hart Island near Long Island somewhere to do autopsy rotation. He could not even think about seeing the dead people, let alone dissecting the dead bodies. He could not imagine such audacity Samantha has with her tiny body and small hands. In fact, he did not like her job and wished that she would quit being a pathologist. He would always think about what else did she touch with her hands when she brings food to him. He would gag even thinking about that. Ed could not stand seeing blood, human organs, and all the terrible things. In fact, he would pass out.

Ed agreed to meet Dr. Shei's daughter Lifang, tomorrow. They needed to convince their daughter to meet him, since they had not yet told her about Ed. She apparently has a dark skin boyfriend in England who they do not like or approve. It looked like they had a different idea about Lifang's life, and it was definitely not with that boyfriend. Ed was not sure if the boyfriend was black or not, but he was not going to ask them. Ed had known that some Chinese are more discriminatory against the blacks than the white people, including his parents. He could see why Dr. Shei would be adamantly against her daughter seeing a black boyfriend and aggressively seeking someone like Ed to be a potential son-in-law.

Ed did not mention to them he has a girlfriend who is a mixed Asian person. He thought it would be better to go along with their request to meet with Lifang and then gradually invade into the lab space where Dr. Shei works.

"Well, I'd love to see your lab and really tour the level 4 area and get some education on how you sequenced the coronavirus from the bats," Ed said, and Dr. Shei agreed to do so if he meets with her daughter the next day and goes out for a date.

"It's a deal!" Ed said and left the house. He could not believe all the conversations they had were in Mandarin, and he was impressed with his own linguistic skills.

He was somewhat glad that none of the speculations from Ed's team members were true. He was happy that Dr. Shei was not interested in Ed personally, nor asked him about the American intelligence or intentions.

He couldn't wait to tell the real reason why Dr. Shei invited him for a dinner when he gets back to the hotel.

CHAPTER 26

Casual date

April 15, 2020

Ed met with Lifang the next day for a date. They started in the late afternoon, strolling around the nearby park, which was sparsely populated. The sidewalks of the park were filled with white and pink cherry plum tree flowers and Saucer Magnolia in its deep magenta colors. It was beautiful to walk in a crispy sunny weather, a perfect spring day, except he was not with Samantha.

Lifang was a cute, short, delicate, skinny and lovely Chinese woman. *Any man would find her attractive*, Ed thought. She was rather spunky and at times abrasive in her usage of language, especially when she spoke English.

Lifang said that she did not want to meet with Ed that day, but she decided not to fight back so strongly with her parents. Lifang felt that the criticisms her mother was facing both nationally and internationally were too much to bear, and she wanted to be a good obedient daughter for at least one day.

She came to Wuhan recently to celebrate her mother's belated birthday. She was going to come to Wuhan during the Chinese New Year, but obviously she could not come during the lockdown and there were no flights to China at that time.

She told Ed that she had a boyfriend who is black in London. They met in college and were living together for two years, but she obviously did not tell that to her parents. He was a musician, played saxophone professionally at night in a jazz club.

She worked at a prominent laboratory in London, mainly in the production line for the influenza vaccine as a research assistant.

Currently, her work was focusing on the research for the COVID-19 vaccine. She liked her job somewhat.

She did not want to be like her mom—visible, famous, and exposed to the public in both positive and negative ways. She wanted to enjoy her life living as a "normal woman" as a mother, wife and in London. She eventually would like to marry her current boyfriend, but knew that she would face an unbearable amount of opposition from her parents. She had some pressure from her mom to also climb up the ladder to be a director of the vaccine lab in London within the next five years. She laughed as she was saying this to Ed. It was obvious that Lifang was stressed out from her parents' expectations, including who she should be married to.

Ed did not mention much about himself and did not tell Lifang that he also had a girlfriend. He just wanted to listen to Lifang. They actually had a nice time. Nothing romantic or special about their meeting; it was just a pleasant, honest and casual date to know a little more about each other as a friend.

They had a hamburger and french fries for dinner. Ed took her back to Dr. Shei's home early in the evening, walking rather slowly, so they could talk more. Lifang knew that Ed also did not want to date her, and his interest was to visit the WIV lab where her mom worked. She said she would speak to her mother to get that arranged.

CHAPTER 27

A proposal

April 17, 2020

Half of Ed's team left Wuhan and returned to the US. Ed was still in Wuhan to visit Dr. Shei's lab alone. The rest of his team were excited that Ed was finally invading into the space and getting some information from Dr. Shei.

There was a growing speculation that the coronavirus was "spilled out" from the Wuhan lab globally. Especially, the US government and the president's administration continuously claimed that the novel coronavirus originated from the WIV laboratory supported by "enormous evidence" without sharing the evidence, despite scientists all around the world who condemned conspiracy theories.

China made the largest amount of medical supplies, including PPE, and controlled the supply and shipments to the world. During the pandemic, China provided welcomed shipments of medical supplies to the world, including the US. Initially, the US administration praised China for the act, but now, there was growing blame and criticism as the US death tolls increased with COVID-19.

By going into the WIV lab at the actual place where the viruses were kept, Ed would have a rare opportunity to know what exactly happened, perhaps. No one was able to access the lab. Only Ed from the US would be the first person to visit inside this lab.

Dr. Shei was kind to take Ed inside. They went into the level 4 lab spaces, all prepared with several layers of personal protection gear. Dr. Shei spelled out every detail of her discovery. Ed did not have to probe her much. She took him as a future son-in-law and personally walked with him and informed him regarding her work. The only condition was that he could not take photos.

What he learned about the coronavirus which caused the COVID-19 were as follows:

In 1912, German veterinarians had a case of a feverish cat with an enormously swollen belly caused by coronavirus. At the same time, the coronavirus caused chickens bronchitis, and pigs an intestinal disease that killed almost every piglet under two weeks old. At that time, the pathogen that caused all these animal sicknesses was not known, until the 1960s, when researchers in the United Kingdom and the United States isolated two viruses with crown-like structures causing common colds in humans, and animals had the same bristly structure, studded with spiky protein protrusions. Under electron microscope, these viruses resembled the solar corona which led researchers in 1968 to name the pathogen as coronaviruses.

The coronaviruses are relatively big, 125 nanometers in diameter, contain an extraordinarily long (27-31 kb) RNA genome, relatively large for the viruses that use RNA to replicate, the group that accounts for most newly emerging diseases. What really stands out for the coronaviruses are their large genomes, which is the largest genome of all RNA viruses. Their genomes are three times or more larger than those of HIV and hepatitis C, and more than twice influenza's.

All viruses have the ability to mutate, which can be advantageous for viruses. The unique quality of coronaviruses is their genomic proofreading mechanism, which keeps the virus from accumulating mutations that could weaken it. Many antiviral drugs can thwart viruses such as hepatitis C, but in the coronaviruses, the proofreader can weed out those changes, and the drugs fail to subdue. Not only that, coronaviruses can often recombine, swapping chunks of their RNA with other coronaviruses. When two distant coronavirus relatives end up in the same cell, recombination can lead to formidable and more deadly versions that infect new cell types (not only the respiratory cells) and jump to other species.

Scientists are now aware of seven strains of coronavirus that infect humans. Among the four that cause common colds, two (OC43 and

HKU1) came from rodents, and the other two (229E and NL63) from bats. The three that cause severe disease, SARS-CoV (the cause of SARS), Middle East respiratory syndrome (MERS-CoV and SARS-CoV-2) all came from bats. There is usually an intermediary; an animal infected by the bats that carries the virus into humans. With SARS that caused an epidemic in 2003, the intermediary is thought to be civet cats, sold at live-animal markets in China.

The origin of SARS-CoV-2 that causes COVID-19 is still an open question. Because the virus shares 96% of its genetic material with a virus found in a bat in a cave in Yunnan China, it is most likely coming from bats.

The intermediary may be the pangolin which had a coronavirus with a unit called receptor-binding domain in the spike proteins almost identical to the human version, and this is central to their success in entering human cells. The Yunnan bats' virus does not have this receptor-binding domain, and hence the bats probably are not able to directly infect people.

Some researchers suspect, however, the pangolin was not the intermediary because the coronavirus found in the pangolin is only 90% genetically similar. There is a need for continued surveillance and increased vigilance towards the emergence of new viral strains by zoonotic (animal) transfer.

Why some people have a very different degree of experiences who had exposure to the COVID-19 is still unknown. Most people start manifesting their symptoms in the throat or nose, producing a cough and disrupting taste and smell, and then end there. If the virus works its way down to the lungs, it debilitates that organ and causes death by the immune system reacting to the virus.

SARS-CoV-2 is much better at infecting people; the virus can infect the lungs, intestines, heart, blood, sperm (as can MERS-CoV), eyes and brain. Once in the blood system, the damage to the kidney, liver and spleen are observed in people with COVID-19, triggering an excessive immune response known as a cytokine storm, which can lead to multiple organ failure and death.

According to scientists, the mechanism of SARS-Cov-2 to infect the human cells is to breach the protective membrane of human cells using its spike proteins. First, the protein's receptor-binding domain latches on to a receptor called ACE2, which sits on the surface of the human cell. ACE2 is expressed throughout the body on the lining of the arteries and veins that course through all organs, but it is particularly dense on the cells lining the alveoli (air sacs) in the lung and small intestines.

The host (human) cell snips the spike protein at one of its dedicated 'cleavage sites', exposing fusion peptides—small chains of amino acids that help to pry open the host cell's membrane so that the virus's membrane can merge with it. This causes leakage of the host cells and other viruses such as HIV, Ebola, Hantavirus can enter. Once the invader's genetic material gets inside the cell, the virus commandeers the host's molecular machinery to produce new viral particles. Then, that progeny exit the cell to go on and infect others.

So far, the COVID-19 outbreak, in terms of the virus success point of view, has done a remarkable job. It knows no boundaries between countries, races, ages, and borders.

The outbreak involves the case-fatality rate (CFR), defined as the percentage of deaths among all cases. Currently, the estimated global mortality is reported at 4.7% but this varies widely by location from a high of 10.8% in Italy to a low of 0.7% in Germany.

The ultimate strategy for controlling this pandemic will depend on a safe and efficacious vaccine. The race against the vaccine development began globally, and currently there are mainly 3 candidates in phase 1 human trials: a messenger RNA vaccine and 2 adenovirus vector-based vaccines. The estimated timeline for availability of an initial vaccine is between early and mid-2021.

Now, Dr. Shei said she is very much interested in working with a new technique in development of the vaccine with Ed in Abby Laboratory in the US, and her daughter's company in Britain to manufacture the products. The deal is that she will provide all the necessary information, including the virus in tissue culture to Ed, who then will develop the vaccine in the US. Once it is developed, the FDA process of the phase studies including human trials will happen in the US. Dr. Shei already has a possible vaccine that she developed and tried in Rhesus monkeys, and had tremendously promising findings, but it requires Ed to finesse the vaccine and carry out human trials in the US.

Once it is proven successful, the British laboratory will manufacture by fast-track and produce in massive numbers, around 300 million vials to be distributed around the world. The reason for the collaboration with Ed in the US is that the intellectual property and financial gain is not independent from the Chinese government, and she will lose everything. She wants Ed to share the honor for the discovery and share the financial benefits with her.

Dr. Shei would not trust any of Ed's team members, but only Ed, because they were both Chinese. She said that the novel coronavirus came from Wuhan, China and she and Ed, both Chinese, would have to come up with the solution to the problem by having a vaccine from China. In that way, China would redeem its honor and save face. She would show how powerful China had become in the world and the US was not the only superpower country She wanted Ed, a Chinese American, to be a part of this glory to end the pandemic.

Ed was in shock, almost disbelief at the position he found himself in with Dr. Shei. In fact, he recognized that he did not even have to convince her to reveal her work. She was practically giving him everything she discovered in 30 years of her life and placing it on his lap to carry on and complete the work. How could he refuse the proposition?

Dr. Shei said that she was thinking about providing Ed with the virus culture to be carried to the US on the airplane Ed was going to take, illegally. Otherwise this could not be done in regular shipping, not only because the virus could not be shipped by using any transportation system, but it is a property of China which could not be given to any country or any person.

She said she had been thinking about this when Ed showed up the first day of meeting.

The primary problem was how to package the virus. There were two major issues; one was to make sure the viability of the virus in tissue culture would not get damaged which meant it required dry ice or cold ice for the entire trip which meant about a 13-hour flight to the US and two to four hours of airport transportation time, give or take. The second issue was the airport security; how to get it done under the radar of the two countries.

The meeting lasted the entire day. She gave him a USB that looked like a pen in secret. She said it had all the scientific information about the virus and the vaccine. She told Ed not to share about the virus transport and the USB with his colleagues and had given him both in confidence.

They both went a separate way and will later resume discussion of the transportation of the virus.

At this time, Dr. Shei had given Ed a tremendous number of things to think about. Ed recognized that Dr. Shei was now extremely vulnerable. She really had to trust Ed to carry on with her proposition in secret. Whether or not Ed sees her daughter was secondary, and what Dr. Shei really wanted was to carry on the scientific project with Ed in the US. Ed was in the right place in the right time. He felt a tremendous responsibility of carrying the hope of the world, the vaccine in this devastating pandemic time.

He placed the USB inside the computer bag he always carried and slowly walked to his hotel. He was thinking about what to tell and what not to tell his team members who were still with him. He had to make sure not to slip his tongue, and hence, he decided not to have a drink.

Later that night, Ed's remaining team members gathered in the hotel to have a late dinner to debrief. They always had one or two glasses of wine or drinks to accompany food.

One of the people who remained was the media reporter who found out that the Wuhan Institute of Virology (WIV) organized a 10 day conference during October 15-25, 2019, the International Workshop on Biosafety Laboratory Management and Techniques, hosted by the Chinese Academy of Sciences (CAS) and the Ministry of Foreign Affairs of China, and it was successfully held in Wuhan, Hubei and consisted of 24 foreign scientists from 22 different countries who participated in the workshops.

During the conference, China was telling attendees they are committed to promoting international cooperation in biosecurity, actively providing bio-security public goods to the international community and strengthening the capacity-building of the developing countries, aimed at building up global bio-security defense in cooperation with all countries.

During the 10 days of training, they covered biosafety laboratory management, bioethics and biosafety policy, laboratory management systems, biological risk assessment, preservation and transportation of virus resources, and experimental practices. In addition, the WIV also held a seminar on Code of Conduct for Biological Scientists, and organized visits to the Microorganism and Viruses Culture Collection Center and Wuhan National Biosafety Laboratory.

They emphasized the fact that the global outbreaks of emerging infectious diseases have shown an upward trend which seriously endangers human health, economic development and social stability, and stressed the point that a scientific research support platform is needed for countries to respond to sudden public biosafety emergencies and prevention of biosafety risks.

Through the conference, attendees learned about China's biosafety management experience and their willingness to give full play to be bridges to better publicize and promote the training results, to further strengthen bilateral scientific research cooperation, and jointly fulfill international biosafety responsibilities for prevention and control of infectious diseases.

Ironically, one month later, China saw COVID-19 cases that brought a global pandemic from the same area, Wuhan. And as soon as the SARS-like deaths were occurring, the same government was oppressing doctors who tried to tell the world about what was happening in China.

What was remarkably interesting is that at least two international diplomatic personnel who visited the WIV in 2018 cited there were inadequate safety protocols and improperly trained personnel, especially in the level 4 laboratory. Supposedly, one of the lower level research students had died in the lab in mid-November 2019, which the WIV and the Chinese government had wiped out from records. So, it was not in early January or late December Wuhan had the first death.

The reporter speculated that the patient zero of COVID-19 was not from the seafood market but from an accident in the WIV lab. One of the paramount evidences was WIV had three days of absolutely no cell phone activities in mid-November, around the time the research student died, which meant that the WIV must have shut down the entire facility.

Ed was fascinated with these findings, albeit a rumor, and what that could mean with Dr. Shei, who probably knew about it and did not tell Ed anything about this.

Could he really trust Dr. Shei? She seemed very open and willing to share her knowledge about this virus and even find a vaccine for global use, but was she using Ed somehow to gain her interests to benefit China, or was she a victim of oppression from the Chinese government? Was she really only interested in financial gain by providing information to Ed, or was she trying to manipulate the US government to enhance China for their gain? To whom should Ed share this information? Ed could not trust anyone on his team to share the USB. He did not even want to open it using his personal computer.

He needed to call his boss at Abby Lab in DC, but he did not know if that was even a good idea. Does he go directly to the CDC Director or even the President of the US with this information? How could he possibly get in contact with such authorities?

His life could be endangered by the Chinese government if they found out he had this USB. Where could he hide this USB? Was Dr. Shei testing him? Was she a spy and somehow wanting Ed to be imprisoned in China?

Ed obviously did not debrief any of the information from his visit to the WIV, especially his conversation with Dr. Shei today, but only shared what the Biosafety Level 4 Lab experience was like. He gave an estimate of about 50-60 people working in the level 4 lab areas from a total of 200-300 workers in the WIV and how uncomfortable the protective gear really was.

CHAPTER 28

Crime scene investigation

Samantha received a phone call from the coroner's office for her to report back to the hospital. Luckily, she lived only a few blocks from the hospital and so she walked fast.

A medical examiner, Dr. Stevens, was going to a possible homicide scene investigation, and remembered Samantha was in rotation with the coroner's office that week. Dr. Stevens took Samantha in her Hyundai car and drove to a grungy apartment in a poor, dangerous, and known to be a drug addict boulevard area of the Bronx. Police were already there and the coroner's van. Dr. Stevens gave Samantha personal protective equipment (PPE).

She, unlike Dr. Falkner, not only prepared and brought an extra set for Samantha but also carefully instructed her on how to put on the gear while she was putting them on in the car.

Samantha always liked Dr. Stevens when she gave several lectures on Forensic Medicine during her residency program. She was a middle-aged, tough looking female physician who taught several lectures and demonstrations of typical autopsies to both medical students and residents in the Bronx. She was one of the popular pathologists and known for her extremely tough questions on the final exam for medical students.

She was not particularly a warm, fuzzy and sociable person but was clear in her verbal communications, and loud, so that there was no misunderstanding in what she was saying.

"What I have heard about this case is that a man in his 50s was found dead by his landlord, who went to his apartment unit because he had not paid his rent for more than two weeks. The landlord was bugging him since the beginning of April. He said he would pay two days later, then another two days later until yesterday when the landlord went up there and knocked on the door and finally opened the door because there was no response from the tenants. He lived with his elderly mother who was in her 80s. He was known to be a drug addict for heroin and sold it and other drugs to others around town.

"The landlord called the police this morning and had found two bodies there. The landlord said that the last time he saw the man was about three to four days ago. The 80-year-old mother was not capable of coming up and down the steps of the apartment and the landlord rarely saw her. Obviously, the building is extremely old and lacks an elevator.

"We do not know if it is a double homicide or suicide situation, whether or not a gun was involved; essentially nothing at this point.

"So, your job is to just observe what I do, and do not touch anything, do not move anything, and don't create any scenes. Just tag along right behind me and I will try to explain what is going on as I gather some information. Got it?" Dr. Stevens said.

"Yes," Samantha answered.

She already had a clear picture of what is going to happen when she goes up the stairs to the scene and appreciated the clarity from Dr. Stevens.

As they went upstairs and then under the yellow tape around the door of the unit, the first thing Samantha noticed was a stench; she was gagging. The bodies were already decaying. The elderly mother was lying down on the bed in a supine position with a thick blanket on top of her.

The 50-year-old man was sitting on the floor, next to the kitchen table against a chair with drug paraphernalia.

The elderly body was in a more decomposed state than the man in his 50s and maggots were found on her opened eyes. On top of that, the apartment unit was so horrific, dirty, unorganized, excessively accumulated with things of no actual value, a classic sign of hoarding disorder. Everything was disgusting and smelled awful. Kitchen sink had a pile of unwashed dishes with pieces of dried food particles and flies were everywhere.

Samantha threw up for she could not bear the smell and the frightening sight of two people's deaths. She ran out of the unit into the hallway and threw up her entire breakfast from that morning.

Police and coroner's officers were laughing at Samantha, but she could not help it. She had seen horrible sights including many dead bodies, freshly cut, still warm organs with the surgeons and other bloody things in her life which did not bother her too much, but she could not stand the smell of decomposed bodies.

Unfortunately, Samantha could not stand to go back again, so Dr. Stevens gave the car key to Samantha and told her how to undress the PPE without contaminating. Samantha felt guilty wasting the precious PPE, but she got out of the gear except for the N95 mask and then she got inside Dr. Steven's car. N95 should diminish the smell, but it must have not fit tightly around her face today. Samantha was definitely not helpful for Dr. Stevens, but was a burden.

Samantha sat there waiting for Dr. Stevens to come out and still gagging because the smell was in her brain now. After about an hour, the bodies were brought out and shoved inside the coroner's van. The police and Dr. Stevens came out right after that and talked for a while in the street.

Dr. Stevens finally came inside her car and asked Samantha if she was okay. She said, "I know it is hard, some residents cannot face this kind of thing. It's ok. You just are not made to be a forensic pathologist. But you have so many choices in pathology, and this is not for you. Well, we have to do the autopsies on those two bodies today. Are you up for it or do you want to skip it?"

"I will try." Samantha herself was doubtful of doing autopsies, but she felt so bad not having stomach enough to face it. She had seen so many bodies on Hart Island, so why couldn't she face another two?

Dr. Stevens smiled and said, "You can take off that N95 mask now. We'll see if you can do this."

They drove back to the coroner's office. They cleaned up so they could gear up again, back into the PPE. Samantha realized it was a disadvantage to have long hair and she should cut her hair very short like Dr. Stevens to be practical, especially during the pandemic time. It was cumbersome to hide all her hair inside the bonnet.

"Well, I applaud your courage to face these two dead bodies again, Dr. Parker. I will make sure you get two milestones checked; one for decomposed body and one for the crime scene."

Samantha thanked her and proceeded to do the autopsy with her. With the proper negative-pressured morgue, and a tightly fit N95 mask under the bright light of a medical examiner's autopsy table, the smell was not as bad as Samantha feared.

Dr. Stevens first put the bodies in a CT scan to make sure that there were no gunshot pellets. She examined to make sure the skin surface did not show penetrating wounds, lacerations, or blunt trauma to the bodies. She then collected blood, stomach contents and vitreous fluid samples from the back of the eye by using long needles and syringes and ordered toxicology and COVID-19 tests. She then opened the chest in a V-shape, cracked open the rib cage and took out the organs. She did a full examination, including the brain by using the electric bone saw to open the skull.

Samantha was gagging a little when she saw maggots falling out of the eye sockets of the elderly mother's body. She knew that this particular image will forever implant in her brain, no matter how much she wanted to erase it from her memory. They completed the two autopsies within five hours. Dr. Stevens gave her a brief summary of her observations and opinions of the cases to Samantha at the end.

"By the looks of the scene and the autopsy results, I feel that the elderly mother died earlier than the son. She died of pneumonia, most likely COVID-19. I know that she had a blanket cover on the top of her body and the decomposition starts earlier because of the warmer temperature created by the blanket but the fact that she had maggots in her eyes tells me that she died much earlier than the son, most likely two to three weeks.

"The son died of a drug overdose, maybe a suicide. The reason why I say that is that he did not call police, 911 or any help even though his mother had died. His rigor mortis was gone by the time we were there, and the landlord said that she saw him three to four days earlier and that timeline fits well. He probably died three to four days ago.

"With COVID-19, the two were inside their home, and he most likely did not have too many customers buying drugs from him and ran out of money to pay the rent. Of course, that is my hunch and not bulletproof evidence. I do not think this is a double homicide case. One died of COVID-19 and one by possible suicide.

"I will bet that the son had the virus and transferred it to his mother. I am sending in the COVID-19 tests on both. The COIVD-19 is affecting the elderly populations in a dramatic and detrimental way. We are seeing it next door from the nursing homes.

"Well, Dr. Parker, I say you got lucked out on the crime scene because you did not have to see bloody crimes. Sometimes it is worse than the decomposed body with maggots, trust me!" She smiled to Samantha.

Samantha was admiring Dr. Steven's competency and efficiency, not just her professionalism toward the trainee who really did not help her much. She was quite different from Dr. Falkner, who really did not communicate his intentions. Samantha appreciated the female attending in terms of the quality of education and attitude toward the residents.

Samantha could not help but to compare these two medical examiners who appeared to be in a similar age, probably assistant professors, comparing in their teaching abilities and the cars they drove. Samantha heard that male physicians make 10-20% more than female physicians, even in the pathology field, and wondered if that was true between Drs. Falkner and Stevens.

Samantha also noticed that she much preferred to learn from Dr. Stevens and felt she probably was more competent than Dr. Falkner, but she admired Dr. Falkner more deeply for reasons she could not explain. Maybe it was because she had known Dr. Falkner more personally and in a romantic way. Samantha was realizing the intrinsic bias she had against the female pathologist, even though on a competency level, Dr. Stevens might be superior.

Samantha felt embarrassed to feel this way, especially since she was also a female pathologist.

She ran into her apartment and took off everything quickly and dumped it all in the laundry hamper, including her sneakers and went into the shower. She thought she should just throw out all her clothes and shoes. In this rate, she would need to go shopping for clothes and shoes soon, because she was throwing away things after the horrific autopsies performed this month and she did not want to keep any items to be reminded of those memories. She could not stand her hair having that decomposed body smell. She took a long, hot shower.

She would need to cut her hair herself, very short. She missed seeing Dr. Falkner and wondered what he would say about her short haircut.

CHAPTER 29

Phone call

April 18, 2020

Samantha was glued to reading The New York Times every day, mostly about COVID-19 stories. The moment she got up and made her coffee, she was looking at her computer screen and reading news. Today, only 540 new coronavirus deaths occurred, 606 from the day before, instead of 799 on April 9, which was the highest count for New York City. A downward trend, finally, but still so many people in New York City were dying. Advanced age, men more than women, and a high number of underlying diseases such as high blood pressure, diabetes, cardiovascular diseases, obesity and chronic lung disorders, asthma or chronic obstructive pulmonary disease, and neurodegenerative diseases were linked to more severe disease and death.

She thought about what she observed on Hart Island and Dr. Falkner's manuscript data, and the similar conclusions on who were more vulnerable to die with COVID-19.

Samantha was waiting for another phone call from the Bronx coroner's office to observe an ambulance experience, but she was not looking forward to that call. These days, almost all the ambulances were used to transport the COVID-19 cases, and she did not want to get added exposures.

The ambulance workers were not well equipped with the proper PPE. Most of them just wore thin paper gowns, always blown aside by the New York City wind, often captured in the images from newspapers, and probably not wearing N95 masks but just surgical masks. There were shortages of PPE in her hospital and everyone was keenly aware of not wasting even gloves. She was counting the number of COVID-19 exposures through her autopsies she had done and wondered if she would be tested positive if she got the COVID-19 test. But due to a shortage of nasopharyngeal swabs and the reagents, the lower risk hospital workers which included those in the pathology department were not given the opportunity of COVID-19 testing.

The funny thing was, someone like Samantha should be listed at the highest risk for exposure because she was often handling the dead bodies with most likely the highest concentrations of viral particles, aerosolized with bone saws doing invasive procedures like cutting the lungs filled with the virus loads, and her long hours during the autopsies, all adding up to that conclusion.

Perhaps she already had the COVID-19 infection, but because she was a healthy young woman, she did not have any symptoms, a so-called "asymptomatic vector" who could be the deadliest type of person.

She was glad that she was not going out on the street or to her workplace, exposing other people unknowingly.

She thought about her mom, who should come to Miami soon. Emily mentioned her arrival within four to five days the last time she spoke to her. Samantha asked her if she should go to Florida to meet her there when her mom disembarked from the ship, but Emily said no, because every time they dock at the port, they take so many days to just get disembark for some reason. Then Samantha would be staying in Miami just waiting. Emily said when she gets out from the boat, she will just go to the airport and buy a ticket to San Francisco. These days, the airplanes were practically empty, and it would be easy to buy a ticket to fly. Once Emily was in San Francisco, then Samantha could visit, maybe in late April or early May if Samantha's rotation schedule was feasible, her mom said.

But in May, Samantha was to have her surgical pathology rotation when no residents were allowed to take any vacation time off. She had not told that to her mom yet. Maybe she would just have to catch a redeye flight on Friday night and come back to New York City on Sunday evening if it had to be in the month of May. For the month of

April, she would just ask to take a one-week vacation to visit with her mom. She hoped her residency director would be sympathetic enough to send her off to deal with the loss of her father in Spain and to arrange the funeral. Emily and she would need to discuss the funeral arrangements. Samantha had no idea what to do for the international processes of getting the body back to the US.

She was searching for information about this when she received a phone call. It was Dr. Falkner. His voice was very weak. "Hi Sam, how are you?"

"Hi, Dr. Falkner, why is your voice like that?"

"I am home, actually, pretty sick. I think I might have COVID-19. I tested positive last week."

"Oh, No!"

"Well, I am home resting. Hopefully, I will recover soon. I just wanted to hear your voice."

"Are you able to get up? Are you able to eat and drink?"

"Yes, I am fine, I am ok. I was wondering how you are doing. How is your rotation? I hope you are not doing autopsies. Are you?"

"Yes, I did two this week. I think they were both COVID-19 cases, unfortunately."

"I am worried about your exposure to COVID-19. You worked with me for two weeks already."

"I am fine so far. Dr. Falkner, I probably will test positive, anyway. Don't worry about me. I am worried about you. There is no one to get you anything. Do you have some medication?"

"Yes, I do, and I took some. You know how most doctors self-medicate and we are not good patients," he chuckled.

"Don't you think you should go to the hospital?"

"No, I am not at that stage, at least not yet. I do not want to go to my hospital, anyway. I'd rather die at home than be at the hospital where I work and be in the ICU with a ventilator."

"Do you want me to go there now?" Samantha asked.

"Oh, no, I will be fine. I was worried about you whether you are okay, and that's why I called,"

Dr. Falkner said in between coughs. Samantha wanted to ask him whether he called his wife to tell her he was sick, but she did not. She did not want to ask that question for some reason. In fact, she hesitated to talk about her and admit that his wife and son existed in her reality. They hung up the phone.

Samantha realized he was actually calling her to see if she was down in her bed getting sick with COVID-19, not just telling her he was sick. But knowing that he was sick, and him being alone in the house, she could not help but to think about the worst scenario. He could pass out and die in his bed without anyone to take him to the hospital. He could fall in his bathroom since he could be very weak due to lack of fluid and food intake for many days.

She began to pack a few things in a duffle bag, at least for the weekend to be with him. She would just have to take a chance to miss the phone call from the coroner's office for the ambulance experience. Or she could just make an excuse by saying she was sick. She could not believe that she was going to see Dr. Falkner again. She thought it was the end when she shut his car door last Sunday.

CHAPTER 30
Miami offshore

APRIL 18, 2020

The cruise ship arrived in Miami in the evening, but the ship had anchored a few miles offshore from the dock. The captain informed the passengers and crew via intercom that they needed to be anchored there for a while until further notice from the US Coast Guard. The captain also said there were currently 123 passengers and 150 crew members on board, and some people were extremely ill and needed medevacked off the boat. There were 10 dead bodies on the cruise ship, which the captain did not announce.

The captain was in communication with the US Coast Guard officers, constantly saying that the sick needed medical care and ventilators and pleaded to disembark the dead, but the US ports were delaying their response. The US Coast Guard helicopter dropped testing kits onto the ship, asking all remaining people onboard to get tested.

The captain abided by the orders and the two remaining doctors performed the nasopharyngeal swab tests again, even though all the passengers had supposedly tested positive in Barcelona a week ago. All 150 crew members were tested this time. Four hours later, the helicopter airlifted off the testing kits. By this time, several news media helicopters were circling over the ship.

Evidently, there were over 20 cruise ships offshore near Miami and Fort Lauderdale experiencing the same situation, drawing worldwide attention since the cruise crisis struck. Emily's ship was the smallest. Some cruise ships had 6,000 passengers and over 4,500 crew members, all stranded at sea. Most of the passengers were confined to their rooms, surviving on dwindling supplies of food delivered to their cabins.

The US ports, the state governmental officers, the CDC and the cruise ship industry were required to put forward a new comprehensive plan to address a range of concerns, including surveillance and reporting of illnesses on board, testing procedures, onboard medical care and evacuation logistic, but all parties were taking so much time to have uniform policies. This had been going on since early March of this year, and every cruise ship was facing the same sluggish speed to disembark the passengers.

The captain imagined that the test results would come back in three to four days and then they could disembark the US citizen passengers first, required to stay in nearby hotels for 14 days to quarantine. All cruise line trips were now suspended until further notice from the US government.

The captain and all crew members who were still under contract would face a choice: Leave with the guests and risk future employment prospects with the cruise company; or remain onboard for the nine days left on his/her contract and have the cruise line cover the cost of their return home.

Most crew members chose the latter option. All other cruise lines were facing a similar binding contract policy but were still working through the details about the repatriation of crew that were not required to remain on board the ships for essential operations during the period when cruises were suspended.

The captain was telling the passengers only a few pieces of information at a time and not the whole picture what would happen to them and the crew. But the rumors circled around the ship very quickly despite the fact everyone was confined to their room.

Emily's source of news came from Mahalia. Emily was calculating how long arrival in San Francisco might take; four days to wait for the test results, and 14 days of quarantine in a Miami hotel will add up to 18 days, which would be May 6. Emily was glad she told Samantha not to meet her in Miami on the weekend of April 18 when she was originally expected to dock in Miami.

Emily was constantly talking to Mahalia these days. She was her only lifeline for human contact. Emily was very fearful of going out to take a walk or even to exercise because she did not want to meet those nasty British accent speaking people.

She was wondering if they were American citizens because the captain said only the American citizens could disembark at this time in Miami. Emily was secretly hoping they were not American citizens and get stuck on the cruise ship for another nine days with the crew members. She was shameful to think such nasty thoughts and quickly prayed for forgiveness to God. She should not wish bad things upon other people.

Emily could not figure out why an additional nine days for the crew. What would they do within that nine days they were kept on the ship? A NO SAIL order from the CDC came in, which meant cruise ship operators must transport their asymptomatic crew members directly to non-commercial transportation and then to their respective homes. This meant the captain and the cruise company must come up with a solution to get everybody home. The crew members were from all over the world. Mahalia said to Emily that she was definitely staying on for nine days because she needed the money for her family in the Philippines. Emily and Mahalia exchanged their phone numbers and home addresses.

They were no longer having filet mignon for dinners. Food sources became not as abundant as before, and because Emily's ship was the smallest, they probably were not getting the main attention. A large cruise ship such as a Diamond Princess Cruise Liner required tons of food because they had thousands of people on board.

Emily was content with what she could eat. She just wanted to be off the boat and go to her home. Emily did not want to call her daughter Samantha too often because she had nothing positive to say these days. She just left a text saying she was offshore close to Miami, unable to dock yet, but she was doing well.

CHAPTER 31

Chicken noodle soup

It took Samantha two-and-a-half hours to arrive at Dr. Falkner's house by train and bus. She knocked on his door. It took a long time for him to answer. "It's me, Samantha."

He opened the door and was shocked to see her there. "What are you doing here? What happened to your hair?" he asked.

He was wearing thick flannel pajamas. He looked pale, cold, and was shivering. He did not even bother to lock the door behind Samantha and went back to his bed. Samantha locked the door and went into his bedroom on the second floor. Nearby his bed were several bottled waters, Tylenol, Theraflu powder packages, his cell phone, and a bottle of red wine, half emptied. His kitchen was clean. He obviously had not eaten anything. For how long, Samantha did not know.

"Have you eaten anything?" Samantha was looking into his garbage can, which was also pretty clean as she asked him. He did not bother to even answer her. Samantha found a chicken noodle can of soup from his pantry and poured it out into a bowl and microwaved it. She brought the hot soup into his bedroom with a spoon. He took it and slowly ate it. He was coughing a lot while he was eating.

"I don't want you to get this nasty virus from me."

"I know, but I probably got it by now, anyway. I had to come. I would worry sick if you stay here alone."

"How is your mom? Is she back yet?"

Samantha was impressed that he was asking about her mother when he was so sick himself. It told her he was really thinking about her.

"She is still somewhere in the Atlantic Ocean. She was going to call me when she gets to Miami."

"I just realized when I am lying in bed thinking, this virus affected all of us in such significant ways. I did not have to go to Hart Island and handle so many dead bodies, you did not have to come there either, your father passed away from COVID-19, your mother is stuck on a cruise ship and left her husband's body in Spain, my wife and son cannot come back here and I cannot go to Italy to fetch them back.

"I also heard some inmates who buried the dead on Hart Island died the other day, and one of the contract workers who you came with on the boat on March 31st." Dr. Falkner said all these with severe coughs in between the words.

Samantha took his temperature after he finished talking. The thermometer said 100.3 F degrees.

"You have a fever. I think we should go to the hospital."

"No, please, Sam. Since you are here anyway, will you stay with me this weekend? Maybe you can pamper me, get me food and some water. Here is the key to the car. I have not done any grocery shopping for more than a week. There is really nothing much left in the refrigerator. You can find the money; my wallet is on the kitchen table. Thank you for coming, Sam."

Again, Samantha did exactly as he commanded. It was strange that she always found herself doing what he commanded without any argument. She rarely obeyed anyone's commands, even if those were from her parents.

"Sam, cover your face with a mask and wear the hood. There was an incident. Some kids kicked an Asian woman near the grocery," he said as Samantha was walking out from the bedroom.

Again, she did exactly as what he said, feeling overwhelmingly sad that such incidences actually happen. She was devasted that people can be so ignorant about the situation and discriminate against Asians in times like this. She thought somehow, she was immune to racial discrimination. Aside from her straight dark hair color, she had many features of the Caucasian race, such as fair skin, green-tinged light brown eyes and tall nose.

Samantha did not have any adversary incidences in the grocery store. She brought two bags of groceries back to his house and began cooking dinner. Chicken noodle soup with carrots and celery. That is what the Americans eat when they were sick, not the bean sprout soup with kimchee or rice congee. She smiled when she was chopping the vegetables.

She brought the soup she had made to Dr. Falkner. He had been taking a nap, but he got up to eat. He was perspiring on his forehead. He said, "Please wear a mask. You can find them in the closet just before the door." He was pointing to the closet and Samantha did exactly as he said. He ate hot soup and said it was good. She watched him eating and was happy that he was eating what she had made. She was having the same bowl of soup with him.

"I cannot smell or taste this. It looks wonderful. Thank you, Sam."

"No need to mention, Dr. Falkner."

"David, when are you going to say David?" he smiled.

"I am not sure. I am not used to call you by your first name."

"Sam, here is what I would like you to do. Please listen carefully," he said as he was setting aside a bowl of soup which he had not finished eating. "I called my wife last Wednesday when I got real sick. In fact, I was not able to go to work since Monday. I was able to talk to her this time. She is obviously devastated with the news. She is trying to come back, but I am not sure if she can buy a ticket. If she comes, she will come by herself, not with my son."

After a long pause, he said, "I am not sure if I can live till then. I have this strange feeling that I will not make it."

Samantha was crying, listening to what he was saying. He was saying things with so much difficulty, with coughs and sad emotions.

"Sam, don't cry. Listen and please do as I say. My wife does not know much about finances. She just has a credit card that she uses and purchases things. She thinks the money just happens to fall down from the sky. When she gets here, and again, I do not know when, this is her phone number. Please call her sometime next week. Tell her the bank accounts, life insurance, 401K, 403B, all the retirement accounts and life insurance policies from work and the personal ones are in the drawer here." He was pointing to the bedroom dresser.

"Give them to her, and the account passwords are in this laptop computer under the file name Anthony, which is my son's name. It is an encrypted file and she will need the password, which is his birthday. My wife's name is Greta Falkner. Obviously, she does not know you. Tell her what you want to say about who you are. A lover, resident, I do not care. Can you do that?"

"Am I your lover?" Samantha asked. It sounded strange that word came out of his mouth.

"Yes, you are. I was thinking about you a lot these days, lying in bed. I had nothing to do except think. I was sorry that I did not treat you well the first time I saw you. I was really disappointed that you were a female resident. I am not sure why. Now that I think about it, you did the same amount of work, maybe more than the previous male resident I had in March. In fact, I had a wonderful time being with you and I got a chance to know more about you. Me being of German heritage and my wife, an Italian, I never really had to think much about what Asian people go through in this country, but through your lens, I saw a glimpse of Asian American experiences in this country, which was wonderful to me."

Although what he said to Samantha was touching, she thought she really was not a true Asian American. She always thought she was more American than Asian. She was surprised why Dr. Falkner identified her as an Asian person.

"Who cut your hair?" Dr. Falkner said.

"I did, I didn't want to deal with my hair. It smelled like a dead body and it was cumbersome to hide it all when I was wearing PPE."

"You did a terrible job, indeed. I loved your long dark brown hair. Will I be able to see your hair grow again?"

Samantha did not know what to say. She looked at his eyes filled with tears.

Dr. Falkner became so weak and emotional. He really was thinking that he may not be able to survive through this sickness. This made Samantha sad and frightened.

"Why do you say such a thing? Of course you will see my long hair again. It grows so rapidly."

"Sam, do you ever feel that you know the end is coming? I just feel that. I know my end is coming. I had some strange dreams. I saw both my parents in my dreams. They both died when I was in my teens from a car accident. I lost both of them on the same day. They were driving to New York City from Long Island.

"We've always lived on Long Island. I grew up not too far away from here. I had a strange premonition that they might go away. I kind of knew that they would die in the morning when I was going to school," he said in his deep thoughts.

Samantha was getting more nervous.

"I really have no one. No brothers or sisters. If I die, I will die here alone. Until my wife comes back from Italy, no one will know that I am dead. In a way, I am glad to know you in so many ways. I am grateful to you that you came here to see me today. I thought that last Sunday was our last encounter because I knew you meant it when you said that was the end. Something about you, I know when you have made up your mind, you really mean it," he sighed and continued.

"If you and I met in a different circumstance, in a different time, or if we had more time to know each other, I would not know what I would do with my marriage. Maybe it was good that my wife left me. I'd want to be with you. I can't stop thinking about you. I don't know, if I had known I would die so young, the hell with the publications, I would sleep around more with many different women and maybe find a different soul mate!" He chuckled.

"Am I just a different woman to you?" Samantha asked.

"No, I don't mean that. I knew you would take it that way. Most women would think what you just said. I know I was the first man you've ever slept with. I was honored that I was your first. It meant a lot to me you gave your soul and body to me. At first, I could not believe that I was the first man because you are very attractive. These days, it would be hard to find a virgin in their late 20s. I am not saying this to make fun of you. I mean that I felt privileged. I know from my residents in our hospital how young people are these days," he continued. "I would have loved to take you to see the world together, traveling Europe, to see a Safari in Africa, the pyramids in Egypt, the Arctic ocean to see the aurora borealis," he said.

"Would you have done that with me, not your wife?"

"Yes, with you."

"Why?"

"I am not sure why. I was thinking about that, why definitely with you and not with Greta. I think I was rushing into getting married with her. I was lonely. I had no one. I wanted to have a family of my own very quickly. After my parents passed, I grew up alone, handling all kinds of stresses of life all by myself, and I thought I needed a family of my own. I am not sure if I really loved my wife. Nor can I say I knew her much, really. She always wanted to inherit her winery business from her parents.

"They have a big family, Catholics with 10-12 kids. Not only that, they have their extended families, cousins, nephews, nieces; I don't even know who's who there. They just have a huge family gathering almost every day, eating great food and drinking their home-grown wines. Life is quite different there. Their priority is different, and I have always liked that. I dreamed about having my family dinner like that someday.

"When my wife came here to live in the US, she soon recognized how different and lonely my life was. I think we drifted apart the moment we got settled here on Long Island. It was just a matter of time when she would go back to Italy and I knew that it would come. She and I had nothing in common. She did not know medicine, and I did not know much about the winery. I just like to drink wine. Her ambitions were so different," he paused.

Then, he continued, "Then I saw how we worked together, no need to talk much, you just seemed to understand and carry on with the projects without many questions. We have so many things in common, and we are going through this pandemic crisis with enormous amount of psychiatric pressures, seeing truckloads of dead bodies, literally truckloads. Seeing such sights together will change anyone. And you were there, with me, silently crying with me and it shocked me to see how futile life really is. How can I possibly share that with someone verbally? I can't even explain what I saw and how I felt. But you were there with me watching those cheap coffins, forklifted and dropped in a massive grave. How can I put that in words what I felt by seeing that? We are all born with so many bright hopes with the bodies given to us. And at the end, it just gets dumped in a mass grave site, no one bothering to claim them, no one loved them, no one cared enough to give decent funerals. I realized that I am not too different from them. I am here alone, no one will know I died here and maybe I will get dumped on Hart Island too. Then I met you. I am not saying you will need to give me a proper funeral, but you are someone to who I can say, 'I am dying,' at least. Someone to love me or care for me like bringing this hot soup." His tears dropped onto his cheek.

He said, "Yeah, I want to take you on all these trips. I want to see you getting old with me. Sam, I want to know if you need money, please take whatever you'd need before you give out the rest to my wife. I don't know your circumstances, but that's the least I can do for you."

"No, I have enough. That's not what I want," Samantha said.

"Also, please publish the work we have done. I finished the manuscript. You know where the files are from the laptop."

"Please do not say as if you are dying," Samantha said.

"Sam, I am getting tired now. You sit there six feet away and tell me what you think about God."

"I am a Christian," Samantha said.

173

"I know, you told me. So, I want to know more about your God. Would he love me?"

"Yes, He does, all you have to do is pray to Him, that you are a sinner, but now you believe in Jesus Christ as the Son of God, your Savior and that you proclaim that by saying it out loud to me. Then you will be saved from the eternal death."

"I will pray that now, and I am saying that Jesus is my Savior, the Son of God."

He cried when he said that. "I believe that. Stay here till I fall asleep. Thank you for telling me about God. I am so happy that I met you, Sam."

Samantha watched him for a long time. He looked peaceful sleeping. She went out to the couch and found some blankets and slept.

Next morning, bright sunlight came through the windows. Samantha got up to make some coffee, fumbling along to find the espresso coffee. She forgot to buy more from the grocery and felt lousy that the espresso coffee had run out.

She went into the bedroom to check on Dr. Falkner and found him dead.

CHAPTER 32

True love

April 18, 2020

Samantha was terribly stressed dealing with a panic situation when she found Dr. Falkner dead in his bedroom on the morning of April 17. She called 911. The police and the coroner's officers came rather quickly, within 10 minutes. Samantha told them the specifics; why she was there, the status of Dr. Falkner the night before and answered all the questions they asked. The coroner officers recognized Dr. Falkner, and they were in shock to see one of their own dead and confirmed that he was not at work since Monday, presumably due to COVID-19 infection.

They took him to the place Dr. Falkner worked, the Long Island Coroner's Office to perform an autopsy. Samantha could not imagine how "the bitch" Dr. Falkner mentioned would respond to seeing one of her colleagues dead. Not only that, she and other colleagues would have to perform an autopsy on him. The policy to perform an autopsy was required when a body was found outside the hospital or medical care facility to document the cause of death and rule out foul play.

Samantha called Dr. Falkner's wife. It must have been nighttime when she answered the phone.

"I know you do not know me. I was working with Dr. Falkner. My name is Samantha Parker and I am his resident. Dr. Falkner is dead with complications due to COVID-19. I was told by Dr. Falkner before his death to contact you, and once you come to the US, he told me to instruct you how to access the finances." That was what Samantha said.

She did not divulge the relationship with Dr. Falkner as a lover. Dr. Falkner's wife did not cry. The phone call was rather short. She did not tell Samantha when she would come or ask more specifics about how and where he died. From Samantha's perspective, Dr. Falkner's wife was somewhat indifferent about the whole thing, and her reaction was not what Samantha expected. She probably was too shocked to receive the news in the middle of night, only half awake.

Samantha copied his manuscript from his laptop for her to finish and submit it to the New England Journal of Medicine. Dr. Falkner had not told Samantha his son's birthday to access his encrypted financial file or his iPhone password. So, even if Samantha wanted to get some money, she couldn't. But Samantha was not going to take money from him, anyway. She was merely curious how much money he had. It would have been better if he used some of it to travel as he wished, all over the world, had he known he would die at such a young age.

What good is it to leave all that money by working such long hours after graduating from medical school, and residency training for another five to six years?

Samantha remembered the words in the Bible, the words in Ecclesiastes say:

The words of the Preacher, the son of David, king in Jerusalem. "Vanity of vanities," says the Preacher, "Vanity of vanities! All is vanity." What advantage does man have in all his work Which he does under the sun? A generation goes and a generation comes, But the earth remains forever. Also, the sun rises and the sun sets; And hastening to its place it rises there again. Blowing toward the south, Then turning toward the north, The wind continues swirling along; And on its circular courses the wind returns. All the rivers flow into the sea, Yet the sea is not full. To the place where the rivers flow, There they flow again. All things are wearisome; Man is not able to tell it. The eye is not satisfied with seeing, Nor is the ear filled with hearing. That which has been is that which will be, And that which has been done is that which will be done. So there is nothing new under the sun. Is there anything of which one might say, "See this, it is new?" Already it has existed for ages Which were before us. There is no remembrance of earlier things; And also of the later things which will occur, There will be for them no remembrance Among those who will come later still.

Ecclesiastes 1:2-11

There is an appointed time for everything. And there is a time for every event under heaven—A time to give birth and a time to die; A time to plant and a time to uproot what is planted. A time to kill and a time to heal; A time to tear down and a time to build up. A time to weep and a time to laugh; A time to mourn and a time to dance. A time to throw stones and a time to gather stones; A time to embrace and a time to shun embracing. A time to search and a time to give up as lost; A time to keep and a time to throw away. A time to tear apart and a time to sew together; A time to be silent and a time to speak. A time to love and a time to hate; A time for war and a time for peace.

Ecclesiastes 3:1-8

I know that there is nothing better for them than to rejoice and to do good in one's lifetime; moreover, that every man who eats and drinks sees good in all his labor—it is the gift of God."

Ecclesiastes 3:13

Samantha was glad that she met Dr. Falkner and especially glad that she would be able to meet him in heaven when she also passes away. Miraculously, he made a confession to God the night before he died and made peace with Him. And God was using Samantha as a vessel for the task. She was glad to come to his house before he died. He did not die lonely. He was afraid of dying alone. Even though Samantha may have taken a great risk of her own health, she was happy that Dr. Falkner received a gift of eternal life before he died.

Samantha could not understand her own behaviors, which even led to a romantic relationship with him. She had never experienced the attraction she felt, with reasons she could not articulate in her mind.

They started off the relationship in a wrong way; disliking him immensely and hating the feeling of trapped under the male authority. To Samantha, it was not just the physical attractions, but the way he made her feel with total acceptance. No matter what, how, or who she portrayed herself, he accepted her without additional demands.

She did not put on her makeup nor comb her hair nicely. She talked about her innermost feelings of being an Asian American to him without getting any judgmental comments. She introduced him to Asian cooking, and he gladly experienced it with her. In fact, he liked to try different cuisines.

She did not have to impress him with her accomplishments and degrees like the way Samantha felt toward Ed's parents. There were no underlying expectations and performances Samantha should measure up to. No strings attached to certain conditions Samantha should meet. She just felt free to be who she was with Dr. Falkner. Is that called love or is that just to embrace, she did not know. Whatever it was, she felt comfortable, and she wanted to be with him.

Such a feeling was never found when she was with Ed. Even though Ed said he was not judgmental like his parents, Samantha felt that she was not good enough for him. Ed and his parents were quick to point out what was lacking in Samantha. Samantha also felt rebellious toward this because for her, being Chinese was not that great. They were not superior over any Asian countries. Ed's family did not have money, in fact. Ed had to get an ROTC scholarship to graduate with all his education.

Samantha was born in a family of money; her father was a prominent OB/Gyn doctor, and her mother was independently rich from her parents in Korea. Her grandparents from her mother's side owned a technology company in Korea for a long time, and they were filthy rich.

Samantha was not honest enough to know or did not want to be honest with herself to know why she felt pressured the whole time she was with Ed.

But now, she had another romantic relationship with Dr. Falkner to have the comparison, and she recognized why she was not totally happy with Ed. Once she was sure about what she wanted from a romantic relationship, she knew what she needed to do with Ed. Eventually, she needed to be free of that oppressive relationship. Perhaps finding another man like Dr. Falkner would be difficult, but now she knew what to look for in her romantic relationship.

It only took her two days to process all these thoughts. She was caught up with details of taking care of practical and necessary things, such as moving Dr. Falkner into the hospital coroner's office. There was a moment she had, just sitting down in his lovely library, and she missed him terribly. She began to cry blindly looking at the window. The waves were crashing into the dark rocky cliffs. She realized that this would be the last time she will stand here in his house expressing the true emotions about him. She would not be able to cry in front of his wife, for it would be illegitimate and inappropriate.

Samantha decided not to reveal her true relationship with Dr. Falkner to anyone. It was indeed a truly short relationship in terms of time, but the deep love and respect that she felt knowing him and knowing herself through the experience would take a long time to be erased from her memory.

Samantha received a text from her Mom that she had arrived Miami offshore, unable to dock. Her mom had never texted Samantha before. She knew how to call and send photos via text and email but had never texted a message to Samantha.

Samantha therefore knew that her mom was not yet comfortable to talk to Samantha about her situations. Samantha had been reading that many cruise ships were stuck at all the borders, including Miami and Fort Lauderdale on the east coast, and Los Angeles and San Francisco on the west coast. Samantha was glad that she had not yet flown to Miami. It would be awhile until her mom could dock and fly back to San Francisco.

CHAPTER 33

The transport

April 20, 2020

Ed had another dinner meeting with Dr. Shei in her house. This time, however, it was only with Dr. Shei, to discuss the method of transport for the virus in culture. While Ed was thinking about the potential transport methods these past days and nights, Dr. Shei said she already had it figured out, which Ed was extremely glad to hear.

She said everything was already prepared for Ed to take the virus: She had prepared several syringes containing the virus in RNA stable media and labelled as Insulin. Many people carry their insulin onto an aircraft and ask the crew to place it in the refrigerator on the plane. The syringes are in a box, inside an insulated styrofoam container that also contains plenty of dry ice to last for 15-16 hours, but the cool temperature in the refrigerator will further maintain the longevity of dry ice.

Ed must lie that he has Type I diabetes and will require to self-inject during the flight after meals, if someone asks, Dr. Shei told Ed. Under no circumstances should a syringe be broken—by dropping, for instance— because once the virus content spills, it may kill the entire crew and passengers.

She said it may kill because she was not sure; she has never tested whether the virus in her laboratory has the capacity to transmit the disease into humans because the virus was directly extracted from bats. In order to infect humans, the virus may require a zoonotic vector such as pangolins. But if anyone finds out that Ed and Dr. Shei have tried to transport the deadly virus on the airplane, it will cause international disasters, and their careers or even her life will be over.

Knowing all the information Dr. Shei just shared, Ed realized COVID-19 most likely did not originate from her lab.

Ed asked about PPE to handle the box. "If the Biosafety Level 4 requires PPE to handle the virus, how can I just touch the box with bare hands?" he asked.

Dr. Shei said the box in the styrofoam, and the syringes would prevent seepage, and she told him never to open the box to show, even if someone asks. The box itself will be labelled as Insulin, and the crew members just need to trust him. She assured Ed that the syringes are double pane glass, and even in the worst situation to show what is inside the box, the virus will not seep out unless he breaks a syringe.

Dr. Shei agreed that Ed should tell this only to the CDC director once it gets transported successfully to Atlanta. Ed was flying directly to Atlanta, not to his home in Washington, DC. The first thing she said Ed should do is go to the CDC lab and replace the dry ice packages.

Dr. Shei said Ed must be involved in making the vaccine from his workplace in DC and never relinquish the responsibility to the CDC or to the American government. The CDC would most likely provide funding to successfully develop the vaccine in Abby Laboratory, where Ed must take the virus samples. Ed was to make a contract with the CDC and Abby Laboratory, along with the lab in Britain to mass produce the vaccine vials.

The estimated timeline for the entire process should be completed in December 2020. Dr. Shei predicted that another huge surge with COVID-19 would happen this fall, starting in September or early October, even if the world had successfully obeyed the lockdown orders.

Wuhan and South Korea were seeing more than a handful of new infections again with COVID-19, and she suspected it would be a common pattern throughout the globe, especially if the US opened businesses earlier than others due to economic pressure. So, the curve of COVID-19 would show a steady plateau or even an increase, and not a decreasing trend.

Ed asked her intention of choosing him for the task. Dr. Shei did not answer that, she just smiled. Ed asked her if there was a young researcher's death on November 17, 2019, before the novel coronavirus was even known to cause COVID-19, and she adamantly denied. She said the virus she sequenced would most likely have the potential to infect humans, but it was not a bioweapon she created, nor was there an accidental spillage from the WIV that spread the disease into the pandemic levels.

Ed was to fly back to the US on April 22. Dr. Shei asked him to fly in first class. Ed told her he was not at that level of flying first class. In fact, none of his team members were flying first class.

The team members who left a week earlier were at the Director level, so they all flew first class. Dr. Shei thought it would be better to fly first class with the viral sample, since the crew members typically were more attentive to serve the first class passengers and did not ask many questions. She even offered to give him money to buy the first class ticket, but Ed told her it would look strange to his team members. They might suspect more if Ed did that because as it was, even now, they were suspicious of Ed meeting Dr. Shei privately like this.

Dr. Shei understood and told him to deflect the attention to her daughter, who Dr. Shei wanted Ed to have a romantic relationship with. He realized that Dr. Shei was very calculative and a smart woman who thought through every aspect of things. She would not tell her true intentions; why she was doing this specifically with Ed.

Ed felt like he was in one of the 007 movies. He found himself in a situation that he never dreamed of. He felt extreme weight over his shoulders with many responsibilities. Ed's team had two missions; to see the WIV level 4 laboratory and get a sample of the virus. Ed had achieved these missions, but he was not able to tell this to his team members.

CHAPTER 34

Maximum mental capacity

Samantha got a phone call from the police officer on Long Island who wanted to meet with Samantha because he said she was the last person in contact with Dr. Falkner before he passed away. She was not a murder suspect or anything like that, but they just wanted to perform a formal interview with Samantha.

The police officer told her that the coroner's office conducted a thorough autopsy on Dr. Falkner over the weekend by his colleagues, and that Dr. Falkner had a massive pulmonary embolism arising from thrombi located in the deep veins of the lower extremities, which was one of the related complications of COVID-19. His lungs weighed two times the normal male lung weight. This was a fast and silent killer.

Because of his young age without any pre-existing high-risk factors, he could have fought the virus but once the cardiovascular and peripheral vascular complications occur, stroke, heart attack and in this case pulmonary embolism caused an immediate death. He was only 41 years old.

Samantha thought anticoagulative therapy may have helped him to avoid blood clot if he had come to the hospital, but his stubbornness to avoid going to receive health care cost him his dear life.

The police officer agreed to meet her at her apartment later in the Bronx at 6:00 pm.

Samantha had to go for the ambulance pick up experience today, Monday at 10:00 am. The case was a fatal motor vehicle accident of a 19-year-old male who died at the scene in his red sports car. The impact was with a hazmat truck carrying hazardous material—gasoline.

The truck driver was describing the scene as a kid driving 95 miles per hour on an empty highway while passing his truck in the same direction, losing control, and colliding with the front left tire of his truck.

The truck driver was trying to bear to the right as he saw the car approaching and colliding, and the truck rolled over due to this sudden maneuver, spilling the gasoline, hitting the highway metal guardrails, causing sparks and an explosion, catching the sports car on fire and killing the kid.

The kid's car was in front of the truck when both cars finally came to a stop. The truck driver got out and tried to pull the kid out but could not open the door on time because suddenly, in that moment, the gas tank of the sports car exploded. The truck driver had severe second-degree burns and was airlifted to the nearby hospital.

The coroner's office and the ambulance were going to the scene of the fatal accident and Samantha was to go with the ambulance. She was not sure why the ambulance was going to the scene if they already knew the kid had died, but she tagged along anyway. At least it was not a COVID-19 case.

The ambulance drove at least 80-90 miles per hour. Inside the bumpy ride, they were to wear their PPE. At times, Samantha's head touched the roof of the ambulance as she sat in the back seat. It was extremely difficult to wear any gear under the circumstances. Stopping at the scene, all three health care workers in the back of the ambulance got out, along with the driver.

Samantha saw a completely charred car with a body inside the driver's seat. She could not recognize even the color of the car. The residual smoldering smoke was coming out of the car. The firefighters and police officers arrived before the ambulance and had put out the fire. The ambulance pulled out the gurney, and the firefighters pulled the body out and placed it on the gurney. The hair, nose, fingers and shoes including the toes were all charred and gone. It was absolutely unrecognizable except to say he was a human.

The smell of burnt human was undeniable, and it smelled not too far from barbeque meat. Samantha began to throw up again.

One of the firefighters came to Samantha to make sure she was okay. "You must be new," he said gently holding Samantha.

She could not take it in any longer. She began to wail. She did not know exactly why she could not take this life anymore. She had lost her father, and her lover with COVID-19. She had seen miserable deaths when she went to the murder investigation scene.

Now she faced seeing the charred body beyond recognition, and she just could not take it any longer. She sat on the highway, wailing. A few police officers and the ambulance workers also came asking her if she was okay. Samantha realized that she was making another scene, obstructing the work that all these people needed to do.

One of the policemen said that she should just sit down in his police car and take a drink, so she followed. She sat in the back seat of the police car and drank the bottled water he gave her. Samantha had met her maximum capacity to take in things of life, which she had never known before.

This was how far she could go, she realized.

She was surprised that she was not as strong as she once thought. A tough, stoic doctor who could take bloody scenes, cut organs without any problems; deal with life and death situations in a rather cool manner with her sound judgment intact.

She even noticed she was blaming this 19-year-old kid; why couldn't he just stay home under the lockdown state order, why do people behave in such non-responsible ways during the pandemic, why are they so selfish, do they realize their actions they take today can cause other people detrimental effects later on, why did this kid drive so fast, just because the highways are empty does not mean he can drive that fast, and why was she in this moment of her life facing and seeing such an ugly side of humanity.

All the self-pity came to her at once, and she felt miserable. She needed to see some counseling for sure. She thought about going back to her program director and tell him what had happened to her and try to seek psychiatric help. She was taking things in, and the responsibility of her mother's well-being, and her father's funeral arrangements as though she was in charge of everything when she does not have a faintest idea how to go about doing anything.

She was definitely not going to perform this charred kid's autopsy, which was brought to the coroner's office at her hospital.

She just stayed inside the police car. Finally, two policemen came and drove her to the Bronx hospital. She got dropped off and went to see Dr. Wells in his office. He was not there. He was working remotely from his home these days. Samantha forgot about that.

She called him and told him everything she was facing and feeling. He thought it would be good to admit her for one night in the psychiatric unit for observation, which she agreed to. Dr. Wells said it was not unusual for the health care workers to face this tremendous pressure, even to the degree of suicide these days.

He said that Samantha does not have to finish the autopsy rotation from that day on and she needs to take care of herself first and then take care of her mother later this week. He will even excuse her from doing the surgical rotation in May and to switch with someone. Dr. Wells said that he would arrange everything for her and to just take deep breaths and rest for a while.

The complication of getting admitted to the psychiatric unit surfaced because Samantha was exposed to COVID-19 when she was with Dr. Falkner, the medical examiner who died due to COVID-19 complications and who Samantha had spent the last two weeks with. Dr. Wells instructed her to go to the Employee Health Department to get tested for COVID-19 with a nasopharyngeal swab test today and go back to her home to wait for a phone consultation from one of the psychiatric doctors.

Samantha did as Dr. Wells suggested. She came back to her apartment and threw herself onto the couch. She lay down there until she felt asleep.

She was dreaming about Dr. Falkner when a doorbell rang. It was two police officers from Long Island; she had completely forgotten. It was already 6:00 pm. She had not eaten except her breakfast that day and later lost by vomiting at the scene. Samantha noticed one police officer was a woman who she had never met, and the other was a male officer she had seen at Dr. Falkner's house.

Samantha did not offer even water to them. She was famished and did not have energy to face them. She grabbed some bread and yogurt from her refrigerator, saying to them she had not eaten anything. They waited for her to finish. They were polite about that. Samantha had multiple missed phone calls and text messages in her phone; it might be the psychiatric doctor who tried to call her, she thought.

"You are the last person who stayed with Dr. Falkner, and we need to ask you some specific questions. Is that okay?" the woman police officer said.

"Yes," Samantha said, sitting on a chair, still drinking the last drops of her bottled water.

The two police officers moved and sat closer to Samantha around the kitchen table.

"Please tell us why you were there," the male officer asked.

Samantha told them she was there because she received a phone call from Dr. Falkner that Thursday and she went there to see him. She was a resident working with him for two weeks prior in April and knew where he lived. She had to talk about Hart Island experiences and that she spent some nights at his place to commute to Hart Island together.

The two police officers looked at each other when Samantha said that, jotting down every word Samantha was saying. Samantha felt a tension but did not admit her relationship with Dr. Falkner beyond that statement. Samantha explained that she took care of Dr. Falkner the night before and he ate some soup and took some medications and he went to sleep that same night.

The following morning, she went back to his bedroom and found him dead and called 911.

The policeman asked to see the phone call from Dr. Falkner on Thursday from Samantha's cell phone, which she found and then showed. She had not deleted the phone records, and she felt relieved about that.

Samantha found out from their conversation that Dr. Falkner's wife was asking who and why Samantha was at Dr. Falkner's house at that time, and the police decided to investigate, or at least have a formal interview with Samantha. Samantha also told them that his wife called her—actually, she called her first because Dr. Falkner said to contact his wife. Mrs. Falkner and she talked briefly, and they were to meet each other after the funeral, scheduled for April 25.

The police took all the information and appreciated Samantha's cooperation. They said that they may come back at a later time if they have further questions, which Samantha agreed to. They left Samantha's apartment.

Samantha looked through her cell phone and texted back the psychiatrist, who introduced herself as a good friend of Dr. Wells: Dr. Song. She was also the program director for the residency program in the Bronx department of psychiatry, and she said she would love to talk to Samantha via Zoom. Dr. Song said she had already heard about Samantha's situations through Dr. Wells.

Samantha texted her back saying tomorrow would be better.

Dr. Song immediately texted back, "Fantastic, how about 9:00 am?"

Samantha agreed to have a one hour confidential consultation by telemedicine, which had become the first modality of many physicians during the pandemic time. Samantha was a little relieved that Dr. Song was an Asian doctor, a Residency Program Director in her same hospital. She could confide with her in many aspects.

CHAPTER 35

Greed of cruise lines

April 22, 2020

Emily found out for the second time that she had tested positive for the COVID-19. She had already tested positive at Barcelona. It was not surprising for her to get repeated positive results. The captain announced via intercom that all passengers and crew members must remain on the cruise ship for 14 days.

This was what she expected. From her cabin, she saw many sick patients medevacked by helicopters, probably to nearby Miami hospitals. She also saw the dead bodies covered inside plastic bags getting pulled out and transported by US Coast Guard ships.

The cruise ship supplies had been diminished and meals for all the living people became a logistical nightmare. This was not just on Emily's ship but all 20 or more cruise ships off the US coasts with tens of thousands of people. Amazingly, Washington, DC chef José Andrés, known for his humanitarian relief efforts in disaster areas, had directed his attention to the quarantined cruise ships and their coronavirus-infected passengers and crew. Emily heard that this man with a heavy Latino accent started to distribute food to the people stranded aboard ships through his nonprofit World Central Kitchen. An off-site kitchen was set up at the port by Andrés' team, who were preparing and delivering meals for the guests and crew, along with videos showing the team's work.

When Emily saw this video and how Andrés' team worked on a massive scale to feed the people he did not even know, she was touched by the enormous humanitarian act. Some people like him were stepping up to save others in such a dire period of a pandemic time, despite the risk he and his team might face and the negative affects financially, and physically with infection.

When many people were becoming unemployed, Andrés' team was hiring more workers to help feed other people; three meals a day. The quality of food was not poor at all. It was delicious with precious meat, fish, bread and vegetables.

Whenever Emily received her portion, she ate with Mahalia, with tears of the gratefulness they felt. They always ate after a long prayer to God, thanking Him for the hot meal Andrés' team prepared and asked God's blessing to them.

On the other hand, there were several who were signing a petition being distributed through the cabins among passengers who were recruiting large numbers of people on Emily's ship. Some were saying they should join a lawsuit against Carnival Corporation and their portfolio of several large cruise lines, which accounted for nearly 70 percent of the global cruise industry's revenues.

Cruise lines were facing an unprecedented legal storm when coronavirus outbreaks on board their ships began leaving thousands ill, and many people dead. Most of the cruise lines knew the pandemic was spreading, but cruises continued through February and early March, with the industry only suspending new voyages when the CDC issued a NO SAIL order on March 14.

The agency cited concerns over high transmission rates on cruise ships, and signs that passengers getting off the vessels were spreading the disease in communities far from the water.

Emily heard to date, at least 69 cruise passengers had died from COVID-19. While the number of deaths on cruises was a fraction of the rising global toll, critics alleged the crisis on board the ships reflected an industry culture that prioritized profits over lives and routinely disregarded passenger and crew safety.

From the reading of the petition letter, it appeared there were a multitude of people who faced illness and death of their loved ones, remarkably similar to Emily's situation. Passengers on cruise ships had already filed a class action lawsuit in Florida, seeking compensation from cruise lines that had directed its sales staff to downplay the severity of the disease in order to keep bookings by saying "Coronavirus in humans is an over-hyped pandemic scare."

The cruise operators had not expected to see litigation on this scale before. Most passengers were angry at the cruise operators for a failure to warn and a failure to be transparent, and they had ample proof of negligence.

When the dust settles dealing with COVID-19, it will be class action lawyers who benefit the most, Emily thought.

The Cruise Lines International Association (CLIA) said the industry responded to an "unprecedented crisis based on the information that was available when it was available and always under the guidance of prevailing health authorities," and in addition, the cruise lines stated that "they took immediate and aggressive action in response to this crisis with policies and protocols that went above and beyond the actions of other industries."

The CLIA defended itself by saying they had submitted proposals to the US government on a framework for resuming operations, including more stringent boarding procedures, monitoring capabilities and quarantine arrangements.

The US government had expressed concern that allowing passengers who had tested positive with the coronavirus to leave a ship would put the US at risk of accelerating the coronavirus' spread and contemplated to leave them on board because bringing them ashore would increase the number of official cases on American soil. The passengers and crew members, however, could not stay on board the ships forever.

The crew members were facing new challenges because cruise lines were registered in foreign countries and locations such as Caribbean tax havens, allowing them to skirt labor and environmental laws in Europe and the US. Most of the crew members were not receiving protection of minimal wages, health insurance benefits, or work hour limitations; exploitation continued without anyone noticing it.

Emily was seeing firsthand how Mahalia was being treated on the ship. She was not even earning the minimal wage per hour. The money was a pathetically small amount, which Mahalia was very happy to get. She was supporting her entire family with it.

How did the US get to be so abusive and still continue the exploitation of slavery, she thought.

The US government banned cruise ship travel until July 24, 2020 and still, cruise firms were reporting a surge in bookings when more operations resume in early August. They were enticing the customer with a credit of 125% of points or a free trip on their next booking within the same cruise line. Some passengers really loved cruises and had already booked their next trips, despite the COVID-19 experiences they recently had. Emily could not understand this.

She also received a letter from her cruise that they would refund fees and credit her 125% points toward her next trip if she paid now for the next trip. She promised herself that she would never go on another cruise.

Emily was just frustrated that she could not be on US soil and endured the quarantine processes, again and again. Now, it looked like 14 more days on the ship, and another 14 days in Miami hotels. There were talks about being transported to the CDC in Atlanta for another quarantine, and Emily was not sure if that was in addition to the 14 days in a Miami hotel quarantine or instead of the Miami hotel quarantine. Whatever it was, she just wished that these days were moving faster. She just wanted to be at her home in San Francisco.

She thought there were always two forces working in an opposite manner; one good and one evil.

So many good things happen in very tough times, like Andrés who gave his time, money and effort to feed the people on the cruise ships.

And there were so many greedy people, like some cruise operators and companies who sought profits at any cost. The cruise lines should have stopped traveling around the globe in January or early February when they knew that there was an epidemic in Wuhan, China.

No one knew if the epidemic in Wuhan would become a pandemic around the world, but on February 11, 2020, WHO announced a name for the new coronavirus disease as COVID-19, and on March 11, WHO announced that the COVID-19 outbreak was a global pandemic.

It was then and there Emily's ship should have turned back and returned to San Francisco from wherever it was. If the captain had returned to the US on March 11, Robert may not have faced his death.

He died on April 6. Robert was doing very well on March 11. If he had proper hospital care in San Francisco, he may have lived and fought the coronavirus infection.

Emily signed her name on the petition letter. She had to provide her home address and phone number. She wrote clearly and legibly to make sure no one would have any difficulty reading her handwriting.

CHAPTER 36

For whom the bell tolls

Ed was at the airport in Wuhan. He had the box holding the virus culture, and the Montblanc bag with his computer and the USB Dr. Shei had given him. Dr. Shei provided an ID stating he had Type I diabetes and he must take insulin shots. Ed had no idea such things exist to carry insulin shots onto an aircraft. Ed had never carried a fake ID or an Airport Information Card, which was necessary when carrying insulin and devices necessary to monitor glucose levels. Everything was too risky for him. He was already regretting taking this risk.

For whom the bell tolls, he thought.

A thought came to his mind to just turn back and return the items to Dr. Shei. He was sweating heavily. His team members joked with him saying, "Is he carrying a bomb and why does he look so nervous and sweating when the temperature is pleasant at 62 F degrees and he is traveling very light."

He had only one reasonably sized suitcase and one carry-on bag. He wished that he was cool and nonchalant as a 007 spy movie star, but he was far from it. He was disappointed in himself. He might as well say and admit that he had illegal drugs or a bomb he was carrying into the US.

Ed checked his suitcase, which went through the X-ray machine, and he was now walking toward the airport security before boarding the flight. The TSA allowed for diabetes-related supplies, equipment, and medication—including liquids—through the checkpoint once they had been properly screened by X-ray or by hand inspection.

Ed packed all the insulin supplies together in his carry-on bag and not in his checked luggage, as it could be affected by severe changes in air pressure and temperature.

The viral cultures were divided into two syringes of 5 ml each in the box. It should easily pass the general rule prohibiting passengers from bringing liquids over 3.4 ounces through security.

Accessories required to keep insulin cool, such as freezer packs or frozen gel packs, were permitted through the screening checkpoint. But people with diabetes should also take, aside from their insulin, other medications such as Glucagon, and other liquids and gels, including juice and cake gels which would end up well above the 3.4-ounce limit.

A physician prescribed the insulin and needles by providing a professional, pre-printed pharmaceutical label identifying the medication which Dr. Shei had prepared.

Dr. Wang's name was printed on all the items. Ed had never met Dr. Wang.

Ed was informed that all these items could go through an airport metal detector and they were designed to withstand common electromagnetic interference but could not pass through an airport body scanner.

Ed took his computer and the insulin box out of the carry-on bag and placed them on the metal detector conveyor, along with his belt, watch and shoes.

He went through the checkpoint and came to collect his items when one of the TSA requested Ed to open the box. The insulin syringes were in freezer packs with a small amount of dry ice, and an adjacent small container held orange juice, glucagon medication, and cake gel. All of them were carefully labeled with the pre-printed pharmaceutical label with Dr. Wang's name.

The TSA requested to see Ed's Airport Information Card, which he pulled out from his wallet. Then Ed was allowed to pass through. One of his team members asked Ed, "I did not know you had diabetes. I don't think I remember seeing you carry that stuff in Atlanta." Ed did not answer, but just gathered his items back into his carry-on bag and went toward the gate. He could not believe he actually made it.

Ed had no idea how complicated things were with airport security systems that diabetes patients must go through. Some people may have an infusion set, placed under their skin with tubing and they must request an alternative pat-down screening process and not go through an airport body scanner since Medtronic had not determined advanced imaging technology to be safe for insulin pump or Continuous Glucose Monitor (CGM) devices.

Finally, Ed boarded the airplane and promptly asked the flight attendant to put the box in the refrigerator. She looked for the labels and smiled. She took it and put it into the refrigerator, saying, "Let me know when you need it!" Ed sat in his seat. Sweat was now dripping down from his forehead.

Why did he have to take this kind of risk? Was he doing all this for the benefit of the US government or for his own glory to develop a vaccine against COVID-19? Why was he chosen for this task? Was he just placed in the right place at the right time? What was he going to do with this, anyway? Is Dr. Shei correct about releasing the information to the CDC director, and if so, why? Does he even have this kind of ambition to develop a vaccine to save the world?

Who is he anyway? Wouldn't it be ideal to just marry Samantha, have a few kids and be a man of the house for the rest of his life, working in some lab?

He had no desire to be a sacrificial lamb for anyone, including the US government. He did not sign up for it and he had no reason to do this task but ended up taking the risk, anyway.

One moment at a time, Ed thought.

He was relieved to safely sit down in the airplane. The next task for him was not to forget about bringing the box with him when they land. Since he was not really a diabetes patient, it would be very easy for him to forget about the box. He imagined what would happen if he left the box on the plane. His name and Dr. Wang's name were all over the box. He set an alarm on his cellphone to remind himself to pick up the box.

The airplane was only a third filled, and the people were all scattered about and wearing masks. The passengers were all tested for temperature before boarding near the entrance of the airport. Ed realized that the danger of the coronavirus contamination was everywhere, reminding him to be mindful of what he did, especially touching his face.

He got out the hand sanitizer and wiped his surroundings.

CHAPTER 37

Greta Falkner

April 23, 2020

The flight from Italy to New York was suspended on February 29, 2020 and re-scheduled to April 25, 2020. Samantha had learned that Greta Falkner was to be back in the US on the 25th to arrange the funeral for her husband.

Apparently, Greta had given her approval to perform an autopsy on her husband on April 18, when he was moved to the Long Island coroner's office. In order to perform an autopsy, the next of kin, (in this instance Mrs. Falkner), had been required to sign and fax her approval to the coroner's office from Tuscany, Italy.

So, Greta Falkner knew that her husband was dead before Samantha called her. Several days after their first conversation, Greta called Samantha asking exactly who Samantha was to her husband, and how did Samantha know about their finances. It would have been puzzling for Greta to get a phone call from Samantha, a woman resident, whom her husband never mentioned.

Samantha now realized why Greta Falkner never revealed her sadness or any shocking emotion when she called Greta the first time. Everything must have been surreal to Greta.

"How do you know my husband?" is what Greta constantly asked Samantha. Samantha kept her answer the same as before, that she worked with Dr. Falkner doing autopsies at Hart Island and that they were writing a manuscript together. Samantha told her she stayed in his house to take care of him the night before he died, because she had to. Samantha went to the home after she received a phone call from Dr. Falkner that he was sick and went there voluntarily to check on him. He never asked Samantha to be there.

Dr. Falkner told Samantha to inform his wife how to access their financial information, and that was exactly why Samantha called Greta Falkner. Greta asked Samantha to meet with her after the funeral service on April 25, which Samantha agreed to do.

When Samantha left Dr. Falkner's house on April 18, she left all the car and house keys inside the house and his wallet in the exact same places where she had found them and locked the door from the outside. She also cleaned up everything including the dishes they had used. She made sure that she did not leave any trace of her belongings.

Samantha was hesitant to meet with Greta Falkner, but she was left without a choice except to meet her. She hoped Greta will not have her sixth sense; a woman's sense to detect what had happened between Samantha and her husband.

CHAPTER 38

The box

Ed landed in Atlanta. Getting out of the airport with the box was no problem. No one checked the contents of his carry-on bag. He and all his team members had to report to the CDC first. It was good to be back in America. Ed did not forget to bring the box back with him. He could not sleep nor eat much on the aircraft and there was no way that he could forget about the box; all he thought about was the box while on the airplane.

All the what-ifs.

During every turbulence the plane had, he panicked, thinking what if the syringe burst or broke? He was jumpy the whole trip, and even during the CDC meetings. All Ed cared about was to find a refrigerator and more dry ice.

His team members were wondering about his strange behaviors and questioning why they did not know Ed was a diabetes patient before the trip to China.

They were all tested for COVID-19 with a nasopharyngeal swab on the day they arrived at the CDC and were to remain in the CDC facility until the test results came out. If a test result was negative, then one can fly back to wherever one needs to, but if the test result is positive, one needs quarantine for 14 days in the CDC. The test results were expected to come out the next day.

Ed called Samantha as soon as he saw a chance to call. She was not energetic as usual. She said there were a lot of things going on with her. She told him about her father's death on the cruise ship, that his body was actually in Barcelona, Spain. Her mother was stuck Miami offshore, and her miserable autopsy rotations. She didn't cry when she was talking about these things, but Ed noticed that she was somewhat different.

Ed obviously did not tell her what had happened to him during the trip to China, but he couldn't wait to see her. He promised Samantha that he would drive to the Bronx as soon as he was allowed to move around and told her he may need to stay in the CDC for 14 days.

Samantha didn't seem to care about when she could see him and was rather indifferent toward Ed.

Ed also contacted his boss at the CDC, who organized the entire team to have a private meeting. Ed requested to see the CDC director alone, and the boss said that would not be possible unless Ed had a specific reason why he had to meet with the CDC director.

The CDC director was in Washington, DC these days, attending the President's Administrative COVID-19 task force meetings. Ed asked to see him in Washington, DC, because he also lived there, informing the boss he had essential information which he must discuss directly with the director, and left it at that.

His boss contacted the CDC director, and they were to meet sometime next week if Ed was free to go to Washington, DC.

Ed and his team members were transported to lodging in the CDC. As soon as Ed got to his hotel room, he placed the box inside a small refrigerator after he had emptied all the liquor contents. He also added ice from the ice machine to cool down the temperature inside the box. He couldn't wait to hand this box off to someone quickly.

All he wanted to do was to just give that box away to someone else. He would not relax or sleep as long as that box was in his hands.

CHAPTER 39

Engagement ring

April 24, 2020

Luckily, Ed's nasopharyngeal swab test turned out to be negative. A few team members tested positive and were extremely disappointed that they must stay at the CDC for two more weeks. Ed immediately got a rental car because there was no way Ed was going to fly, risking the identity of the box while going through the airport security checkpoint again. He realized that it would be faster to arrive to DC by air, but he was simply scared to death of going through the TSA security.

It would be approximately 10 hours to drive if Ed did not stop much. He did not know if the virus will survive an additional day or not. He drove as quickly as possible to get out of Atlanta. He bought an icebox from a convenience store, filled it with a bag of ice and his styrofoam box, placing it on the floor next to him on the passenger side, securing and snugging it tight with his bags.

The meeting with the CDC director was not yet set. Ed was going to put the box in his workplace, definitely inside the Level 4 Biosafety lab after he spoke to his boss Dr. Allen first thing on arrival. He could not access the Level 4 Biosafety lab without the approval of his boss.

He left a voice message for Samantha that he was going to drive to New York, maybe on the weekend to see her. He could not wait to talk to Samantha. They had not seen each other for months. He was going to spill the beans to her, the whole thing.

He could not wait to see her response after telling her he transported the virus to the US from the WIV in China. As soon as he could drop this damn thing off, he would drive to the Bronx.

Maybe he would buy a diamond ring and propose to her this time if he could shop for it. He did not know if the stores were open to buy a ring. He was happy thinking about giving this ring to her and seeing her facial expression. He was thinking about putting the ring into a cake he would bake in her apartment. Samantha would cut it with a knife, finding it by the clinking sound of the ring.

He had to orient the cake with something on top to make sure of the angle Samantha must cut the cake to find the ring. He was imagining all the happy moments that they would face together. He was going to make a multilayered chocolate cake Samantha always liked.

For Ed, the thought of having Samantha as his bride was more solidified as he was facing the enormous challenge transporting the virus from China. All he really wanted to do was get married to Samantha and have a family of their own.

Ed was smiling all the way on his drive to DC.

CHAPTER 40

The funeral

April 25, 2020

Samantha dressed in a black suit with pants and a white blouse. She liked a traditional look. She was used to wearing scrubs for so many months and it was strange to dress up, but she had to because she was attending Dr. Falkner's funeral.

She took the train and bus for two-and-a-half hours to arrive in Long Island and then to a nearby church where the funeral was to be held. The train and bus were pretty much empty.

She saw Mrs. Falkner sitting in the front row wearing a black dress and black hat with dark sunglasses. She was stunningly beautiful, especially with her long blonde hair. Because of COVID-19, the church was occupied by only a dozen or so people attending the funeral.

The casket must be closed, and people were appropriately distanced in their seats. Samantha sat in the very back row. The two police officers Samantha saw at her apartment were there. Dr. Falkner's boss, who he referred to as a "bitch" was also there and she delivered a short speech about his work at the coroner's office.

Surprisingly, his wife did not say a eulogy. The preacher gave a very brief message and prayer. The service was rather short.

His body was to be buried in a grave site not too far from the church, a walking distance. The casket was carried by four men to the car, and his wife also rode in the car to the gravesite. The rest of the handful of people walked. They gathered around the already dug grave site, and the casket was placed on top of the two poles. After a short prayer, a single rose was thrown onto the casket by each individual who attended.

The people dispersed after that. It was truly a short funeral. There was no gathering in his house for even a meal because of the strict rules not to gather in a closed space.

Samantha and his wife were to meet in his house after the funeral. Samantha was walking to the house when the black funeral car pulled over near Samantha. It was his wife, rolling down the window asking Samantha to ride with her. Samantha got into the back of the car in the seat next to his wife, risking the social distancing.

At least Samantha was wearing a mask.

It was just a few blocks when they got out of the car. They walked into the house. Samantha felt strange not seeing Dr. Falkner inside the house. His wife offered a glass of water to Samantha and she took it.

"So, tell me again, how do you know my husband?" Mrs. Falkner said.

"I was working with him as a resident for two weeks."

"So, you told me that David said to you to tell me how to get the finances from this laptop computer." The laptop computer was on the kitchen table where they both sat.

"Yes, I can show you where it is."

Mrs. Falkner gave the laptop to Samantha.

"It's this file under your son's name, Anthony." Mrs. Falkner walked around and stood behind Samantha.

"Just double click," said Samantha, and Mrs. Falkner did as Samantha said.

"Now, the password is your son's birthday, which Dr. Falkner did not tell me." Samantha turned her head, looking away from the computer as Mrs. Falkner typed out some numbers.

"It does not work," Mrs. Falkner said. "Maybe it is the entire year, two thousand…" She tried typing the entire year.

"Yes, it opened."

Samantha got up from the chair and said, "That is all I needed to tell you. I am going to catch the bus now."

"Oh, please sit down, I can drive and take you to your home later," Mrs. Falkner said.

"No, I rather take the bus and train."

"Please, sit, I need to know more things from you."

Samantha hesitated but sat.

"Tell me again, how did you meet my husband David?"

"I met him at Hart Island, working."

"When was that?"

"On March 31st."

"What were you doing there?"

"Burying the bodies and doing a few autopsies as Dr. Falkner instructed."

"And did you commute with David from this house together?"

"No, I slept in Hart Island."

"So, how do you know where this house was when you visited David after his phone call saying that he was sick?"

"Well, I spent a night here one time and commuted with him." Samantha felt harsh interrogation and did not know how to cover up things any longer.

"I see, did you sleep with David?" Mrs. Falkner was intensively watching her, trying to catch any signs if she fumbled.

"No," Samantha lied.

"So, you came back from where you were; did you say it was the Bronx you came from?"

"Yes."

"What day did David call you he was sick?"

"Thursday, April 16."

"And you stayed here that night?"

"Yes."

"And you found him dead the next morning?"

"Yes."

"Where did you sleep?"

"On the couch."

"I found someone took a shower in another bedroom downstairs. Did you take a shower?"

"Yes, I did."

"Yeah, it wasn't the way I decorated and put things in that bathroom and the bedroom. I know what and where I put things. David never walked into that bedroom. He does not know many things I do in this house, you see?"

Samantha was getting a red face and flustered as she tried to answer all her questions. "I did sleep in that bedroom one night, but on April 16, I slept in the couch because I wanted to hear well if Dr. Falkner needed something from the second-floor bedroom."

"I see, a nice resident."

"Did my husband like you? He must have, if he brought you into this house." Mrs. Falkner smiled.

"We were working on a paper for publication."

"I see, well, he was rather stuck on the idea of publications. His work was his everything. He worked more than 60 hours a week for years; well, since we got married. He never had time for me and Anthony.

"I always thought he had an affair with his boss, the one who gave a eulogy today. Well, it does not matter anymore. He is dead," Mrs. Falkner said rather coldly.

And she continued, "Well, I need to sell this house quickly. I need to go back to Italy. There really is no reason why I need to stay here anyway, especially when David is gone. He really did not listen to me, anyway. I wanted to go back to Italy and attend to the winery, but he wouldn't have it. He cared only for his career.

"Now, look what happened to him.

You, young lady, watch out about your career, it means nothing when you die like this. He was a workaholic! What did that mean to him now?"

Samantha felt sorry for Dr. Falkner who had such a cold, unloving wife, who did not even show tears at his funeral and saying futility of being a good pathologist. Samantha could not help herself crying for Dr. Falkner. Mrs. Falkner watched Samantha cry as if that was something unusual.

"I respected Dr. Falkner. He was a good medical examiner. He taught me something about being a decent pathologist in the pandemic time and how to contribute to the society as a doctor. I think he was a wonderful man!" Samantha said.

She gathered her bag and left the house. She stopped and looked back on the beautiful house, trying to store all images of the house where she found her ideal man in her life.

David Falkner might never be found in Samantha's life once more. She felt sad that he lived in this beautiful house without a loving relationship with his wife. It was too late for him to live a life with his soulmate who could let him be the way he is.

Samantha also realized that Mrs. Falkner knew about their relationship when Samantha began to tear up.

Mrs. Falkner did have the sixth sense.

CHAPTER 41

Unwinding the stresses

April 28, 2020

Samantha had several Zoom psychiatric consultations with Dr. Song every other day since April 20. She was surprised to see Dr. Song was in fact a Caucasian doctor who married a Korean American physician and adopted her married last name as Song. Although Samantha did not see her face to face in person, Dr. Song appeared to be in her 50s, a mature, calm and sympathetic person.

Samantha was glad Dr. Song was also a residency director and accustomed to dealing with residents' issues. She already felt much better just talking to someone on a regular basis. Dr. Song was incredibly supportive of what Samantha was going through.

Dr. Song also told Samantha news of what was going on inside the Bronx hospital and the affiliated medical, dental and nursing schools. In mid-April, the hospital faced a $500 million budget gap for the current fiscal year, attributed to declining revenue and higher costs linked to preparation for a surge of COVID-19 patients.

Due to COVID-19, most health care providers had stopped the delivery of many health care services in their tracks by shutting down almost all non-essential surgeries, procedures, and in-person medical visits. This cut off revenue generation for hospitals, health care systems, and private practices. The estimated losses were now anywhere from $300,000 to over $1 million a day. In total, the American Hospital Association (AHA) estimated US hospitals and health systems would experience over $202 billion in losses between March and June 2020.

Dr. Song also said the Bronx hospital was trying to procure PPE at exorbitant mark-ups and continued to pay essential vendors and contractors. Reimbursement for telemedicine, low-interest or no-interest loans, and federal relief (CARES Act) were supposed to provide some assistance, but how the monies will be allocated was difficult to understand and lacking transparency.

The hospital administration eliminated new hiring, pay increases and delayed capital spending, but still faced a $500 million deficit. And hence, it would require the furlough of 1,500 workers, or about 13% of the hospital's staff.

The medical center was also furloughing 3,500 employees, more than 19% of the workforce at its school of medicine and dentistry, school of nursing, the medical faculty group, and in its health sciences division, who provided administrative support for the medical center's clinical and academic enterprise.

The department of psychiatry was affected even though patients, families of CVID-19, and faculty doctors were needing mental health care during the pandemic. The department announced 10% partial furloughs for doctors and 20% full furloughs for ancillary staff.

Full furlough meant an employee did not work at all until the furlough ended, while partial furlough meant an employee worked fewer hours.

At the peak, she was witnessing the COVID-19 crisis overwhelm the hospitals, who were in dire need of physicians on the frontline. However, amid all of this, hospitals had to furlough thousands of employees, demanded that staff risk their lives while they cut their pay and requested volunteer staff, and yet failed to provide adequate PPE.

Some nurses and doctors had spoken out about lacking adequate PPE and over-working their shifts to 15 hours, but the hospital administrators were punishing those that spoke up against the system.

Other hospitals were laying off their employees.

Even worse was that some of these same CEOs, administrators, and executives were being compensated with million-dollar salaries or more.

Dr. Song was very perplexed how health care workers could be fired, furloughed, or asked to take pay cuts as they put on PPE to care for critically ill patients at great personal risk.

Dr. Song was sure the department of pathology was affected in a similar way. Dr. Song shared some of her stresses because she was the one to choose who would be furloughed in her department. She said she was mostly working at her home, which was good because she did not have to face the faces of those employees who were getting furloughed. She was not the most popular person in her department right now.

She needed psychiatric care for herself, but she had nowhere to turn to. But she was happy that Samantha was reaching out for help.

Samantha also found out from Dr. Song that doctors already had among the highest reported suicide rates, more than double the general population according to some surveys, but with the COVID-19 pandemic, suicide rates were expected to rise.

Just a day before, a young doctor who worked in New York City committed suicide. She was putting in 18-hour days and sleeping in hallways that patients from ambulances could not even access because it was so busy. She had been on the front lines for weeks, handling the onslaught of cases.

New York City had been recording nearly 300,000 cases and more than 22,000 deaths at that time. On April 22, the US reported the highest single day death toll for any country: more than 2,600, mostly from New York City.

Dr. Song also said recently, a 23-year-old rookie Emergency Medical Technician (EMT) was put to work on the Tactical Response Group within the busiest COVID-19 areas of New York City. He worked for less than three months in his new career since graduating in January.

He was found dead with an apparent self-inflicted gunshot wound to the head by the river near Astoria Park without leaving a suicide note. He had started working for the New York City Fire Department Bureau of Emergency Medical Services in the Bronx; Samantha's neighborhood. He was generally known as a happy kid but told other EMT colleagues he did not like his job because he was seeing "people passing away right in front of me" and that the deaths were weighing on him.

Dr. Song also mentioned that physicians were prone to experience burnout and could consequently suffer from mental health issues, including depression and substance abuse.

Dr. Song did not think Samantha needed psychiatric medication. She said Samantha needed to grieve for the loss of her father and deal with her unknowns, like how to deal with her mother's cruise situation.

Samantha did not have guts to tell Dr. Song about the relationship with Dr. Falkner and the loss. Samantha only said that her attending from Long Island's coroner office where she worked for two weeks had died last week due to COVID-19. Dr. Song said it was interesting that the pathologist had died from COVID-19.

As usual, other doctors thought pathologists were the last doctors to face any danger for viral exposures simply because pathologists were not out there on the front line dealing with patients like in the Emergency Departments or the ICUs.

Even though Samantha could not share every aspect of herself, she was so happy she had a lifeline out there who she could talk to. She was in desperate need of someone, just listening to her. Dr. Falkner had that job duty before, but now he was gone.

Samantha was dealing with the loss of her father, her mother's strict lockdown and quarantine in Miami, her loss of Dr. Falkner, the investigation and his wife's suspicious looks on her. Now, new sights she had to endure for a murder investigation and ambulance experiences during the autopsy service in her training program all overwhelmed her mental capacity.

She realized that she had not even processed the mourning of her father yet. Even though she was facing an enormous amount of stress, and reached her maximum mental capacity to handle life, what strengthened her to live with hope was the fact that she was with Dr. Falkner in the trenches during the pandemic time.

Now he was gone. Her sadness deepened as she was feeling her body aching and a headache. She knew that it must be the coronavirus. She must have gotten it from Dr. Falkner. She was glad that she took a week off to de-stress and relax. She slept for many hours, which she could do these days.

CHAPTER 42

Breakup

Ed pushed the doorbell at Samantha's apartment. He had texted twice while he was driving that he was coming to see her, but he had no response from Samantha. He intended to visit her last weekend, but he couldn't. He used that time to take care of the important logistics of storing the virus at his workplace. First, he spoke to his boss, Steve Allen, PhD about smuggling the virus from the WIV.

Dr. Allen was shocked. He could not believe that Ed risked transporting the virus on a commercial flight and heavily criticized Ed. Now, Dr. Allen was involved in dealing with the aftermath, so he too was in turmoil. They met every day to strategize their plans. Neither of them slept much while thinking about the situation.

First, Ed was successful in storing the virus in the Biosafety Level 4 Lab, which Abby Laboratory was well known for. That part, at least, was not an issue. The next step was to discuss the situation with the most appropriate person or persons in the US government.

At some point in their discussions, Dr. Allen became excited about their laboratory having such an opportunity and privilege to develop a vaccine, yet confused why Dr. Shei would hand over this precious information to Ed.

Finally, Dr. Allen agreed that they should meet with the CDC and NIH directors to get funding support, and he would recommend that Ed lead a team to develop a vaccine. Ed's title would change to Scientific Director of Vaccine Development, and his promotion announced today, April 28, by Dr. Allen via email. With the change of Ed's title, his salary would be doubled.

Ed was thrilled about that and excited to accept the challenge and responsibility. He would oversee a team of 90 scientists on the development of a vaccine against COVID-19. It would be a fast-track development timeline, since they already had much needed background information from the WIV.

Ultimately, there were some benefits for Ed taking the considerable risk of transporting the virus, while Dr. Allen was a bit concerned about Ed's huge jump in promotion from associate research director to a scientific director who would oversee 90 scientists, but Dr. Allen said he would handle the explanation.

Ed could not find any jewelry stores open in Washington, DC, or New York City. He bought a bag of groceries and a dozen red roses and finally arrived at Samantha's apartment. He rang the bell twice, but there were no sounds from inside. Ed called, and he heard her phone ringing on the other side of her door. She finally picked up the phone after the 10th ring and said, "Hi Ed, I am not feeling well, and I do not want to open the door."

"Please open the door. I am right here," Ed pleaded.

"No, I might have COVID-19."

"I don't care, let me see you."

"No, I am not opening the door. Please go back."

"Please, Samantha, let me see you."

"No, I am not opening the door. Ed, why is that I need to tell you more than once?"

"I came back from China. I haven't seen you for months. Please, just open the door."

"No, Ed, I said go back to DC and call me from there."

"No, I will not. I will stay at your door until you open." Ed began pounding on Samantha's door.

Neighbors began yelling from their doorways, "Stop that pounding, and stop talking from the hallway!" *Typical New Yorkers, saying what they want to say without hesitation in loud voices,* he thought.

Ed pounded again and again on her door. One neighbor stepped outside a nearby apartment and said, "Hey you, there, stop pounding. The lady does not want to see you. Get your ass off!"

Ed said, "She is sick inside and she will not open the door!"

"Hey, get the heck out of here, or else I will call the police!" the neighbor shouted.

"Samantha, please open the door!" Ed pleaded again.

"No, go away!" Samantha replied.

Ed was heartbroken and put his face on her door as he slowly slid to his knees and sat outside her door.

He stayed there for a moment and said, "Okay, I will go, Samantha. I drove 12 hours to get here. I will leave something outside your door I brought. I will go to my car parked right outside and I will call you from there. Okay?" Ed got up slowly, looking at the neighbor still watching him.

The guy felt sorry for Ed now and said, "That a boy! She will like the flowers. You come back later!"

Ed looked at him and gave a bitter smile as the neighbor's door closed. Ed left. Samantha waited about five minutes and then opened the door. She found the dozen red roses and a bag of groceries and took them inside. Then she called Ed.

"Ed, thanks for the flowers and groceries. I appreciated it, but I will not see you today, for I am afraid that I will also make you sick. In fact, I have been thinking, Ed, that we should not see each other anymore."

"Are you breaking up with me now?" Ed was in shock.

"Yes, Ed, I am sorry, but we were getting farther apart from each other. We came too long; we are not able to come together any longer."

"What are you talking about? Samantha, this does not make sense. Maybe you are too sick now, you are not yourself."

"Oh, no, I am myself for the first time, Ed. I now know what I want. I am very sure now."

"No, please don't do this on the phone. Let me at least see you." Ed was crying.

"Ed, please listen, and do not cry. I meant to do this quite a long time ago, but I did not have courage to do this. What I say, I am sure of. Don't think this is a joke."

"Is it because I am not a real doctor? A medical doctor?" Ed asked.

"No, that has nothing to do with it."

"Samantha, I can become more famous and richer than a medical doctor. You just watch what I will do. It will be less than a year, and I will make you proud of me. I will make so much money that you do not need to work as a doctor anymore!"

"Ed, this is what I mean, I do not want my boyfriend to be rich and famous. And I need to work if I am to be happy with myself."

"What else do you want from a man, then?"

"You never really understood me, Ed. This is a precise reason we should just go on with our own lives. I am really tired of explaining to you who I am."

"What have I done so wrong? Samantha, I only loved you and waited for you."

"Yes, I know Ed, you have not done anything wrong. It's just that I am grown up. I am different now. I need to move on. I am deeply sorry that I am breaking up with you over the phone. I am truly sorry, but I cannot see you anymore."

"Samantha, please listen to me. We have known each other for almost 10 years. This is not an ordinary relationship. You need to think through things. You are not well, obviously. Let's talk again. Okay, I will not come up to your place now, I will just drive another 12 hours back to DC. But we need to meet and talk about this when you are not sick. Okay?"

"I am not saying this because I am sick. Ed, you have never taken me seriously when I am talking to you. That is one of the reasons I cannot be with you."

"Samantha, I've always been faithful to you. I haven't seen any other woman in these 10 years!"

"Yes, I understand, and thank you for your devotion toward me. I think it is time for you to see other women and explore. Ed, there are so many women who will love you."

"I don't want any other women, I just want you, Samantha." Ed cried again.

"Ed, please, I think you will appreciate me saying this in the future. You will see how glad you are not seeing me then. We are not a good fit for each other."

"Samantha, is there another man in your life?"

"Yes, there is…" Samantha said.

"Who is it? When did you meet this guy? Is he a medical doctor?" Ed was angry.

"I do not want to say anything. Ed, please, you will find another woman who can support you and adore you because you deserve that. You lack nothing! It's not because you are not a medical doctor. You should know that."

"What is it, then?"

"Ed, I am getting tired. I will hang up the phone now. I need some rest. Thank you for everything you have done for me over the last 10 years and thank you for the groceries and flowers. Safe driving to DC, and I am so sorry."

With that, Samantha hung up the phone.

Ed was heartbroken. He could not believe his girlfriend of 10 years just broke up with him. She did not even have decency of doing it face to face, regardless of her sickness possibly due to COVID-19. He did not care if he got infected with COVID-19. His heart was aching to a point of suffocation.

He sat in his car, holding on to his chest as if he was having a heart attack. He cried out loud. He couldn't believe he was sobbing for a woman. He felt shameful that he was so broken for a girl. If his parents had seen him like this, they would not be proud of their son. But he couldn't help feeling devastated, and sadness overwhelmed him.

He had not thought about or made preparations for Samantha actually breaking the relationship. He believed that they would get married, regardless of his parent's silent disapproval. Once they have a few babies, his parents would forget about what they thought before and mend the relationship with Samantha and everything would work out.

He did not know Samantha had it in her to be this strong, and so determined to break up.

What bothered Ed was she said she had another man in her life. He did not see this coming. She never told him she met someone new. Then it occurred to him that was not something she would share with her boyfriend.

But he could not help to imagine who this person could be; was he someone he already knew, and what was it about the other man Samantha would fall in love with, despite Ed was her boyfriend for the last 10 years? Ed regretted not marrying her a long time before and not having a sexual relationship with her. Perhaps she could have gotten pregnant and then would have been forced to marry him out of wedlock. There were many opportunities for him to have sex with her over many years, but he was saving that for their special time on their honeymoon.

Samantha also wanted to keep her virginity until she wore her wedding gown, and she wanted to be a good Christian woman. Ed wondered if she had slept with this new man. Ed shook his head and tried to shake out the thoughts of her having sex with another man. Everything that just happened was not real to him.

He gathered his strength and started to drive back to DC. He was determined to change her mind. Once she got better, she would come around, for sure. He would call her when he returned to DC, where he would work and focus on developing a vaccine. He would call her once he succeeded to some degree in achieving this goal, and then perhaps they could reunite.

He would not give up that easily. Not over the phone, not on their 10-year relationship they had built together.

Yeah, she is really sick and will come back to her senses once she gets better, he concluded.

Samantha was exhausted with her headache, and body aches after she hung up the phone with Ed. She was glad not to have irritable dry coughs while talking to Ed. As much as she liked the flowers, she could not bear looking at the dozen roses for the next week.

A dozen flowers to remind her of the cruel breakup she gave him over the phone, so she threw the flowers in the trash.

She looked at the grocery bag, containing mostly items for baking. She put them in her small pantry.

She noticed his car was still parked outside. She went back to bed. She noticed Ed did not come back to pound on her door again. She felt sorry for Ed. This was not the way she imagined ending their long relationship; such a heartless way, but she needed to do this at some point. Whichever the method was, it was indeed a heartless breakup.

She hoped that Ed would be strong to hold himself together and move on with another relationship that would enrich his life and build his confidence as a man. She regurgitated what Ed was constantly saying about his inadequacy.

For Ed, it was the fact that he was not a medical doctor. Samantha did not think that was such a big deal, but to Ed, that was an unfathomable barrier he could not overcome for her to accept who he was as a whole. How sad that really was.

It did not matter to Samantha whether he was a medical doctor, famous, rich or capable to bring enough income for her not to work the rest of her life. In fact, she was independently rich through her family, and she did not need to work for the rest of her life, if she chose. She did not need a man for that reason.

She wanted her man to accept the way she was, just as she was, not to demand more than who she was and let her grow up at the pace she needed to grow up, to be there to accept and hold her.

She realized that she may never meet such a man. Maybe David Falkner would not turn out to be the man she imagined if he lived a long time with her. But for now, Samantha was fully satisfied knowing David Falkner was that man for her, albeit just two weeks in her life.

CHAPTER 43

The manuscript

April 30, 2020

Samantha gathered all the manuscript material written by Dr. Falkner and herself and put it together to submit to one of the top journals in medicine. The findings were from a total of 20 autopsies that Dr. Falkner had done over a two-month period of time. His last contribution to the body of knowledge in medicine was about death from COVID-19, which also caused his own death.

The first sentence Dr. Falkner wrote was: The only predictable aspect of this pandemic is that it has been unpredictable with COVID-19.

In his summary, he writes that the COVID-19 adverse impact extends beyond the respiratory system, and is actually a disease of the endothelium, the cells lining the blood vessels. The endothelium is found all over the body and the virus attack the endothelial cells, causing small blood clots in the entire body. The end products and results are the manifestation caused by the small vessel blood clots; most commonly the respiratory tract in the lungs. Lungs seem to be especially hard hit. If the clots are found in the heart, then it causes cardiac dysfunction, arrhythmias and heart attacks. If the clots are found in the arteries of the brain, then it will result in strokes. A form of strange rashes on the skin, red and swollen wounds that look like frostbite on the patient's fingers and toes are results of the blood clot in the peripheral skin. The blood vessel constriction, which causes ischemia—a reduction in blood flow— can lead to swollen, painful digits and tissue death.

On autopsy, the small vessels of the lungs, bowels, liver and kidneys of COVID-19 patients are choked with blood clots. D-dimers, which are left over when the body breaks up blood clots, are high on the blood test.

Myocardial injury which causes heart attack, strokes and venous thromboembolism in deep vein in the leg can travel to lung causing pulmonary embolism are significantly associated with fatal outcome of COVID-19.

Approximately 37% of the autopsy samples had acute kidney injury and kidney failures needing dialysis. The coronavirus can infect the lining of the lower digestive tract, causing diarrhea and other gastrointestinal symptoms. The presence of virus in the GI tract raises the possibility that it could be passed on through feces and causing fecal transmission, especially by aerosolizing during the toilet flushing. But it is not yet clear whether stool contains intact, infectious virus, or only RNA and proteins.

Of the two pediatric cases in early teens and infant, the clinical findings were atypical Kawasaki-like syndrome with high fever, skin rash, and abdominal pain. On autopsy, rash, eye redness (conjunctival injection), dry or cracked mouth, redness of the palms of the hands and soles of the feet, and swollen glands were found. Under microscopic examination, the coronary arteries and cardiac muscle showed chronic inflammation.

It is clinically atypical because more than 80% of the children who get Kawasaki disease are younger than 5 years of age. Whether the virus itself is causing the clotting or the host immune system attacking the body or more damage is not known; however, the autopsy findings in all the organs examined found inflammatory cells. This hyper-inflamed state is itself a well-known risk for blood clots. The inflammatory cells can cause cytokine storms, which can result in a condition called disseminated intravascular coagulation (DIC), where patients both bleed uncontrollably and clot too much at the same time. The coronavirus infection can start in the lungs, which is ground zero as the entry point, but it then travels into the bloodstream, infecting and causing inflammation of the endothelial cells, causing endotheliitis. Patients with certain conditions like high blood pressure, diabetes, and heart disease stress the endothelium. It is no surprise then, that people who have these conditions are also the people who get the sickest when they become infected with COVID-19.

The findings from the autopsy results in Dr. Falkner's cohort was that the coronavirus can affect multiple organs with increased inflammatory cells, which may cause multi-organ failures. The photo images of all the organs with chronic and acute inflammatory cells and blood clot, (thromboembolism) within small vessels are presented with the figure legends which Samantha had worked on. She organized the whole paper and submitted electronically. The paper authorship was just two; Samantha Parker MD as the first author and David Falkner MD as the last author. She hoped that the peer reviewers will be gentle and accept the manuscript without too many harsh criticisms.

Even though she was still sick, she worked to publish the paper, and she felt good about carrying out something that Dr. Falkner wanted to achieve, his own paper. She had done one thing substantial for Dr. Falkner. This was a part of him where even his wife could not help, possess or control. Samantha was hoping Dr. Falkner would be proud of her and happy with what she did for him.

Samantha was feeling much better than a few days ago and she would be ready to go back to work on May 1. Her hospital now measured the temperature from every person who was entering to work. They also provided one surgical mask per day to wear at all times. She measured her own temperature, and she did not have a fever. She never had a fever when she was sick for several days. She called her resident director Dr. Wells regarding her conditions, and he asked Samantha to get tested for COVID-19 and if it came back positive, she would need to quarantine herself for 14 days. Samantha went to her hospital employee office to get the test done. She was able to get in from the entry checkpoint, for she did not show a fever. The result would be out within three hours because they had test results read within the internal pathology lab.

CHAPTER 44

Grandmother

May 1, 2020

Ed's grandmother died. She was 92 years old. Ed's mother called, and she wanted Ed to go to Brooklyn to find her body from one of the U-Haul trucks rented by the Brooklyn funeral home so that Ed could arrange for cremation.

Ed's parents would drive from Ohio where they lived to arrange a proper funeral which was scheduled to occur on the weekend of May 3. Ed's parents did not want to take the airplane or the train to avoid COVID-19 infection.

They chose Ed to drive to New York since Ed was not really on the frontline like his two brothers. One of them lived in Washington, DC like Ed, and the other lived close to Ohio and was in his residency. To Ed's parents, what Ed was doing (developing a vaccine) was not as important as being one of the medical doctors who were facing the patients with COVID-19.

Ed did not bother to explain to his parents what he was doing recently because that would end up with another hour of futile discussion.

Ed was the first son who needed to take care of all family matters, anyway. So, he needed to drop everything and attend to the family matter. No further question or discussion needed.

After he had a breakup with Samantha last week, he was focusing on building his team of 90 scientists, brainstorming, studying the genetic codes of the virus from Dr. Shei's USB, testing the vaccine Dr. Shei already made in mice and strategizing who would do what portions of the tasks.

His boss, Dr. Allen, had arranged a meeting with the CDC and NIH Directors for early afternoon on Monday, May 4. Luckily, both of them were in Washington, DC and the meeting was arranged at Abby Laboratory.

Dr. Allen had told the two directors what they had in their possession, so they were happy to meet with them. The CDC did not realize the task force of 11 people they sent actually accomplished their goals from the Wuhan, China trip.

Ed and Dr. Allen had tremendous power and ammunition to demand what they needed from these two directors because they all had a common desire: End the pandemic.

Now, Ed had to leave the team from Abby Laboratory to take care his family issues. He did not have any other options because Ed knew that he had to do what his parents asked, no matter what he was personally dealing with.

There would be no negotiation between him and his parents.

Ed told his boss all about the situation and then took off, driving back again to New York City. Of course, his parents told Ed that he must drive, not fly because they were afraid Ed might catch COVID-19 in the airport or airplane.

They knew Ed had recently traveled to Wuhan, China, but that would be a different story to his parents.

That was the government issue, not a personal issue, as if the government issue had a special immunity against the virus.

Ed knew better not to fight with his parents. He just needed to come back for the important meeting on May 4.

The funeral service was on May 3, so he had to leave right after the funeral. They were going to have the cremation done, followed by a family gathering in the Brooklyn funeral home. The cremation remains would be carried by Ed's parents to Ohio and buried in the Buddhist temple there.

Initially, Ed's parents lived in Brooklyn, New York, where they enrolled as PhD students when they came to the US. Ed's grandmother soon followed her daughter after she lost her husband in Beijing, China.

They were all well educated in China. Ed's parents finished their PhDs in Beijing where they met from one of the top schools, but when they came to the US, they had to repeat their doctoral programs.

Then they both held jobs at Ohio State University as research scientists in medical fields. Ed's grandmother decided to stay in Brooklyn and lived with her Chinese friends. Four older Chinese friends chipped in their money to buy a small house to live independently and away from their children to avoid burdening them. Ed's grandmother was one of them.

They bought the house with cash, for they did not understand the concept of a mortgage. She did not want to move to Ohio, where there were no Chinese people. She was happy being with other Chinese-speaking friends, Chinese grocery stores in walking distance and playing mahjong all day in the house.

One by one, her friends died, and she was the last one standing in 2017. Ed's parents then decided to sell the house, divide the property money among the four families, and moved Ed's grandmother into a nursing home nearby. She still did not want to leave Brooklyn, and she knew other Chinese friends in the nursing home. She lived in the Brooklyn, New York nursing home for the last three years.

On April 28, workers at a nearby Dollar General store alerted police to a foul smell and some leakage coming from a U-Haul truck parked on Avenue M. The police found nursing and funeral homes had rented four trucks to hold about 50 corpses. The rental company U-Haul had reportedly cut ties with the Brooklyn funeral home that was caught storing dead bodies inside their unrefrigerated trucks.

A U-Haul spokesperson defended their position to the media by saying, "This is a wrongful, egregious and inhumane use of our equipment, and our trucks are designed for household moves. Properly caring for the remains of people's loved ones requires vehicles suited specifically for that purpose. Our trucks absolutely cannot be rented for this reason."

Ed later learned the funeral home could not obtain a large refrigerated truck prior to this incident; not because they were lazy getting one, but simply because there were no more refrigerated trucks available in New York City.

The funeral home was absolutely packed with dead bodies and in their defense, they had no other choices. They were later cited only for failing to control the handling of their dead bodies.

They finally got relief from the city and later transferred the bodies into a refrigerated truck. Death tolls in New York City nursing homes at that time were estimated to be at least 6,700, and no one would ever get a complete and accurate count.

Ed had no idea whether his grandmother's body would be found in the refrigerated truck or in the funeral home at this point. The bodies were shifted and moved quickly during this time. His task was to identify his grandmother's body before his parents and his brothers all arrived in New York City. He had a very tight schedule; he would need to drive today, find the body tomorrow, have the cremation done on the same day or Sunday morning, then have a short funeral service, then drive back to DC on Sunday, arrive on Monday early morning around 2:00 am, sleep for a few hours and then go to work in the morning to discuss the 1:00 pm meeting. He would have maybe five hours of sleep before the meeting.

He was calculating all these timelines and hoped that no other complications would occur.

He could not believe that the nursing home stacked the dead bodies in a U-Haul truck. His grandmother would be decomposed inside of the truck and he was hoping that the funeral home or nursing home would have a tight and orderly system tagging the dead with the proper names.

Otherwise, Ed may not be able to recognize his own grandmother.

He definitely would not and will not see the decomposed and smelly body to identify his grandmother. He could not handle such stress.

He wished that he was driving with his brother from DC, in case Ed had to identify the body of his grandmother. But his brother couldn't accompany Ed because he was going to take a redeye flight on Saturday night despite the long lecture from his parents not to fly since he was on call Friday night.

The last time he had seen his grandmother was about 10 years ago. He was embarrassed that he had not visited her more often, especially when he had been seeing Samantha who lived in the same city. He could have made more effort to see his grandmother when he had visited Samantha. He was driving again to New York City, and this time, he knew he could not see Samantha.

CHAPTER 45

Goodbye to wedding gown

May 6, 2020

Emily finally disembarked from the cruise ship on May 6. Because she had tested positive on April 22, she had to stay on the ship for 14 more days of quarantine in her cabin. She was moved to a nearby hotel in Miami for retesting. Emily thought she would be able to fly on May 6 back home to San Francisco. She was one of about 150 passengers who checked into a single hotel for retesting. If she got another positive result, she would need to quarantine another 14 days in the Miami hotel, then she needed to get negative results on two consecutive days of retesting with nasopharyngeal swab.

Before she checked into the hotel room, the health care workers were in the lobby testing all passengers from her ship. They were all lined up, six feet apart from each other.

Emily had seen thousands of people lined up to get into different hotels from the cruise ships. The Miami coast guard was trying to gather all passengers from each ship into one hotel, but sometimes it was not possible. The Princess Diamond cruise ship was so big and still had one thousand passengers on board; therefore, those passengers were scattered throughout several Miami hotels.

It was good to land and disembark from the ship. The only sad part was to say goodbye to Mahalia. They held together, crying until Emily had to disembark.

Emily was on the ship so long, bobbing a little constantly, that she felt dizzy and unstable with her gait on the land. She had been on the ship for a total of three and a half months. Her hair was now long and white. She could not recognize herself. She normally dyed her hair every three weeks or so, but she was not able to take care of herself.

She regretted having so many pieces of luggage because she could not handle all that weight. Many people helped her get the luggage into her hotel room. All she needed now were a few comfortable clothes, sneakers, and bathroom items. She wished to throw away all the fancy clothes and shoes she had brought. She did not know what to do with Robert's belongings.

She called Samantha from her hotel room to update her. Samantha was doing her surgical pathology rotation, but said she was not too busy. Samantha somehow had tested negative for COVID-19. Her rotation was done in a nontraditional way. Samantha would preview the slides and make a diagnosis in the report, and then her attending pathologist would sign out remotely from home.

They were constantly Zooming.

There was really no direct contact with her attending pathologists. The only time Samantha was with someone else was when she was cutting the specimens and reading the slides in the common-area residents' room. They had glass shields attached to their cubicles and wore facial masks at all times. They looked like Biosafety Level 2 Laboratory workers, Samantha told her mom, laughing.

Samantha asked her mom what would happen after she stayed in Miami for another 14 days and then tested positive for COVID-19. Emily was not sure how to answer that question. No one asked such a question. Emily just hoped that they would release her. She could not even think to stay in Miami for another 14 days.

Samantha said she recently broke up with Ed. Emily did not say much to that. Emily just wished that her daughter was happy, and it did not matter much to her if Samantha was no longer with Ed. In fact, Emily was happy that her daughter knew what she wanted in her life.

Emily told Samantha that she got a call from the ship informing her that Robert's body would be cremated in Barcelona and then sent to Emily's house in San Francisco by aircraft. Ironically, Robert's remains might be there by now. Spain could not hold bodies of foreign travelers who died with COVID-19 for more than two weeks, so they sent Robert's body without anyone's approval or signature.

Emily said it was definitely not a normal time during the pandemic, and they both agreed Spain's decisive policy was refreshing, and were relieved of handling what to do with the body. Spain could not have contacted Emily for her approval or signature since Emily still had been somewhere in the Atlantic Ocean traveling.

Also, Spain and other countries were experiencing thousands of deaths due to the pandemic. There were few if any officers or workers to contact each and every person involved between countries.

Samantha and Emily both chuckled to know that Robert might be on their house doorstep. Emily was exhausted by her ordeals and she could no longer care about anything. Emily told her daughter she was going to donate all the stuff from their cruise luggage, except her jewelry. Emily was sad to tell her daughter that even the 50th anniversary wedding gown and Robert's tuxedo would be donated because she did not have the energy to carry the suitcases back with her. So many things changed with a new forced normality and reality.

Samantha told her mom she could fly in early June to see her in San Francisco. Emily completely understood Samantha's rotational schedule, and she never forced or demanded her daughter to obey Emily's desires. They talked about having a small funeral in early June at the church Robert and Emily attended, and to bury the remains in the nearby cemetery.

They both cried, missing Robert. It would be so different without him. Samantha reassured Emily that she would take care of the finances and at least make it reasonably simple for Emily to handle a few things like writing checks when she received bills.

CHAPTER 46

Vaccine

Ed and Dr. Allen met with the CDC and NIH directors. They were both very interested in Ed's progress with Dr. Shei at the WIV. With Abby laboratory being the top institute of virology and Ed being a top scientist, it made perfect sense for Ed along with 90 other scientists to develop a vaccine. They were enthusiastically promoting the idea and would provide financial support to Abby Laboratory.

The National Institute for Allergy and Infectious Diseases would partner with Abby on this vaccine. The NIH asked Dr. Allen and Ed to formally and quickly apply for grants and promised to expedite the grant approval processes. Both directors asked about the viability of the coronavirus that Ed brought from China. Dr. Allen and Ed answered that only 10% of the virus survived and they were now successfully cloning the virus in their lab.

It would be important to have much access and production of the virus to work on future diagnostic tests, drugs, and vaccine development.

No one was able to clone the virus until Ed had come up with the idea to insert synthetically engineered DNA and the entire SARS-CoV-2 genome into yeast. Then Ed sat and watched yeast cells do their magic, gluing together the overlapping sequences on the fragments to turn them into full-length genomes. Just two days later, the team was able to check the yeast, now blossomed into dot-like "colonies" on a plate, for signs of the virus's genome.

Dr. Allen especially thought how incredible Ed was in terms of his creativity and ingenuity and felt that Ed was the most valuable player in his company. Both directors were also impressed with what Abby Laboratory was able to do in the enhancement of the scientific discovery. Ed's natural talent, creative mind, and his courage to bring the virus from the WIV was particularly impressive. They said Ed would be the "savior" of all humankind in the world and would be a Nobel prize winner if he was successful in developing a vaccine.

All the conversations were very productive, except no one discussed Dr. Shei's interest. Even to Ed, she seemed to be a disappearing shadow.

When Ed asked about her specific request to use a manufacturing facility in London, they just ignored it and went on with the conversations, stating that the race for a vaccine was already well underway globally. Ultimately, they may have several vaccines with slightly varying efficacy profile characteristics around the same time. Then it was a question of which vaccine would the global convergence circle around and would countries and health systems start paying attention to one or two as compared to everyone scrambling to get their own vaccine.

Most viral vaccines now use attenuated virus, or inactivated live virus.

Attenuated vaccines use a weakened form of the virus that causes a disease. This kind of vaccine prompts an immune response without causing disease. The term attenuated means that the vaccine's ability to cause disease has been reduced.

Inactivated vaccines use a killed version of the live virus that causes a disease. This kind of vaccine also causes an immune response, but not infection. Inactivated vaccines are used to prevent the flu, hepatitis A and rabies. However, inactivated vaccines may not provide protection that's as strong as that produced by live vaccines, and hence, it often requires multiple doses, followed by booster doses, to provide long-term immunity. Producing these types of vaccines usually requires the handling of large amounts of the infectious virus.

A recent vaccine development method uses genetically engineered DNA or mRNA nucleic acid that enables a vaccine to give instructions for making copies of the S protein. And this was a method Ed and Dr. Shei used. The coronaviral genome encodes four major structural proteins: the spike (S) protein, nucleocapsid (N) protein, membrane (M) protein, and the envelope (E) protein, all of which are required to produce a structurally complete viral particle. The S-protein copies prompt an immune response to the virus and therefore it is an ideal method to create a vaccine.

With this approach, no infectious virus needs to be handled. While genetically engineered vaccines are in the works, as of today none have been licensed for human use. Most of the coronavirus vaccine developments use this genetically derived method. Rapid genetic sequencing of new pathogens and the identity of the genes encoding structural proteins can form the basis for vaccine immunogen development. Also, rapid isolation of human monoclonal antibodies has been helpful in defining epitopes that are the targets of protective immunity.

Development of a vaccine and its widespread availability historically takes 15-20 years, if the process proceeds smoothly without major biological or logistical challenges, and historically used attenuated or inactivated live virus methods.

The first step is for the vaccine to be tested in animals to see if it works and if it is safe. This testing must follow strict lab guidelines and generally takes three to six months. If the laboratory animals are alive and well and develop a suitable number of antibodies specific to the vaccine, then testing in humans is next, and in three phases. Small phase I clinical trials evaluate the safety of the vaccine in humans. This can be shortened to three months.

During phase II, the formulation and doses of the vaccine are established to prove the vaccine's effectiveness.

Finally, during phase III, the safety and efficacy of a vaccine needs to be demonstrated in a larger group of people.

Even if vaccine regulators fast-track some of these steps, it is unlikely that a COVID-19 vaccine will become available sooner than six months after clinical trials start. More realistically, a vaccine may take 12 to 18 months or longer to develop and then test in human clinical trials.

Once the vaccine has been tested successfully with humans in all three phases, then mass production is needed. Platform manufacturing technologies imply that the method for generating and presenting a vaccine immunogen can be applied by purification and analytical assays. Then, additional time is necessary to distribute and administer the vaccine to global populations.

It is likely that two doses of a vaccination will be needed, three to four weeks apart because people have no immunity to COVID-19. People would likely start to achieve immunity to COVID-19 one to two weeks after the second dose of vaccine. The numerous pharmaceutical companies, governments and other agencies working on COVID-19 vaccines need to come together, stripping the red tapes intra and internationally to eliminate redundancies and infighting due to financial and recognition greed.

Ed and the three leaders had a small set of research questions which now remained:

Historically, most likely all phases of the clinical trials were performed with a younger population, who could rapidly produce large numbers of antibodies. The most detrimental effect of COVID-19 occurs in the older population who may not respond well from a vaccine. Historically, older people do not respond to vaccines as well as younger people.

Another question was how long would the vaccine be effective, and would it prevent re-infection with the same virus? There were rare cases of re-infection reported with coronavirus after a period of months or some years. An effective COVID-19 vaccine would need to provide people with long-term infection protection.

From Dr. Shei's work and other scientists' publications, the animal model with coronavirus vaccine showed success in development of virus-specific antibody responses, but some viruses did not generate adequate protective natural immunity, such as HIV-1. Therefore, would the virus-specific antibody responses against coronavirus provide robust protective immunity? The preliminary findings suggested that virus-specific antibody did provide at least partial protection by humoral and cellular immune responses in rhesus monkeys. They all concluded the data was promising that a vaccine against COVID-19 infection would work.

The meeting took place over three hours of focused concentration without any break except for water, and they were all tired from the mental exercises. They went down to the cafeteria and replenished their sugar levels in the brain. During the quick dinner, all four men were very encouraged to develop a vaccine, especially having the vaccine mRNA structures Dr. Shei had provided and tested in rhesus monkeys now in their hands.

They discussed about $480 million dollars in funding to support the efforts. Ed and Dr. Allen were thrilled for Abby Laboratory. There were approximately 100 different laboratories currently racing to discover a vaccine, both from commercial laboratories and academic university settings, all in different stages of vaccine development. It appeared that Abby laboratory was at the forefront of them all. Now, what they needed was about 10 healthy volunteers from among college students who were willing to be human guinea pigs. They were not worried about getting this done.

Ed was relieved to make the meeting on time. He really did not get much sleep; maybe two hours or less prior to the meeting. He contacted Dr. Shei's daughter, Lifang, in London and updated her on his meeting and to inform Dr. Shei. Lifang said that China was already in the process of testing a vaccine in 108 volunteer people. The results would be out very shortly. Ed was now more puzzled why Dr. Shei gave him her secret cocktail of the vaccine he brought to the US. Perhaps she gave it to Ed in case China would not follow through on appropriate processes of releasing a vaccine globally to the public.

Perhaps she gave it to Ed for him to alter some RNA strands to better target the S-protein, making it–more effective in the function of the vaccine in the US. Maybe the Food and Drug Administration (FDA) would not accept the vaccine products from China unless the US could validate the data from the study through an onsite inspection, and to accelerate that process, Dr. Shei had provided the information to Ed.

After all, The US would not trust a vaccine made in China to be valid unless the foreign clinical studies were conducted under an Investigational New Drug application (IND) ("non-IND foreign clinical studies") as support for an IND; or a New Drug Application (NDA), Abbreviated New Drug Application (ANDA), or a Biologics License Application (BLA), collectively known as "marketing applications" or "applications for marketing approval."

This amendment was added in 2018 from the FDA, and it was intended to help ensure the protection of human subjects enrolled in non-IND foreign clinical studies and the quality and integrity of the resulting data.

Lifang said, "Well done!" to Ed, and that was exactly what her mother wanted, without further explanation. Once the NIH provided multi-million dollars in funding, then other private sources would pour in billions of dollars to Ed's company. Ed and his company's recognition and success would be beyond imaginable.

It would be much more than an individual medical doctor could achieve by providing care for COVID-19 patients. The magnitude of rescuing the humanity was beyond the level of what Ed's parents would ever know. Finally, they would be proud of Ed's PhD degree and every praise would start with Ed's name. He knew the futility of getting acceptance and approval from his parents, but to him, saving face for his parents would be the proudest moment in his life. He would do everything to achieve that.

And for that, he would go to New York City or wherever his parents wanted him to go, no matter how inconvenient that time might be. Being the firstborn son comes with enormous responsibilities in Asian family cultures.

He could not believe what he had to go through last weekend, testing the value of his family duties. On Saturday, he eventually found the body of his grandmother while going through the stacks of bodies stored in the refrigerated trucks and in the funeral homes. It took five hours to find her body. Her body was indeed one of the bodies originally stored in a U-Haul truck. It was decomposed heavily with incredible stench. He had to verify the identity of the body before they could cremate it. The funeral home tried their best to record the dead bodies, while the sheer volume was a significant challenge for any family member wanting to claim the correct body.

By the time Ed found his grandmother's body, the technicians who perform the crematory process had gone home for the night. Sunday was the only day they rested, and the crematory was not open. The cost for the whole thing was $6,300, but Ed had to pay an additional $1,000 to have one technician come back on Saturday night to perform the cremation because he simply could not wait until Monday to have it done.

All the proper forms were already filled out and signed by a doctor, including a death certificate and written permission for cremation from Ed's mother. Ed had copies of the paperwork he printed out from his smartphone. Ed also had to pick a coffin for his grandmother. The funeral director recommended a specific coffin that would burn easily.

Normally, the cremation service would take place first for about 30 minutes, with an open casket for the family to say goodbye before the actual cremation. But in Ed's case, the cremation occurred first. The cremation itself usually took between one and a half to three hours, depending on the body weight and the type of coffin. Because Ed's grandmother weighed less than 100 pounds and Ed chose a well-burning coffin, it only took one and a half hours. Cooling, collecting and preparing the ashes for the family usually took another one or two hours.

The ashes were then carefully placed in a temporary container for collection. Ed had received a metal container (an urn) with ashes and a separate boxed container holding grandmother's three gold teeth and hip replacement prosthetic implantation devices.

Ed had no idea his grandmother had hip replacement surgeries and gold teeth.

Cremation costs were about $2,000-$4,000, but during the pandemic, funeral directors had increased their prices "since they have to work extra hard," as the director put it. Ed did not care much about the price at that point. He just needed to be back in DC by Monday morning to prepare for the early afternoon meeting at 1:00 pm.

On Sunday, the whole family finally got together for dinner and talked about grandmother; her life, who she was, how she lived and how she died. The nursing home staff said that she passed away from her old age.

They did not emphasize her positive test result of COVID-19 they obtained a week before her death. In that same nursing home, more than 41 elderly patients had recently passed away, along with a staff member in their early 50s. They all died with COVID-19.

Ed's mother was upset about the nursing home staff not being transparent about all the elderly who had recently died while in their care. The whole family was upset, but no one was thinking about suing the nursing home for its inadequacy in caring for the elderly. The entire family could have done more to better protect their grandmother, but they had not done that, and they would not blame anyone in the nursing home.

Ed's mother also said dying at age 92 was not so bad; it was a definition of longevity. Grandmother was a very independent woman who would be satisfied to die like this rather than being a burden to anyone in the family. Ed's mother repeatedly asked grandmother to move to Ohio but grandmother refused, even as recently as about six months ago. She was happy living in Brooklyn.

On Monday morning, they had a short 30-minute service with the funeral director who mentioned that it was now rare to see entire families coming to the funeral home for a service because most were afraid of contracting the disease. It no longer was the norm to have a funeral during the COVID-19 pandemic, and he was impressed with Ed's family coming together to celebrate their 92-year-old grandmother or even to claim her body.

He said so many bodies were now unclaimed; they did not know how long to store the bodies or where to send them, and all funeral homes in New York City were facing the same problem. One thing they were not allowed to do was to cremate an unclaimed body, due to concerns family members might come back later to claim the body.

Cremation would be most helpful to decrease the vast amount of real estate the bodies occupied in the funeral homes. He respected Chinese and other Asian people's cultures, principles, and values for their elderly. Asian families were most often those who claimed the dead and had a proper funeral and burial.

Ed wanted to leave right after the service, but his brothers wanted him to join the family luncheon, so Ed obliged. Because restaurants were closed for eating onsite at their premises, the family carried out from the best Chinese restaurant in Brooklyn and ate in their hotel. The family reserved a top floor penthouse with several bedrooms and a large living room for their short stay. During lunch, they talked about how each one of them would like to be buried, and end-of-life issues, which was not unusual in recent weeks during the pandemic. Ed's parents asked about Samantha, and Ed's brother asked when he was going to propose.

Ed did not answer this poking question and did not admit they had broken up.

In his mind, Samantha would come around and make up with Ed in the near future.

Ed had two cups of coffee with lunch to be alert during the drive back to DC. They quickly split up after lunch, returning to their homes.

No one wanted to stay longer than necessary in the epicenter of New York's Brooklyn zip code 11239, which had the highest death rate of 612 deaths per 100,000 people, far exceeding any other zip code in the city.

Ed drove home with his doctor brother Eric, who practiced in Washington, DC. It was better to have a companion for the 12-hour drive. Ed had some sleep while his brother was driving.

CHAPTER 47

Getting Mahalia out

May 20, 2020

Emily had served another 14-day quarantine in a Miami hotel. It was like involuntary imprisonment, but with payment for her hotel and her food. Although the hotel did not charge the full price per night, Emily still had to pay for her room.

Every day,-heath care workers came by to test for COVID-19, using a nasopharyngeal swab. Emily thought her deep nose cells probably all died since they scraped off everything around those areas. She tested negative for two days, consecutively on May 18 and 19. She was ready to fly on a commercial aircraft. She was so happy about this. She could finally go back to her home in San Francisco. Mrs. Kong had been taking care of her house, watering the plants in the garden and inside the house, letting the cleaning lady into the home every other week, and was getting Emily's mail.

Mrs. Kong even paid Emily's electricity, gas and phone bills using her own personal checks. Emily was very grateful for Mrs. Kong's kindness.

Emily was so bored in the hotel room, all she did at first was read newspapers and watch news on the television. She had learned that crew members of the cruise ships were facing a very difficult time going back to their homes after all the passengers left. The US government extended its NO SAIL order, and many countries, concerned about the spread of the coronavirus, shut down their ports to cruise ships.

Other countries had also shut down their borders, both air and seaports, leaving as many as 100,000 crew members around the globe in limbo as 30 days turned into 40, 50, 60 and more. Crew members who left at the initial opportunity with the passengers and did not accept a temptation to stay nine days were the smarter ones. There were now an estimated 54,200 crew members on board 85 cruise ships in US waters alone, with no end to the pandemic in sight.

Several crew members had committed suicide, jumping overboard from ships, and protesters from one crew had made a sign stating, "How many more suicides do we need?" On another ship, some crew members held a hunger strike in protest.

The repatriation of people was one of the most fundamental, long-standing maritime rights there was. However, when their own countries had shut down the ports, either by flights or ships, how could crew members possibly go back to their homeland? The cruise ship companies had so far successfully repatriated over 16,000 crew members and they were working with governments and health authorities around the world and asking their crews for patience and understanding in this ever changing global situation.

Emily was in contact with Mahalia every day. As the crew awaited repatriation, she was not being paid but was at least moved up to a passenger's cabin with more space. They received food and drinks without working or serving duties.

Her anxiety became overwhelming by boredom. Mahalia did not know when she could possibly go back to her home in the Philippines. The captain said that the cruise was already fully booked for August 1, with a 14-day trip back to the Mediterranean Sea. He hoped to repatriate all crew members before that time for their short work break, but he had no control over that. The captain was an American and was free to go, but he chose to stay with the crew members, and occasionally disembarked to stay in one of the nearby hotels.

Emily started working on getting Mahalia off the ship. She contacted the US embassy and Philippines embassy to obtain for Mahalia a temporary visitor visa to the US. Both embassies did not allow this to happen because of the pandemic, but Emily would not have it.

She explained that Mahalia was already in Miami; US waters.

She had to sign multiple forms they sent via fax, which she accessed from her hotel business office. She could not believe that she was granted approval and was able to complete numerous complex tasks granting a Filipino woman a one-month visa.

One night she had even taken a taxi, sneaking out from her hotel during quarantine to the US embassy in Miami. She had to pay some money to get that done. With the proper papers and a lot of push with the coastal officers, Emily demanded that Mahalia disembark the boat from the Miami port on May 20.

Mahalia disembarked the cruise ship with only her small suitcase and ran toward Emily. They embraced, crying on each other's shoulders for a long time.

"You say Asians save each other, so I did! You saved me too!" Emily said.

They came to Emily's hotel and caught up with all kinds of events, or lack thereof, from each other. Emily decided she would give Mahalia all of her suitcases full of clothes and shoes when Mahalia could eventually return to her home in the Philippines. Emily told her they would both fly back to San Francisco tomorrow. She had bought two first class tickets. The departure time was 9:00 am the next morning.

Mahalia had not gotten additional testing done since all the passengers had disembarked on May 6. No one really cared about crew members' wellbeing and she did not know her current status. The last time she tested, it was positive, but she never got sick. They decided not to tell anyone about Mahalia's last test result.

The airport took passengers' temperature these days, and Mahalia did not have any fever. Emily told Mahalia that she was able to get her a one-month visa, so Mahalia could stay with Emily in her San Francisco home until her visa would run out. By that time, the Philippines might open its borders and Emily would send her home. Emily told her not to worry about the air fee, for she could do so many things such as that for a friend who saved her life.

Emily was excited to tell Samantha what she was able to accomplish. Emily never thought she was capable of doing such a big task by working with the US embassy to create a visitor's visa. Yes, she did use some bribery, but the point was Emily could do something so big. Now, she was not scared of dealing with finances, such as writing checks, paying the bills, bookkeeping and even following the stock markets. Although the latter was a bit too complicated for her, she thought she could perhaps take some classes and learn things about the stock market with Mrs. Kong.

Samantha was glad to hear her mom getting excited to have her friend Mahalia spend a month with her. She was a little worried about her mother's loneliness without her husband, but because Mahalia would be there with Emily; she was relieved. Now Samantha could finish her surgical pathology rotation without guilt feelings at the end of May. The first week of June, she was going to visit her mother to look at the finances her father had kept and attend to her father's funeral. Her June schedule was much easier since she would be doing chemistry, a clinical pathology rotation, and there would be at least two other residents on the same rotation. Samantha was also thankful to Mrs. Kong, who paid Emily's bills and kept the garden alive while she was away for almost four months.

CHAPTER 48

Being a hero

May 21, 2020

Ed was in deep thoughts as he was having insomnia. He often did not sleep well ever since the COVID-19 pandemic started. He was sitting by his window, drinking chamomile tea to fall asleep. It was very quiet— 2:30 am. No one was talking in the street. No one was driving at this time and hour.

So many things had happened to Ed over the last two months. He was reflecting on how this virus had changed him in all levels of his life. Samantha was not by his side any longer. She was never physically next to him for many years now, but the thought she was not in his life made him sick to his stomach. He did not have his best friend to talk about what was happening to him, both the exciting promotion and the sad losses he faced.

Above all, what kept him awake was the pressure he felt with vaccine development. Ed somehow landed in a situation where he had a heavy burden to carry out the responsibility to develop a perfect vaccine. He had to deliver the task in a timely fashion to stop the pandemic. How in the world did he get here? Why him? His insomnia caused by the weight of the responsibility was tremendously inconveniencing to him, and yet he had so many ideas to alter the package of viral genetic codes to make a perfect vaccine in his head.

Every turmoil in life can be converted into an incredible opportunity. He was dreaming about the scenario where his vaccine would be mass-produced, injected into every human deltoid muscle, activate the immune system and fight back against COVID-19. He smiled at his thought, contemplating the fact that yes, there would be a pandemic, but a scientist like himself would prevail and the final victory would be for humankind.

He imagined traveling to Geneva to receive a Nobel Prize in Science with his family. His parents would be proud beyond their measure to have Ed as their son.

America would be proud of Ed, their hero in curing the pandemic due to this virus that seemed indestructible at one point. Ed would be personally proud that a Chinese American saved not only America, but all people in the universe.

The thought elated him beyond his imagination, and he was hopeful and excited that he contributed so significantly to the global problem. America would never treat Chinese Americans in a negative way, as history had shown in the past. With his creative and ingenious discovery of a vaccine, the Americans would respect and honor him, and would never discriminate against Asian Americans.

Ed may have lost his lifetime friend Samantha, but he had no time to grieve. He needed to pick himself up, focus on the energy he required to make a vaccine before other companies in the US or other country. It was his unique chance to save face for China and his family.

He wanted to be a hero like a superman or batman when he was growing up in the US. Maybe that was every man's dream—to be a hero to someone.

He was smiling at himself.

CHAPTER 49

Naming the disease

May 22, 2020

Samantha was very busy doing her surgical pathology rotation, doing things that had been familiar to her the past three years of her life. It was good to be back to a familiar environment. Doing a routine and even mundane things was a privilege during the pandemic, because nothing was predictable. So many things had changed in a such short timeline.

She lost her father, whom she respected and wanted to emulate. She decided to become a medical doctor because she aspired to be like her father, helping others when they were in their most vulnerable situation, fighting for their lives, grasping hopes through their doctors.

It was truly a unique position and privilege to be a doctor when the patients were lost.

Her father Dr. Robert Parker was her hero in her life. She would not quit being a doctor because she saw the meaning and purpose in her life through seeing her father, how he cared for his patients.

She lost her lover, Dr. Falkner, to COVID-19. David Falkner was her second man she met who was hero to her. Even though his lack of communication skill in the beginning was rather irritating and not impressive to Samantha, his unconditional acceptance of letting her be whoever she was, gave her freedom she never felt before.

Above all, God used Samantha to be there with David Falkner on the last day he was able to breathe and convey and introduce him to Samantha's God. It was truly a blessing experience for her.

Beyond everything in life, the conversion experience David Falkner had was the most important moment for him and for her. No one really knows the last day of breath. That she was there to comfort David Falkner, so she could ease his tension and fear of dying alone was the blessing to Samantha.

Even though she had seen vanity and futility in life after seeing the coffins piled up on Hart Island, to be able to comfort one person at the end of breath was enough reason for Samantha to continue living with hope. The opportunity was given to her by God. She was there at the right time and right place through the autopsy rotation she had to have during the midst of the pandemic time to meet David Falkner.

During the month of April, she had thought about quitting medicine and changing career but there was nothing she wanted to do other than what she was doing today, even though she needed to risk her own very life to do her job as a pathology resident.

The fear of COVID-19 exists no matter which way she turns within the hospital, and the facts about the infectious virus will never change. What can she do today and how can she contribute to bless others?

Her surgical pathology rotation was picking up its volume slowly and surely. The patients were coming back to the hospital for elective surgeries and long overdue cancer surgeries. She was busy cutting the surgical specimens after pickling them in formalin overnight.

Surgeons remove the part of the disease in organs and give these to pathologists. No one knows what it is until the pathologist gives the name of the disease. Most of the pathologists in the US spend time doing this kind of work and not forensic or autopsy pathology, unlike how the entertainment industry and media often portray the pathologists.

Cutting the specimens had become second nature to Samantha now. She enjoyed cutting, unlike other residents who dreaded cutting the specimens. She was very good with her hands in usage of a sharp knife, like a sushi chef. She never imagined vomiting when looking at specimens, unlike the forensic autopsy service. She realized she would never become a good medical examiner dealing with autopsies. That was not what she loved, but she loved surgical pathology. Cutting the gross specimen, she did not mind, and above all, she loved making the diagnosis from the patient's specimens.

Time to time, there were unusual zebra cases in America that demanded literature searches and reading textbooks. It was like a 1,000-piece puzzle she had to solve in naming each disease. The patients would never know which cases would be challenging to solve from the pathologist's point of view and how much time it took to research and study in the business of naming the disease. Pathologists are hidden doctors who give the name of the diseases, which is the starting point on the road to cure. That was perfectly okay with Samantha to be behind the curtain, a hidden hero health care worker. Not all doctors need to be in the front line getting all the glory and recognition from patients.

No one can judge how well someone lived except God, who knows everything. Life without God is senseless. Life is like a mist in the morning, here today and gone tomorrow. It is good enough for Samantha to enjoy looking at a fascinating pattern of cancer cells today.

Samantha was looking at one of the weird cases under her microscope. The patient was a 56-year-old female who presented with abdominal mass. The radiologist said the CT scan of the abdomen and pelvis showed a large cystic and necrotic mass measuring 6 x 5 x 5 cm, possibly connected to either her ovary or intestinal serosa. The tumor cells under the microscope were small spindle to oval shaped nuclei without much cytoplasm. It could be characterized as, small round blue cells.

There were a bunch of differential diagnoses one could entertain. She was very much looking forward to meeting with her attending pathologist tomorrow, and to order other ancillary tests to figure out the name of this disease.

I know that there is nothing better for them than to rejoice and to do good in one's lifetime; moreover, that every man who eats and drinks sees good in all his labor—it is the gift of God."
Ecclesiastes 3:22

Writer's point of view on how coronavirus changed the world

Sophia K. Apple, MD
May 22, 2020

The coronavirus pandemic entered quietly into our spaces without warning, unlike many other natural disasters. And it forever changed our reality and normalcy. There were some warnings, but we underestimated its potency and downplayed it by saying, "It's just another flu, thousands of people die with flu every year." This silent and deadly enemy cannot be seen; we cannot shoot a virus by enlisting military forces to honor our heroes amongst the army, navy and air force.

The formidable enemy crosses all boundaries of countries, red and blue states, all races, religions, genders, ages, education, and economic status, a true definition of an equal opportunity.

This coronavirus hijacked our lives without our consent.

We are consumed with news regarding the coronavirus attacks locally, regionally, nationally and internationally. No other news was emphasized from March 2020 until late May, almost three months straight by this brainless and incompetent packet of RNA strands which had changed and captured the human enterprise.

As of May 22nd, there had been more than 5.1 million infections with the virus and a death toll of more than 335,000 globally. Just within the US, confirmed deaths caused by the coronavirus surpassed 95,000. The negative impact caused by the virus was not just the death rate, but the accompanying collateral economic damage with 23 million unemployed Americans as of mid-April, which translated to an unemployment rate of

14.7%, and growing every week, approaching the highest level since the Great Depression in 1929, ten years after the influenza pandemic.

In 1918, during the worst influenza pandemic, the final global death toll ranged from 17 million to 100 million, depending on the way victims were counted. Almost 700,000 people were thought to have died in the US, equivalent to more than two million people today as a proportion of the population. The predominant population who died were young males, soldiers.

In 2020, the coronavirus pandemic largely, but not entirely, had spared the young and targeted the older population, testing how much contemporary US society valued the elderly.

This virus had changed every aspect of our culture, society, politics, business, economy, and life attitudes. It permeated through so many levels, we could not even fathom.

The culture has changed in fundamental ways. For example, by the way we greet each other; we recoil from handshaking, even elbow bumps to keep the distance of six feet away from each other. Such greetings have now altogether become a no-go, not even smiles hidden under the mask.

Politics have changed; no campaign events with a large crowd, no traveling to every state by candidates, and voting may be changed entirely to mail. The blaming games for faulting others in a delayed response to the pandemic has not changed, however.

Americans also became better at several things. Cooking, being more homebodies, and accustomed to being more introvert by the limitations of going to restaurants and bars.

Education has changed. Most classes are conducted by websites or Zooming. Students without computers will be left out in the dark, which creates a lack of access and opportunities in learning for the poor. Tele schooling is now becoming more of a norm, affecting at least 55.1 million students nationwide.

Traveling, entertaining, vacationing, and hotel businesses have been halted by the virus. Instead, online ordering from Amazon, Walmart, Costco and groceries has been doing well, some with price gouging to follow the fundamental economic rule, "as consumer demands increase, the prices increase." Job security for delivery truck drivers has increased since they are now the lifeline to many.

Our hygiene requirements and habits have been changed; we wash our hands more frequently, something we should learn from obsessive-compulsive patients who have perfected this art. Americans also have become hoarders of hand sanitizer, disinfectant, toiletry and tissue products. In lieu of high fashion clothing, more colorful designs of facial masks are selling better. The definition of personal hygiene has shifted. Both men's and women's hair length have been increasing, including some governors who show up every day on television monitors. The people with sign language skills have also stepped forward and are more visible than before.

What about the attitude? American people naturally tend to focus on two desires, safety and freedom. Hyper-individualism shouts, "Keep me safe and leave me alone."

But we now know that these two desires are interrelated and even conversely related. One cannot be safe unless you do your part in the four pillars of our strategy: hygiene, distancing, screening, and masks. Who would have thought someone (index patient zero) from Wuhan, China could affect the entire global world like today? Can one person change the world? Absolutely. Freedom? Yes, we want that too, but not when it affects other people in such a detrimental way. What we do today is intertwined with how we affect others tomorrow, more than we might possibly imagine.

We have lost our innocence in the trust of being together socially. Hugging, handshaking, talking and singing together, touching and holding hands to comfort others, and even breathing the air in an enclosed space has become risky. Every causal contact has become a calculated risk, as if it is a sexual encounter. The question of who and where have you been recently, crosses our mind before welcoming someone into our boundaries.

The comfort of being in the presence of others has been replaced by the comfort of being alone. All things extroverts flourish in have become a thing of the past.

Nobody can predict when is the end, or the full consequences of the coronavirus pandemic. History repeats itself and we can learn a great deal of knowledge by studying past experiences. Key points from observing the epidemiology of past influenza pandemics, especially from 1918, may provide insight into COVID-19. Length of the pandemic will probably be 18 to 24 months, as herd immunity gradually develops in the human population. Given the high transmissibility of coronavirus, to halt the pandemic 60% to 70% of the population may need to be immune to reach a critical threshold. One thing we can predict with confidence is that it will take time to get back to the normalcy we once used to know. We will soon forget what the pandemic was like. Our memory is short-lived, and amnesia is guaranteed, but the history will repeat itself again by having another pandemic.

The COVID-19 pandemic will end most likely by our exhausted energy and fading memory in dealing with it before the actual virus pandemic is over.

The only sure things in life are death, paying taxes and perpetual mutation in viruses. Currently, the pandemic is far from over. Despite continued rising coronavirus infection rates worldwide, America announced businesses would open and resumption of usual domestic air travel would start on 5/25, and on 6/1 travel on hundreds of general passenger trains would resume. The US will also resume the special train to transport migrant workers. Slowly and surely all the essential and non-essential businesses will open, tiptoeing the balance of sacrifices from the health care workers who actually take care of the residual contagious and sick population. There will be spikes of COVID-19 back into emergency departments and intensive care units.

The government will calculate how many bed capacities are available, rather than how many doctors, nurses, EMTs, janitors and other allied health care workers are risking their own lives and putting at risk their loved ones and their families.

Most health care workers did not sign up to be enlisted as military personnel who understand and train for one's own life to be endangered by their duties. They want to help others who are sick and are trained for that. They did not sign up to risk their lives every day as if they are going to the battlefield on the frontline.

As the pandemic prolongs, the glory and honor of the job being heroes, albeit involuntarily, will soon be forgotten and diminished. The price of paying one's own sacrifice needs to be thought through, weighing the benefits and risks, as we now see many early retirements from health care workers. The younger generation will pick up the tune of "for the whom the bell tolls," and we may face severe shortages of health care workers in the future.

At the peak, we are witnessing the COVID-19 crisis overwhelm the hospitals, and we are in dire need of physicians and health care allies on the front lines. However, amid all of this, hospitals had to furlough thousands of employees, cutting their pay, requesting volunteer staff, and yet failed to provide adequate PPE while demanding that staff risk their lives. Some nurses and doctors are speaking out on lacking adequate PPE and over working their shifts to 15-hour workdays, but some hospital administrators are punishing those that spoke up against the system. Some other hospitals are laying their employees off. Even worse, some of these same CEOs, administrators, and executives were being compensated with million-dollar salaries or more. It is very perplexing how health care workers could be fired, furloughed, or asked to take pay cuts as they put on PPE to care for critically ill patients at great personal risk.

Life goes on as death goes on. More recently, news outlets rarely cover how many deaths occur in any prominent manner, as if 50 dead are not important as 800 dead. As media coverage dissipates, so will our reality of COVID-19.

The tail end of the mess is a perpetual chaotic reality that the virus still left will be cleaned up by the unsung heroes, just like the Vietnam veterans, some with amputated extremities, many still with mental and physical scars.

What the author wishes readers to know

Interview with the author

Q: This is your first work of fiction. Why did you decide to write a novel at this time?

Initially, I was captivated by video imagery from a drone hovering over Hart Island in New York. It was on one of the national evening news programs, showing a few people digging a mass grave with many unmarked wooden cheap coffins placed in a long trench. The image was shown probably less than ten seconds, but it captured my curiosity, which then led me to research this place. And ever since, I was inspired every morning with ideas and images in my head. I would say that God has planted these insights every morning for me to describe and tell stories about them for six straight weeks, sometimes late into the night. As a practicing pathologist, I work close to the morgue at a hospital and saw many dead patients of COVID-19 transported to the morgue beyond the room capacity. Seeing the dead bodies in these plastic bags, I think everyone will change how one approaches the pandemic. It is not a joke. It is real. When facing these corpses, people's perspectives on life and death can alter profoundly. For example, asking questions such as the meaning of life or the existence of God become rather natural. And I tried to portray such moments in the life of a few people in the novel.

I also wanted to document the pandemic of COVID-19 in the year 2020 as a diary of the virus, so that this writing would be useful to look at now and, in the future, when the globe is facing another unknown novel pandemic. The experiences people have during the pandemic in this novel are fictional, but the important aspect to address is how the pandemic brings more devastation to the poor like Bita, Payman and Mahalia (the minorities), and elderly that the society often dismiss. Instead of the fragmented news stories we see during the pandemic, I wanted to put together a coherent account showing how interconnected we actually are in a novel story.

Q: You wrote this novel in six weeks?

Yes, I wrote this book in six weeks from the end of March to mid-May 2020, during which time, I was also working at a hospital as a half-time pathologist. I wrote every day when I was not working in the hospital, six to seven hours a day.

Q: Authors often research on the topics relevant to their writing projects. And you mentioned your research on Hart Island in New York. As a physician, and a pathologist at that, did you have to research on other topics and issues that you referred to in your novel?

Yes, I researched many actual events that I found to be remarkable, such as the little-known history and facts about Hart Island, the chaos in New York City as morgues overflowed and situations like using U-Haul trucks to store dead bodies. Wuhan and the Wuhan Institute of Virology Laboratory were also topics I read extensively about. Also, the shocking and mostly unseen cruise line situations, and vaccine development to name a few.

The scientific findings such as testing, virus characteristics, and mechanisms of death caused by the virus are all true, based on my education and extensive reading of current peer-reviewed scientific literature and media news reports from around the world. In particular, I spent more than 30 hours reading and evaluating scientific journals to get the facts.

Q: Would you point out a few scenes in the novel you tried to capture these profound and life-altering moments?

Seeing God in Mahalia, for example. When Emily was thrown into making the life-and-death decision, and when she was on the verge of ending it all, she encountered Mahalia as God in disguise. A poor Filipina laborer invisible to many and omnipresent in real life. Portraying Mahalia as a God's image in the novel is akin to how I experience God personally.

My God who I worship is not someone high in the sky, a white old man with a long white beard, loudly threatening with thunders, looking down on the humanity and ready to punish all wrongdoing, but a real embodied being that's ready to embrace and accept us in love. When we are in desperate need and acknowledge God humbly without pride, God can be found everywhere.

It is not God who is interested in punishing someone like Samantha who committed adultery with a married man, but God who uses someone like her to save David Falkner. God, who could have used angels or even a donkey to talk to, uses us, humans, to do His saving work. Humans are ambassadors to spread and share our understanding of loving God, just as the virus is spreading during the pandemic.

Q: This is a very intriguing theological perspective you are sharing. And one can even say that you wrote this novel for theological purposes. Do you have other points or issues that you would like to share with readers?

Another personal reason I wrote this book is to introduce Asian American angles. Asian Americans live in the US with innate and unconscious bias. All lives are interconnected and intertwined on the globe. All lives are equally significant regardless of race.

I was doing an autopsy on a black corpse and noticed that beneath the dark skin were the exact same organs and structures as any other human. But the magnitude of racial bias that person must have gone through in his life must have been enormously different just because of his skin color.

This was so unconscionable to me, and I believe God must feel the same. Some people are more privileged just because they are white, and most of them do not even know it. God in His infinite knowledge and creativity enjoys the differences—He even creates all kinds of leaves in a tree, all different. No leaf is the same. God delights in varieties and therefore He created all kinds of different skin colors on the globe.

Why should one face difficulty or privilege because of this?

Q: Did you want to write about the virus as your debut novel?

No, actually I had a totally different idea for the first book.

I wanted to write about a story of redemption (like Les Misérables) in modern day life but the thought of writing on COVID-19 came so strongly that it captivated all my thoughts. I felt like God was giving me images of the current time happenings and I could not do anything else other than to describe the images I saw every morning. Readers may appreciate this book is written to create vividly enriching scenes, somewhat like a movie script.

I wanted to document this incredible pandemic that was happening in my lifetime as a diary. So, this book is based on actual events in many different circumstances.

To make the story more palatable, I made fictional characters to connect with each other, making the story more real and coherent rather than reading random newspaper articles of each incident, as I briefly mentioned before. Periodically, different viruses enter into our world and destroy humankind. Poliovirus came from the US and affected me when I was two years old in Korea. Failure to eradicate polio could result in as many as 200,000 new cases every year, within 10 years, all over the world. There is no cure for polio, it can only be prevented. Polio vaccine, given multiple times, can protect a child for life.

Viruses affecting human suffering is not new, and this situation will continue as long as we live in this world. Coronavirus is a novel virus in the era of 2020. I want the people to understand its power in potency and virulence and not underestimate its influence in our lives. Knowing the invisible and formidable enemy is the first step to prevent the history repeating itself in suffering.

Poliovirus first originated from the US. In 1894, the first outbreak of polio in epidemic form arose from the state of Vermont, in the US, with 132 cases.

In 1916, a larger second epidemic of polio was seen in the United States and in 1933, President Roosevelt was infected with poliovirus as an adult.

It is a devastating virus still prevalent across the globe, especially in the developing countries, causing motor paralysis. It is important to note that I do not condemn the US for its origin, as we should not condemn China for COVID-19. A novel virus will erupt anywhere on the globe, it's a matter of when, and not if. We, collectively, should be better prepared to face this invisible enemy and not let it spread into a greater pandemic level, rather than focus on blaming the particular region or country of the virus origin. We have no time to blame.

Q: Are you happy about the ending of the story?

Yes and no, I know some readers will be disappointed in the ending. It may appear mundane, as if nothing much changed. Yet, almost everyone adapted to the changes and regained their composure in continuing their lives. Small and incremental hopes and changes were necessary for them to make by accepting the altered upside-down realities caused by the coronavirus. By continuing to live in their own lives adapting to the environment is really all we as humans can do, and to be content with whatever the circumstances God provides.

To me, the pursuit of happiness is no more than what Solomon said in Ecclesiastes 3:12-13: *"I know that there is nothing better for them than to rejoice and to do good in one's lifetime; moreover, that every man who eats and drinks sees good in all his labor—it is the gift of God."*

I also wanted to be true to the timeline. At the end of May, we still did not have a vaccine in our reality, but at least a few were promising to be developed.

Q: Do you plan to write more novels? Are you currently working on any writing projects?

There might be a sequel to this book. I also have a blog that I recently started: https://DoctorSophiaOnline.com.

I want to continue writing about the life of a female pathologist. I want to let people know what pathologists actually do; they don't just perform autopsies as the entertainment media portrays.

Q: Does Samantha's character in the book in any way portray who you are?

We write who we are. In many ways, my personal bias and how I think reflects into the characters in the book, not just Samantha but many of the characters in the book.

Q: You mentioned all your proceeds will be donated to people in need. Which humanitarian act(s) will you donate your royalty profits?

I am thinking about donating to a food bank in the Los Angeles area, and Joni and Friends Wheels for the World Program that provide professionally fitted wheelchairs while also sharing Jesus Christ with people struggling with disability. I made a promise to God that if the book was successful, all the profits I receive for current and future writings will be donated to His cause, 100%.

I am satisfied completely in writing novels to make my existence meaningful, purposeful and forget about my own tribulations in dealing with my physical disability, uncomfortableness and emotional pains of everyday life. When I write or practice medicine, I momentarily forget about my own discomfort, lose the actual reality of being a handicapped person which is a desirable escape for me.

Q: What is your recommendation to the public as a physician during this pandemic? What should we do to decrease the rate of transmission and death by COVID-19?

It is interesting to note that the death tolls in Hong Kong are only 6, and Singapore 26 when compared to 122,000 in the US as of June 23, 2020. Hong Kong and Singapore are both busy, bustling cities not too dissimilar to New York City.

The only reason I see that they are having success in fighting COVID-19 is that everyone wears a mask. Hong Kong had several mass demonstrations (for political reasons) on the streets disrespecting social distance during the pandemic time as well. I am shocked by the attitude of Americans who think wearing a facial mask is the symbol of weakness.

This is not the time to show our machoism, but to respect and treat the coronavirus properly. Wearing a facial mask is a sign of strength in an individual and a respect for others. We need to do our part—disinfect, keep personal hygiene by frequent hand washing with soap, social distancing and above all, wear masks in public.

Acknowledgments

Thank you for all your support and hard work to publish this book. To my husband Hal Apple, for his infinite love and care. To Kate Stanwick, for her excellent comments and notations on the manuscript. To Stephanie Robinson, for her professional artwork production of the front cover design.

Thank you for the moral support I received in the initial phase of the book writing. To my sister Dr. Jungha Kim, Charles Johnson, Jeffrey Bell, and Julie Kim who continually encouraged me to believe that my thinking and writing is important, and that I can be a great novel writer.

A special thanks to Dr. Jungha Kim and her interview to convey what the writer wishes readers to know.

Made in the USA
Monee, IL
08 August 2021